Her face was pale, lips without color, her chin coated with sand clinging to sweat.

"Mary ... Jesus, I — "

The eyes opened.

"Death," she said, groaning.

He couldn't tell her she was wrong; he couldn't tell her help was coming.

"No prayers, Devin," she said. "I know. *I* know."

Her head tilted back then, as if she was trying to look at the House of Night, neck straining, her hand whipping away to claw at the air.

One eye was pure white, and the other solid red.

And the flesh of her cheeks was peeling off and turning black.

"An exceptional daylight ghost story, with an atmosphere you can feeling creeping up behind you — one of Charles L. Grant's most considerable achievements."

— Ramsey Campbell

Also by Charles L. Grant
published by Tor Books

Charles L. Grant

FOR FEAR OF THE NIGHT

TOR
HORROR

A TOM DOHERTY ASSOCIATES BOOK
NEW YORK

FOR FEAR OF THE NIGHT

Copyright © 1987 by Charles L. Grant

A TOR Book
Published by Tom Doherty Associates, Inc.
49 West 24 Street
New York, NY 10010

ISBN: 0-812-51834-9   Can. ISBN: 0-812-51835-7

Library of Congress Catalog Card Number: 87-50874

First edition: January 1988
First mass market edition: November 1988

Printed in the United States of America

0 9 8 7 6 5 4 3 2 1

This one is for Jo,
who makes long trips worth the taking,
And also for Steve,
who makes the leaving again hard;
Two good friends indeed,
Despite the ocean and the night.

For fear of the Night,
Men shy from the moon,
And Death seeks His throne.

ONE

THE August breeze cooled as the lights began to die, bulbs and twisted glass winking off in slow segments across the broad amusement pier that stretched its bed across the surf, drawing in the darkness from the dark of the ocean, banishing the day's heat still clinging to the sand. The rides were first, empty and shadowed, and the sagging rainbow strings above the iron-pipe railing.

And last, always last, the Ferris wheel at the far end—outer rim, inner rim, and each side of the square that collared the rusted hub.

And when it was done, the dark nearly complete, neon no longer popping, generators no longer grinding, there was the silence above the hollow throat of the constant surf. No voices. No music. No laughter. No screams. Only the ebbing tide that slapped against the pilings, only the grumbling breakers, and the foam that hissed over the sand in crescents a dull white, reaching, pawing, endlessly feeding.

And the moon on its way toward dawn, the stars over the Atlantic that made the night sky seem lower, and colder, the ocean a rolling mirror that distorted reflection.

The August breeze cooled, and behind the deserted boardwalk and the low buildings that faced it, there were hazed sputtering streetlights, lingering porch lights, a few lights in a few windows, all of them feeble without the boardwalk's matching glitter, all of them melancholy in the quiet left behind when the tourists fell to bed. Traffic signals changed color, but there were no cars to obey them. Pennants fluttered. A balloon bounced along a gutter. From a hallway behind the mask of a warped screen door, a clock chimed the third hour, with no one to hear it.

The railing was clammy at the far end of the pier, and Devin leaned against it and looked down at the waves, saw them rising, falling, heard them split against the barnacled wood that held the pier above the sea. A shrug at nothing seen, and he looked out into the breeze that forced him to squint and saw nothing but black, the horizon gone until dawn; nothing but endless black, and silver fragments, and the occasional flare of startling white when a breaker met a sandbar.

A lift of a heavy eyebrow as if he'd expected something more, then a glance to his right, to the beach stretching away toward the first of the brown-boulder jetties that struggled against erosion. Waves in low tiers. The glint of moonlight off a shell turning slowly in the water.

And to his left, the narrower beach that was framed by this pier and the next, the two marking the range of the area's amusements and food stands, the bars and the gift shops. Six blocks of sand at the foot of a boardwalk just high enough for a grown man to walk under without bend-

2

ing his head. All of it deserted now, even the beachcombers gone home or to their niches in alleys, in doorways, those stretches of shoreline where the police didn't patrol.

The far pier was dark, and always had been, even in full sunlight, and it seemed darker now because only the weak waning moon dared give it shape: charred beams, scorched metal, the remnants of a ferocious blaze that had ravaged it seven days before—the result, the word was, of faulty wiring because someone had neglected to turn the electricity off.

The August breeze; a chill.

Even before the fire had swept it, blackened it, turned all its paint to soot and shattered the tinted glass of its roof, the place had been condemned. At the start of the summer season, the caution signs had gone up, the barriers across the arched entrance. Too many years of neglect, too many reports of accidents that shouldn't have happened. Though the story had been in all the local papers, it was odd, in a way, because as far as he knew, there had been no one to dispute the findings of the inspectors. No proprietor had stepped forward, no lawyer, no landlord.

Condemned in an afternoon, and the entrance sealed with plywood.

He blinked then and held his breath when he thought he saw a sudden gout of flame somewhere in the ruins, realized it was only memory, and his fingers curled to tighten their grip on the railing.

He'd been down there, on the beach, beside the center lifeguard stand, when it had happened, right there at twilight, when the long crown of fire suddenly exploded through the domed roof that covered three-quarters of the structure, and the sunbathers and swimmers had started screaming, started running. Without thinking, he had grabbed his cameras and begun shooting, telephoto zoom and wide-angle lens, kneeling, standing, climbing to the lifeguard's seat and bracing himself with his knees, framing

3

furious black clouds against the pastels of the sky, flames brilliant and bellowing and trapped within the smoke.

And when the film was gone, he'd rushed back to his house and made calls as he was printing, the sweat-slicked telephone cradled between cheek and trembling shoulder, and in the following day's New York and Philadelphia newspapers, his photographs told the story.

A young woman had died, and no one knew why she'd been there.

A weekly news magazine took three of his shots, a Sunday supplement three more.

Her name was Julie Etler, and he had counted her a friend.

The breeze; puffing toward a late September wind.

Before he had learned of her death, he had told himself the disaster had been a long-awaited piece of admittedly perverse luck, the break he'd been praying for since he'd first moved to the shore nearly a decade ago. Getting his name known, and his work. Appreciation for more than simple mechanical skills. Doing something else besides endless birthdays and weddings and high school graduations. He had told himself the money was untainted, and unquestionably needed if he was going to survive come September. He had told himself he was a professional and needed to keep his distance.

But Julie had been found in the middle of the pier, barely enough of her for identification, and nothing burned around her.

There were no nightmares.

But there was memory.

And there was the blackened pier up the beach.

The breeze; it was cold.

Trapped thunder beneath his feet as the tide clawed at the sand.

A young woman not long escaped from her teens, dying as he took her picture, not realizing she was there until it

4

hung in the darkroom, and he'd seen her, he'd seen her . . .

Oh Jesus, Graham, enough, he scolded with a quick shake of his head; and he pushed away from the railing to begin the process of going home—camera capped and slipped into its padded bag and the bag hung from his right shoulder, tripod collapsed and hung by its strap over his left, the futile adjustment of his jacket where the straps bunched the denim and made him feel lopsided. Then he stepped carefully over the thick cables that fed power to the rides and made his way down the center of the pier toward the boardwalk, listening to the rattle of a heavy double chain being drawn across the entrance, beneath the horseshoe of a sign flanked with grinning faces of giant clowns.

He yawned, shifted the heavy bag with a practiced jerk of his shoulder, and pushed the fingers of his left hand back through curly dark hair. Shifted the bag again, and blinked and squinted against the glare of two large naked bulbs dangling over the entrance. The chain was little more than a shadow stretching from the shadowhands of a man smaller than he but with considerably more bulk, his back hunched, his arms long, his short wiry hair perfectly white.

"You coming or what?" the man asked, his voice deep and soft. "I ain't gonna wait on you all night, y'know."

With an apologetic grunt, Devin hurried through the gap and turned as the chain was slipped over a stout hook on one of the sign's supports. "You really expect to keep someone out with that?"

Stump Harragan, in shirtsleeves and Bermuda shorts, yanked the chain to be sure it was fastened, then pulled wide plaid suspenders away from his chest, held them with a smile and let them snap back. "It took you all summer to ask me that, you know that?"

"I like to reserve judgment."

5

Harragan stared at him, one eye permanently half-closed. "What's that mean?"

"It means I just thought of it."

The old man laughed, clapping long-fingered hands as black as the shadows building behind him on the pier. "You are something else, boy, something else again." He nodded at the camera bag. "Get anything tonight?"

"I don't know," he said, shrugging. "Depends."

Harragan scratched the side of his neck. "Pretty girls out there, or are you blind? Suits like the stuff they wear, when I was a kid, they were banned. Sinful. Still are, but what the hell."

"I've got all the bathing suits I need, thanks," he said with a mock shudder. "Me and every other photographer in the known Western world."

"Well, what about the tykes?"

"Cute kids building sand castles are boring. So are dogs playing ball and surfers wiping out."

"Sure are fussy, aren't you?"

"No." He cocked a hip. "Well, maybe."

"You get laid yet?"

Devin only stared.

"All them girls," the old man said with exaggerated rue and the sweep of an arm toward the empty beach. "God, all summer long all them girls just lying out there, in the flesh, smelling like oil and looking like heaven, and . . . you," and he pointed a grimy finger, "are not a monk. You wanna be a monk, go to the mountains. You come to the shore, you gotta meet a girl. That's the way of it, boy. That's the way God wants it."

"You know that for a fact, huh?"

For an answer Harragan tugged a bandanna from his hip pocket, blew his nose, and belched loudly.

Devin laughed as he shook his head in friendly disgust. The old man, despite his weight and the size of his arms, seemed aged, frail, and perpetually cowed; only those who rented space on his pier knew that he owned it. The rest thought him nothing more than a half-witted janitor, a bent-over black man who silently cleaned the daily messes and emptied the trash cans and twice a day washed the boards with a tape-patched hose; they either ignored him or made cracks about him, and only those who caused trouble learned how young and strong he really was, and how short was his temper.

"Hey, boy, you gonna stand there all night, or you gonna buy me coffee?"

"Neither," he said regretfully, a hand over his eyes. "I've been up since eight, remember? I'm going to drop if I don't get some sleep."

"Drop," Harragan muttered. "You got thirty years on me, boy. You ain't gonna drop."

Maybe not, he thought as he waved and walked away, but right now he felt as if he wasn't long for another day. His back ached, his eyes were filled with sand, and his clothes were stiff with the salt the sea spray left behind.

What he needed, if someone was inclined to hand him a miracle, was a solid two-day sleep, without the neighbors' interruptions, without tourists shouting outside his window, without the dreams; what he knew he was going to get, however, as he'd been getting since June, was a few restless hours before the sun brought back the heat and made his airconditioner groan so loudly it woke him up.

The August breeze cooled as the lights began to die, and Tony hugged his knees tightly after drawing them to his chest. He wished he had worn his jeans tonight instead of just a bathing suit, wished again he'd brought a jacket instead of his wrestling team sweatshirt. But that was typical of the way things had gone today. This summer. This year. Apparently one step behind and around the corner from the rest of the stupid world, and having a hell of a time trying to find someone with a map.

He sniffed and shrugged at himself—*what the hell.* He rested a cheek on a forearm and looked over at Kelly Albertson, who was shivering even though Mike Nathan's arm was snug around her shoulder.

"Do you guys have any idea what time it is?" he asked at last, his eyes straining to clear away some of the dark.

"But of course," Mike said, his voice naturally deep, a fair complement to his size. "It's the witching hour, Mr. Riccaro." He laughed evilly and held up both hands, hooking his fingers beside his nose. "Time I was turning into a werewolf, I think."

"You need a full moon for that, dope," Kelly said, shaking blond bangs out of her eyes, the breeze blowing them back.

"A vampire then."

"Midnight," Tony said, shifting from cheek to chin and looking out at the ocean.

"What?"

"The witching hour. It's midnight. This isn't midnight. It's almost dawn, for god's sake."

He felt Mike staring at him, trying to figure out if he was kidding or not. He felt the shrug. He heard the kiss. He heard Kelly giggle and push Mike away.

He rolled his eyes and lay back on the blanket, stretched his arms over his head until he felt his shoulders pop. Two hours ago he had decided this was a stupid idea. One of Mike's class-A boners that seemed to come in waves. For the longest time the guy would be perfectly sane, perfectly sober, the perfect model of a young man who wanted to be a doctor; then wham!, like he was Dr. Jekyll or something, he'd turn loony.

It must be the name: Michael Nathan. There was something about it that made people want to smile.

Last week the idea had been to terrorize the kids at all the day schools over in Toms River. He was going to get them all masks like the Shape had worn in *Halloween*, and they were supposed to stand at the fences or in the windows and wait until someone saw them. Then they were supposed to ease slowly out of sight and run like hell.

The week before that, Mike had wanted them to drive up to the Point Pleasant Inlet and throw water bombs at the fishing and pleasure boats heading out to sea.

The week before that it was something else, he couldn't remember and he didn't care. None of it ever worked anyway, and the only reason they let Mike have his head was because they knew something would screw up before the plan ever got started, and they knew too he was due to return to his old self.

Tony puffed his cheeks and blew out a slow breath.

Tonight, while they'd been walking the boards, Kelly had spotted Devin setting up his equipment, so the idea had been to sneak under the boardwalk to Harragan's Pier, wait for the tide to get far enough out, then make spooky noises. Mike figured it would scare the shit out of the photographer, who was a pretty good guy all in all, for a grownup, and probably wouldn't beat their heads in when he found out what was going on.

The trouble was Mike had fallen asleep, and neither he nor Kelly had felt like waking him up.

The August breeze; a chill.

Above him the boards were black, and grey where they parted to let the dying moonlight through.

Sand fell lightly on his face, spiderlegs looking for a way into his eyes; he rolled onto his stomach and pillowed his arms under his head.

The sand beneath him was cold. And hard. But he didn't want to go home. He'd told his parents he was going to sleep out on the beach, and they'd said it was all right. Everything he wanted to do this summer was all right. It was almost as if they didn't give a damn what happened to him, as long as he kept out of their way.

Kelly giggled.

Mike grunted and stood up, walked out onto the beach and looked up at the sky. "Y'know," he said, "if it rains, we're gonna drown."

Kelly lay back and rolled herself in her blanket, looked over at Tony and grinned at him. "Aren't we having fun?"

"Lots," he said.

In the dark her eyes were bright, her lips glistened, her cheeks shone. He would have seen it even if his eyes had been closed; in fact he had seen it every night for the last two weeks, every time he went to bed and let in the dreams.

Mike, his limp almost invisible despite the uneven sand, began moving across the sand, looking for trash the cleaning crews had missed. Stooping over. Straightening. Pursing his lips and moving on. Tony watched him until he was out of sight, then shook his head when Kelly grinned at him again.

"He's compulsive, you know," he said.

"He's just neat, that's all."

"Neat? The guy vacuums his own room, for god's sake! Every night!"

She laughed and shifted to her back; he wished with a silent groan her blanket hadn't been so snug.

"That's because his mother won't touch it, and I don't blame her. She won't let him out of the house until everything is in its place."

"Nuts. He's compulsive."

"So what does that make you?"

"A slob," he said.

She didn't laugh.

He began digging with one hand, piling the sand between them. "Do you realize," he said as if talking to himself, "that after this weekend it's over? I mean, we're practically out of here, you know that?"

"Don't remind me."

"God, it's gone fast. I woke up this morning and I looked at the calendar and I almost croaked. It's gone, Kell. It's gone. Labor Day's Monday, and then . . ."

She said nothing.

The surf continued to slide away.

His hand reached dampness, a deep permanent chill, and he drew the hand away, dried it off on the blanket and stared at it in the dark. He wondered what it was going to look like in ten years, in twenty. He wondered if it would get thin and hard, like a chicken's foot, when he was old like old Stump; or maybe it would get fat like his father's, stained with years of washing grease off hot grills and mixing sauces and rolling dough into cakes that were eaten by pigs who only wanted to get the hell out, back into the sun.

For a moment he saw himself in the diner's kitchen, standing over the grills, standing in front of the four ovens, standing at the huge sinks where the plates and cups were soaking. His black hair was white, his shoulders were stooped, and the lean frame that usually fooled most of his opponents was thin instead, and getting thinner every hour.

He turned his face to the ground and pressed his forehead into the sand. Please, he prayed; don't let me screw it up.

The breeze; it was cold.

Then he blinked and sat up quickly, startled when Kelly called out for Mike.

Under the boardwalk, the echoes of the waves that slammed against the piers.

They exchanged concerned glances and rolled to their feet, stepped out into the air and scanned the beach.

"Now what?" she said, hands on her hips.

He looked behind and above him, to the triple railing that ran along the boardwalk's outer edge. The benches behind it were empty. There was no sound of anyone walking, anyone running. A gleam from the town's lights that seemed more like fog.

"I'll kill him," she said, heading toward the ocean.

He followed, rubbing his arms to give him warmth, stopping when he came to a ragged three-foot drop, a miniature cliff left after a winter storm. There were no footprints on the wet sand below, and he kicked aside a strand of kelp and jumped down.

He looked toward Harragan's and nodded when Kelly joined him. "He must've gone over to see if Stump's still around."

"The lights are out. He's gone. So is Devin. I heard the Jeep before."

Tony didn't look around.

Neither did Kelly.

"Then he's hiding. The jerk."

They started toward the pier, sidestepping the occasional wave that aimed for their sneakers. He wanted to take her hand, but Mike was probably watching. Hiding behind a piling and waiting to leap out and hear them scream.

But the closer they drew, the more his eyes adjusted to the moonlight, and he could see nothing under there but the arches of kelp where the tide had reached at full, a few broken shells, a weak flutter of paper. If Mike was there, he'd lost a hundred pounds to blend into shadow.

Tony stopped.

Kelly moved on for a few seconds before cupping her hands around her mouth and calling.

The sea threw the name back.

She called again, turning toward the boardwalk.

The sea threw the name back.

When she faced him, hands out, he raised eyebrows and a shoulder—*he's your boyfriend, kid, I can't keep track of him for you.*

"Maybe . . ." she said timidly, pointing up the beach.

Damn, he thought.

"You think he would?" It was a stupid question; these days, Mike seemed in another world.

"It's the moon," she said, forcing him a smile. "He'll do anything, you know that."

He did. And he saw her looking over his shoulder.

Damn, he thought again.

"I honest to god don't know how college is going to stand him," he grumbled as Kelly started toward him. "He'll tear the place apart by Christmas."

Her hair blew across her face; he wanted to brush it away.

"I'll watch him," she said. "He won't be able to make a move without me knowing it."

"Yeah, but you're as crazy as he is."

She sneered and punched his shoulder, grabbed his arm and spun him around.

"Hey!"

"Move, Riccaro, before I break you in half."

And as soon as he let himself see the dead pier, he thought: Julie's dead. Julie's dead. Julie's dead. Julie's dead.

And he shuddered.

Neither of them moved quickly, and Tony kept finding things of intense interest bubbling in the wet sand. Dark shapes that moved, dark remains of the seadead, glints of silver, hints of white, blurring his already strained vision until he had to rub a finger across his eyes.

This is stupid, he told himself; Riccaro, this is stupid.

He looked up as his chest expanded with a breath and saw the pier, saw the black, and saw nothing moving above in the twisted timber, or in the dark below that looked for all the world like an gap-toothed open mouth.

Fifty yards from the devastation, there was a thick rope that ran through loops raised chest-high above the beach. Danger signs were posted along it every ten feet, the words in luminescent paint, to catch the sun, to catch the moon. They stopped when they reached it, and Kelly leaned over as if she were looking over a high fence.

"I don't see him."

"He's not that dumb."

Her left hand took a strand of hair and pulled it across her mouth. "Do you think he wants us to go under there?"

"I told you he's not that dumb," he snapped and immediately regretted it when he saw the look in her eyes. Mike was hers, leave him alone.

He snorted in disgust and headed back toward the

13

blankets. He was tired. He wanted to sleep. In the morning he had to help his father at the diner, and he didn't want complaints about his yawning all the time. Besides, Mike was a big boy. He could take care of himself. And if he was dumb enough to climb over the rope, then he deserved what he got.

Julie's dead.

He stopped and kicked the sand, started again and felt the darkness on his right, rising over his head, after all this time still smelling of seared wood and melted iron when the wind was just right. He didn't understand why they didn't tear it down; his mother was always complaining about it, and about how the children could get hurt, maybe even die. But Devin had said they couldn't find the owner, and since it wasn't damaged enough to fall down on its own, fourteen days had to pass before the town could do the work without permission.

A stupid law.

Julie's dead.

He remembered the funeral—a beautiful day, last Saturday, most of the kids were there, and he in his good dark suit, sweating under the sun while the preacher said solemn words the sea wind took away, Julie's mother soundlessly crying. He had felt the tears himself, but he wouldn't let them fall. He only looked at the casket with the flowers draped across it, looked at Mrs. Etler, looked up at the sky and demanded explanations.

What the hell right had she to go and die on him like that?

What the hell had she been doing on the pier?

He had walked away before it was over, threading his way between the headstones, reading the inscriptions, watching his black shoes grey with dust. The next thing he knew he was at the cemetery's entrance, and across the narrow street a stretch of dreary forest—scrub pine, thorn bushes, no shade at all and filled with the drone of insects, the husk of the heated wind. His hands slipped into his pockets, a glance over his shoulder, and he had walked into the trees, found a sandy path and followed it until it reached the highway that led toward the sea.

But Julie didn't join him, and neither did her ghost.

That's when he'd cried.

Standing on the shoulder, trucks and cars screaming past, letting the tears reach his cheeks, letting the sobs fill his chest with stone.

And when it was done, it was done.

He was alone.

And a hand touched his shoulder.

Tony yelled and threw himself to one side, collided with one of the boardwalk's supports and dropped to his knees. His shoulder burned, his eyes blurred, and he started to scramble away when a hand grabbed his arm.

"Tony!"

He panted.

"Tony! Hey, man, it's me!"

He swallowed bile.

Mike dropped heavily in front of him, searching his face, lips quivering as he yanked back his hand. "Hey. Hey, man, it's me."

"I'll kill you," Tony said, hating the boy sound of his voice.

"Hey, I'm sorry. I am. I just . . . I didn't think you'd freak on me, y'know?" Mike reached out and touched his forearm, pulled the hand back and began poking at the sand. "I'm sorry."

All muscles failing, Tony toppled onto his back. Rage kept his eyes closed, shame had him gnawing on his lower lip. His head rolled slowly side to side, but he didn't say a word until he knew his voice was back.

"You creep," he whispered.

"Yeah," Mike said contritely. "I know."

"You idiot!"

"Yeah."

"You . . . you stupid, fat-headed, no good sonofabitch!"

Mike giggled.

Tony opened his eyes.

"Riccaro, does all that mean I'm not an asshole?"

The punch was thrown before he knew he had considered it; it struck the taller boy in the center of his chest, knocking him to one side, making him yelp. Then he rolled to his knees and waited for Mike to get up, fists high, still panting, wanting to take the bastard's face and shove it into his brain.

But Mike stayed down, and Kelly ran up, throwing herself to her knees and cradling his head.

"Jesus, Tony, did you have to do that? It was only a joke!"

Tony looked at his hands and watched the fists open, the fingers grow limp, the wrists turn and bend; he looked at Kelly and her boyfriend, and over their heads to the sea. Then he pushed himself to his feet and stalked away to his blanket, a black patch on dark sand. A stare until he realized what it was. A sigh he was sure no one heard but him. Then he was down again, on his side, legs drawn to his chest, the blanket scratching his cheek as he folded it across him.

Listening to the surf.

Listening to the wind.

Listening to Kelly crooning to Nathan.

It came to him then—a too-familiar melancholy laced with something he didn't quite understand. It's almost over, he thought; the summer's almost over and I'm going to have to go away and Julie's dead and I'm alone and I'm going to have to go away and never see any of them again.

He closed his eyes and bunched a fist under his chin.

Listening to the surf.

Listening to the wind.

Listening to someone walking on the beach.

A frown until he raised his head just enough to see that the others were lying down, together, and asleep.

Devin must be back, he decided, and looked toward the

water, poised to toss the blanket aside. And froze when he saw a woman standing there, on the other side of the drop. A tall woman. Long hair. One hand splayed across her chest, the other hidden behind her.

His free hand rubbed his eyes while he told himself to wake up.

He couldn't have heard her; she was too far away.

He couldn't be seeing her; the moon was on its way down.

Yet she stood there, and the wind touched her, and he knew who it was.

"You're dead," he whispered, as ice replaced the blanket.

"Tony," the woman said, "I want to see you."

Devin drove at a deliberate crawl south along Seaside Boulevard, the first street parallel to the boardwalk. Once it left Harragan's Pier, it dropped to within six inches of the ground and widened abruptly to provide two rows of metered parking next to the sand. The close-crammed buildings sliding by on his right had been boardinghouses even back in the '30s, two- and three-storied gingerbread Victorians, weathered by winter storms and bludgeoned by the sun; freshly painted every few years to lure the boarders who came to marvel at the tiny yards, at the white picket fences, and the view of the ocean from the uppermost windows.

Sand swirled across the blacktop, obliterating the parking lines, the center line, crunching like ground glass beneath the Jeep's worn tires.

He whistled somewhat off-key without giving a damn, rolling down the window to enjoy one of the few times during the week when the place wasn't crawling with garishly clad vacationers, their pets and their children, when the air wasn't tainted with suntan oil and pizza, beer and cotton candy.

Oceantide was a long narrow town that puffed like a

blowfish on Memorial Day weekend and didn't take another clean breath until Labor Day was gone. To its north lay Seaside Heights, Lavallette, and Point Pleasant; to the south, beyond a closed state park and the ragged inlet where Barnegat Bay met the ocean, were Long Beach Island, Haven's End, and Atlantic City. A honky-tonk town neither better nor worse than any other along the Jersey coast; a refuge from the cities, a place to let off some steam and mark another year gone.

The place he had chosen to make his last stand before growing up.

"My god," he said to the glow of the dashboard, "what is the matter with you, pal? It's summertime, remember? Clear skies, great waves, a tan to make you cry. Jesus, you're acting like tomorrow you're turning ninety." He slapped the wheel once as if it were his cheek. "Stump's right, pal. You need a woman. You need her bad."

The laugh that followed wasn't bitter. Most of the women he knew didn't much care for the round of his face, the slight paunch over his belt, the deeply set eyes that seemed too filled with shadow. Definitely not the leading man type, he knew without deprecation, nor did he pretend to be otherwise; though it would have been nice, some morning, to wake up and discover that he looked better than he did.

On the other hand, there was Gayle, who thought he was just fine, and who slugged his arm not quite playfully whenever he tried to put himself down.

He passed a spotted mongrel rooting in spilled garbage. The dog looked over its shoulder, wagged its tail, and rooted on.

Gayle, he thought, and looked at the clock on the dashboard. Too late to call. As much as she liked him, it was too late to call.

Three blocks to where reinforced sand dunes marked the strait of Barnegat Bay, a right turn, and more Victorians, a bit smaller, cars at the curbs, rocking chairs on the porches, signs on squared white posts advertising rooms to let, by the week or the month.

A blinking traffic light.

The houses now markedly smaller, flimsy bungalows on lots barely wider than their foundations. Mediterranean colors bleached, some of them peeling, most of them nice enough in daylight and perfect in the dark.

The faint sound of rock music from an open window reminded him that he had promised to take beach portraits of a group of young friends; tomorrow, in fact. He grunted a laugh. A rash promise indeed, made without considering what he could better do with his time. It wasn't for a fee either, and he suspected they only wanted to give him an afternoon off. Which was, as he yawned and winced at the cracking of his jaw, all right with him.

He was killing himself with donkey work, he knew it, and so far hadn't been able to do much about it.

But neither had he forgotten that next week marked the time when he had told himself he'd finally have to face his future; there was no time left to pretend he was still fumbling through the throes of artistic indecision. He would either find the courage to grab the offer an old friend had made or end up back working staff on a newspaper, a magazine, or worse—stagnating in a permanent studio office where brides were framed on the walls, and fiftieth wedding anniversaries, and a sign in the window promising lifelike passport photos while the customer waited.

A living; it would be a living, and it wouldn't be much more than that.

And finally, at thirty-eight, he would bury the dream and the good intentions, and grow old before his time.

"So what's so bad about a living?" he asked as he slowed to let a prowling cat have the road.

Nothing.

Nothing at all.

It only scared him to death.

A blinking amber traffic light above Summer Road,

Oceantide's main street. Lined with bars, shops, laundromats, a handful of motels with names like Maya and Surfwind, and on the corner a movie theater whose marquee was lit only on weekends during the off-season, and not much more than that in summer.

Two blocks later he turned left and pulled into the pebbled driveway of the last house. It faced away from the sea—clapboard and white trim, its original color now faded to blotched grey. It had been winterized by the owner fifteen years before, and Devin had bought it before prices blew off the roof.

On the left was a bungalow; on the right, the steep rise of fat ten-foot dunes spiked along the crests with saw grass and a flimsy snow fence that kept only the lazy from the stretch of sand and dunes and wind-twisted trees that was a state park being considered for development of a new town.

When he slammed the car door, the sound was too loud.

When he turned the house key and stepped inside, the dampness was too strong.

When he switched on the light, he whispered, "Welcome home, sucker," groaned, and set the padded bag on the small table beside the door. Then he dropped the tripod on the floor beneath it, stripped off his coat, and stretched his arms over his head until he felt his shoulders pop.

The room was over twenty feet square and paneled in knotty pine. He'd gotten rid of the beach furniture the landlord had left behind, gladly exchanging it for a large, camelback print couch and two heavy armchairs that faced the front picture window, an end table, a glass-top cocktail table, and a carved cherrywood sideboard his parents had given him the day after they'd seen the place. For convenience, he called it the living room and set it off from the rest of the house by a series of tall, open-back pine bookcases that stretched three-quarters of the way across the floor. On the shelves were bound magazines, books he wanted to read more than once, and bits of the beach he'd picked up while roaming.

Behind the divider, on the left, was a dining area lighted by a ship's wheel chandelier; and on the right, a kitchen with a round, Formica-topped table and three matching chairs.

On the walls were wood- and chrome-framed prints of some of his own favorite photographs, most of them black-and-white, a few in color. They were there less to blow his own horn than to remind him, daily, of what he hoped he had inside him.

Three doors in the righthand wall—the first was the bedroom, the second the bath. The third had been another bedroom scarcely large enough to stand in, the only room without a window. He'd thrown out the bed. It was a darkroom now.

Where Julie's picture was buried in a file cabinet in the corner.

From the refrigerator he took a can of soda, rolled it across his forehead, and pulled back the tab as he dropped onto the couch and put his feet up on the table. A sip, and he reached over to check the answering machine. "Hollywood calling," he predicted as he listened to garbled high-pitched voices while the tape ran back. "Devin, sweetheart, we have forty or fifty million lying around we'd like you to spend. Think you can do it? Fly out first thing in the morning and we'll take a meeting, what do you say, babe?"

A quick look at the door as if he'd been overheard. But he'd been alone for so long, he thought nothing of thinking aloud; at least it proved he wasn't dead.

He cupped his hands behind his head and stared blindly at the low ceiling.

"Devin, Ken here. Ken Viceroy, remember? The guy who wants to make you rich and famous? Getting sun? I doubt it. Getting any? Forget it. Listen, that opening's not going to wait all year. I gotta know by Labor Day, okay?

That's five days in case you've torn up your calendar. So give me a call; let me talk you into it."

His eyes closed. This was the job that would either make him or kill him, and every time he heard Ken's voice a chill walked his spine. He felt the photographs on the wall, almost opened his eyes to look.

"Devin, this is your mother. Call me."

His lips in a brief smile.

"Mr. Graham, you there? Are you listening? This is Kelly. Three-thirty okay tomorrow? Mike says he's gonna wear a tuxedo. Please don't let him do it, Mr. Graham, I'll die if he does. Tony says we have to wear our graduation stuff. Is he lying? It's so hot! He's gotta be lying, right? Are you there? I hate these things."

His eyes opened and his legs crossed at the ankles.

The next two messages were dial tones; he waited them out, too weary to move.

"Devin, this is Gayle. Do you remember me? I don't have any clothes on, I'm alone, and you're out there somewhere with that stupid camera. If you get back before midnight, I still won't have any clothes on. If you get back after, take a cold shower."

He laughed and shifted.

"Mr. Graham."

He sat up abruptly, his eyes narrowed as he stared at the machine, his head slightly cocked. The voice was a girl's, flat, and touched with static.

"Mr. Graham."

The wind scraped sand across the concrete stoop.

"Mr. Graham, I want my picture."

The pane rattled briefly, the refrigerator coughed on.

"I want my picture back."

He pushed himself across the couch and reran the last message, then grabbed the telephone clumsily into his lap and snatched up the receiver. He had almost finished dialing Kelly Albertson's number when he remembered the time and hung up again. He didn't like practical jokes, and

22

he didn't like people who pretended they were calling from the far side of the grave.

"Mr. Graham, I want my picture."

He turned around.

The machine was off.

The August breeze turned cold when all the lights were dead, when the moon was finally gone and the stars too weak to touch the sea; it turned cold, and grew stronger, and gave itself a keening.

The boardwalk creaked as the wind passed over, sand spilling and gathering and running for the edge; Harragan's Pier whispered in rapidly cooling metal, laughed in clanking chains, groaned when the Ferris wheel made a slow quarter turn.

An unlatched door slammed against a wall. Once. The hinges like a nail drawn across a pane of glass. Once again. And the hinges.

The waves rose and broke early, out of the dark, curling and dying.

And the dark pier grew darker, killing the stars, the waves beneath it silent, a plywood board over the entrance pulling away from its screws with a shriek that reached no farther than the shadows on the boards; ash swirled, splinters fell, planks flared tiny sparks like rats' eyes in an alley.

Behind the barrier was a ticket booth standing alone, roof peaked and window caged; no price ever posted, no specials for children.

Below the sill, where money had been exchanged for a ticket or two, a brass plaque untouched by the fire, small enough to cover the length of a young man's hand; the words etched in black, reflecting nothing until something passed it, soundless in the wind, shadowless and small.

And when it was gone, the plaque was crooked, a pendulum swinging slowly, scraping against charred wood, loosening clumps of ash that shattered against the boards and fell between the cracks and were buried in the sand when the wind rode in against the tide.

An hour before dawn the plaque fell.

When the sun rose, the plaque was blooded, and on it, *The House of Night.*

TWO

FIFTY yards north of the dark pier's shadow, the boardwalk dipped and vanished into a double row of dunes
that stretched for another mile, to the end of Oceantide's reach. The beach here was somewhat narrower and
curved slightly outward to the east, and the three-story
houses facing the sea were close together, their ground
floors blinded by the height of the dunes, their porches extending on thick posts from the second story, into the wind.

Behind them was the first of two winding, unpaved
streets that were little more than pebbled alleys separating
the buildings for the mailman's sake. The inland row faced
Summer Road, and these homes were on much larger plots
that in lieu of an ocean view satisfied themselves with low
brick- or cinder-block walls, wind-bent trees, and struggling
green yards that had to be watered several times a day.

Tony glowered at the squared lawn described by the chest-high wall, glared at the lawn mower through the sliding glass door. As he watched a sea gull land in a flurry, peck once and leave, he decided he'd rather be working at the diner because this was the pits. But like a dope he'd volunteered that morning because he thought he'd get back to the beach that much sooner.

He had also been hoping for some peace and quiet, and a chance to think in daylight about what had happened the night before.

What he hadn't counted on were the damned sharp pebbles flying at his shins from under the spinning blades, the harsh grass that stabbed at the soles of his bare feet. Or his goddamned nosy sister.

"Anthony, why aren't you doing what Momma told you to?" a stern voice said from the stairs at the far side of the large room.

He turned away from the lawn and thumbed his nose at the girl who was trying to sound as if she were twenty years older, not letting her know how she'd stopped his heart in his chest. Little creep.

"I'm taking a break, do you mind?" he said, and turned his back again.

Angie, sunbright hair carelessly bundled atop her head, padded across the carpet to stand beside him. "Taking a break from what?" she said, popping her gum loudly and pulling at the top of her striped bathing suit. "I don't see where you did anything."

"There," he said, jabbing a finger toward the righthand corner, "to there," over by the evergreen in the opposite corner, barely higher than the wall. "And what am I doing, justifying my existence to you anyway?"

She looked up at him, eyes wide. "What does that mean, Tony?"

Slowly he turned his head but couldn't tell from her blinking expression if she was kidding or not. He never could anymore; she was learning too fast. "Never mind."

"You always say that."

"You're too young."

"I'm ten years old!"

"Big deal."

"But that's ten years, Tony!"

"And that's too young."

She pouted. "Nuts. It's always too young. I can't even stay in the house by myself."

"Tough," he said.

"Men," she said disdainfully and stalked out of the room. And returned immediately. "Please give me a call when my ride comes. I'll be slaving at the stove."

He couldn't help a laugh, especially when she stuck out her tongue, waggled her shapeless bottom, and vanished again with a kick back of one heel. Then he slid open the door, flipped down his sunglasses and marched toward the mower; five minutes later he dragged it to the base of the house and ran inside. There was blood on his forearm from a thrown twig that should have been powdered in the grind of the blades.

"Jesus."

"I heard that," Angie screamed from the kitchen upstairs.

"Go to hell," he shouted back.

"You go to hell for cursing, you know, and I'm gonna tell Momma!"

Go ahead, he thought, I dare you. And spun about when a car braked in the graveled drive. Instead of calling his sister, he waited, holding his breath and crossing his fingers, while Frances Kueller honked the horn once before getting out and opening the gate in the side wall.

"Thank you, God," he whispered.

Today she was wearing a pale, two-piece bathing suit under a filmy white beach jacket; her long legs were made longer by the heels that she wore, her figure accentuated by the tiny lines of untanned skin that rose above the lines of her suit.

27

Tony unconsciously sucked in his stomach.

Whenever she smiled, he was blinded; whenever she touched his arm, he had to take deep breaths and go find a quiet room where he prayed it wasn't a sin to think about women as old as she.

She saw him watching and waved.

He returned the wave and slid open the door just as she reached it. "Hi! Angie's upstairs, I'll call her."

"Thanks, Tony. You're a doll."

She smiled as he turned to walk away, and he kept his back straight, his stride firm as he made for the stairs that led to the living room just above.

He called for Angie.

She told him to go to hell.

He looked over his shoulder and shrugged—one tolerant adult to another—while Mrs. Kueller laughed.

"Angela, your ride is here," he called sweetly. And listened as she ran to a front window, realized he was telling the truth, and raced down the stairs past him, into her bedroom at the back of the house, and out again, sunglasses on, bulging beach bag on her arm.

"Please don't forget to finish the lawn, Anthony," she said as she left the house, and Mrs. Kueller laughed again, blew him a kiss, and followed in his sister's wake.

"Oh god," he said, and dropped heavily onto the steps. "Oh god, it just ain't fair."

He lay back and sighed for the women who would be too old by the time he was old enough for them to notice, and stared at the ironwork railing that framed the top of the stairwell.

Black iron.

Black wood.

And his stomach tightened with a chill, his toes curling over the edge of the carpeted stairs.

It had been a dream, of course; it couldn't have been anything else. Neither Kelly nor Mike had either seen or heard the woman, and when he had tried to tell them about it after the sun woke them up, they'd wondered aloud with loud laughter if he'd found a bottle in the sand.

By the time he'd returned home, he'd known it was a dream.

Ironwork.

Woodwork.

Charred wood he could smell even here in the house.

"Stop it."

Quickly he snapped to his feet and went into his bedroom. Angie's room was next to his, a bathroom between them, and he stood at the basin and watched himself in the mirror. He guessed there'd have to be signs or something—twitches, pop-eyes, a maniacal smile—if he was really going crazy, but all he saw was Tony, a nice, young fourth-generation Italian boy who was driving himself nuts.

He sneered at himself.

A long shower then to take care of the sweat, another check in the mirror to be sure he was still Tony.

Then he wrapped a towel around his waist, ran a brush through his hair, and returned to his room, shivering at the air conditioning his mother always kept too high. He looked for a moment at the single unmade bed, the dresser, the desk, the stereo, the black-and-white portable television propped crookedly on a pile of magazines. He puffed his cheeks. It was the same. Nothing had changed. This was Tony's place, and there were no ghosts that he could see.

A shirt, then, and jeans, sneakers without socks, and he walked into the family room just in time to see a robin slam into the glass door, fall to the ground, and raise one tattered wing.

"Jesus," he whispered, and ran across the carpet. And stopped as a hand reached for the handle.

The bird struggled to its feet, trembling, eyes wide, and hopped to the grass where it fell on its side.

He didn't want to watch, and he couldn't look away, and the bird rolled back to its feet with a hitch and a shake, and made its way slowly to the tree. There was shade, a dark pool of it, and the robin seemed to lean against the trunk before moving around to the other side.

He opened the door and stepped out, the tip of his tongue pushing the corner of his mouth.

When he leaned over, he could see a blur on the glass where the bird had struck it, a smear of something not blood he couldn't bring himself to touch. Then he ran to the evergreen, grabbed the bole, and spun around it.

The robin was gone.

A feather danced on the grass.

And the telephone rang . . .

. . . the telephone rang, black lightning in the dark, and he groaned as he fumbled for the receiver. When he couldn't find it, he cursed and sat up, fumbled again for the light and shook the sleep from his head when he realized he wasn't in his room.

Another groan, this time for the raucous thunder that rocked gleefully in his head, and he pressed his palms to his temples and tried to squeeze it out.

"Don't drink much, do you?"

He yelled, and in his haste to get out of bed, his legs tangled in the sheets and he cartwheeled off the mattress, landed on his shoulder and rolled over until he was sitting against the wall, hands braced on the floor, his mouth wide to find some air.

The telephone rang.

The bedsprings creaked.

A head rose from the dark and drifted into the fall of light, and Julie smiled cheerfully from behind a damp veil of long hair.

"God," he said.

"No, just me."

A spattering of rain made him look awkwardly up and back, to a window streaked with rain. It wasn't his window. It wasn't any window in his house. God, where the hell was he?

As she finger-brushed her hair away from her eyes, she moved closer to the edge, and he couldn't help staring—her shoulders were bare, and when she lifted herself up to rest on her forearms, the rest of her was too.

He looked down in panic, then grabbed the corner of the dangling sheet and pulled it over his lap.

The telephone rang again and he said, "Aren't you going to answer it?"

"Nope." Her nose wrinkled. "It's my mother, making sure all the windows are closed."

"But she'll think you're not home!"

She nodded. "Probably."

"My god," he said, looking wildly around for his clothes, "she'll come back!"

"I doubt it. She's at a party. She'll just bitch in the morning if anything gets wet."

He couldn't understand how she could be so calm when he was going to die any minute now. Mrs. Etler was going to come charging through the door, guns blazing, and blow him away for seducing her daughter.

He rubbed a hand over his face and, careful to keep the sheet in its place, scrambled to his knees. His clothes were here somewhere, god, he couldn't have left the party naked. And he froze for a moment: party. A last-minute party at Kelly's house. The Albertsons had gone to the movies or something, there was a bunch of kids, and somehow he had ended up . . . in the kitchen? Talking with Julie. Wanting to know why, with only a couple of months to go, she had dropped out of college. She'd laughed and touched his cheek and reached behind her for a bottle she'd taken from the dining room breakfront. She had offered him a drink. He took it and choked, took another and choked again with tears in his eyes, and by the end of the third one had his arms around her waist.

Oh shit, he thought.

He was still on the floor, at the end of the bed, and somehow his shirt had found its way into his hands.

31

"Tony," she said, sitting now in twilight, half of her lighted, half of her dark. "Tony, it's all right." Her hands were in her lap. Shadows from the rain traced across her skin, lingered on her breasts, were banished in the sheen of perspiration across her stomach. "Tony, you didn't rape me, you know."

He wanted to deny he'd thought any such thing. Nothing came out but a groan, and he sagged back onto his heels. Head down. Both hands buried in his shirt. Angry at himself for being drunk when his first time arrived, furious at her for giving him the drink. It was stupid. He was stupid. This was the way college kids did it, and he didn't want it that way.

"Tony."

Calm, he ordered; be calm.

"Tony."

He looked.

She was smiling, the curious one-sided smile with the slight tilt of her head, the one that had entranced him since she'd first moved to the shore. She was older, and he'd only dreamed, but in the dreams being older didn't mean a thing.

"This time," she whispered. "You'll remember this time, I guarantee it."

"Your mother . . ."

And suddenly she laughed, high-pitched, trilling, tossing her hair side to side as if it were a mane as she crawled across the mattress, reached out and grabbed his arm. He resisted automatically. She grinned and yanked him close, so close he could see the freckles that made a starnight of her forehead, the gold in her eyes, the abrupt lines of her nose. Then she took his left hand and put it against her breast.

She kissed him, and he followed her, sliding over her, propped above her, so painfully in love he turned his head to hide the tears.

"Tony," she whispered. "Tony."

The telephone rang . . .

32

. . . and he blinked away that April night as he picked up the receiver.

They'd never made love again, though god knew he'd wanted to, and sometimes he could still feel every inch of her body. Now she was dead. Five days in the ground, where she shouldn't have been; five days when she couldn't tell him why she hadn't let him come back, and why women, somehow, no longer looked the same.

"Hello out there?" a voice said in his ear. "Earth to Riccaro, are you there?"

He remembered the robin.

"Damnit, Riccaro, obscene phone calls are supposed to work the other way around!"

"Sorry, Mike," he said. "I was thinking."

"Oh jeez, my heart, the world's coming to an end. What the hell are you doing thinking in summer anyway? God, that's disgusting."

He explained about the robin; Julie's night faded.

"Dazed," was Mike's instant judgment when the explanation was done. "They do it all the time. They can't see the glass, they see something inside, flowers or whatever, and they think it's someplace they can go. He's got a headache, that's all, don't worry about it."

Tony sprawled on the living room couch so he could look out the picture window at Summer Road and the larger houses on the other side. His foot tapped the armrest; he couldn't stop it, nor could he stop flinching every time a shadow flew past.

"So look, Tony, you still going to the beach? For the stupid picture?"

"Sure."

"What're you gonna wear?"

"I don't know. The usual."

"The usual? Are you kidding, Riccaro? The usual?"

"Sure, what's the matter with that?"

33

Mike forced a sigh. "No ambition, you know that? You ain't got no sense of ambition, and you look like it too. A man with ambition's gotta look the part, man. He's gotta show some style, some class."

Tony grinned. "It's gonna be ninety zillion degrees today. What kind of ambition am I going to have, to be a fireman?" He shifted his gaze to the floor when the windows across the road began to flare the sun back. "Why? You got a plan? I don't want to hear it."

"Why not? Don't you trust me?"

It was his turn to sigh, but it became a laugh he couldn't stop despite his friend's yelling. And when he calmed, a hand hard to his chest to force the giggles away, he heard the silence on the other end, and he frowned. Mike was taking things too seriously these days.

"All right," he surrendered. "Shoot."

"That's better," Mike said, and cleared his throat. "I think we oughta get dressed up. Do it right. Suit, tie, the works."

Tony grinned. "You are nuts, Nathan. You are out of your freaking skull."

"No! No, I mean it, pal, no kidding. I mean . . . like this is going to be the last time, you know? Almost the last time, anyway. Sort of. You want to remember me in a bathing suit, for Christ's sake?"

"Yes," he said. "Now get off the line, creep. I'll see you this afternoon."

Mike sputtered a lot, swore vengeance, and just as Tony was about to ring off, called his name.

"Now what? And I'm not wearing a tuxedo."

There was a pause. "Hey, Tony?"

"Yeah."

"I'm sorry about last night. You know? I'm sorry."

Tony sat up, the telephone heavy in his lap. "Me too."

"We were jerks, right?"

"Perfectly."

"Good."

"Now go away."

Mike laughed, was still laughing when Tony set the receiver gently on its cradle, the telephone on the sidetable, stood up and stretched. He had several hours before meeting the guys to get their picture taken, a present to each other, and he surprised himself by using one of them to walk through the house.

Slowly.

Tunelessly humming.

Wandering through his parents' room where he saw his yearbook picture on the vanity and his father's navy picture on the bedtable, and his own graduation profile facing the bed from the dresser; through the spare room his cousin Charlene was using now; through the Angie-cleaned kitchen where he opened the cupboards and cabinets, peered into the oven, opened the refrigerator and stared; through the dining room where somehow he could smell the last birthday party—Angie's tenth, last month—candles smoking, icing, sharp candies, a hint of wine; through the family room, switching on the television, switching it off, hunkering down to stare sideways at the albums in the stereo cabinet, touching the spines when he found one too old for him to remember right away; standing at Angie's door to count the stuffed animals ranged across her bed, raise an eyebrow at the posters of rock stars and cowboys, take a deep breath and smell the talc and the fresh sheets and the crayons and the perfume his aunt had given her that she couldn't wear until next year.

The house was large enough for them all, and too small for him now.

In less than a week he'd be gone, up to a campus in New England, and the next time he returned he'd only be visiting, not staying.

The telephone rang.

He didn't go into his own room because he knew it too well, and because three days ago he had taken Julie's picture from his wallet and had stuck it in the bottom drawer of the desk, under the clippings of his matches that had made the local papers. She was dead. He didn't need it; he could remember her quite well.

But she hadn't loved him again.

She was dead, and with a grunt he decided that he'd be damned if he'd go away without finding out why.

The telephone rang.

He ignored it. Instead, he stood at the front door and watched the summer traffic crowd by, rubbing one arm as he squinted against the glare. The harsh light bothered him, and he didn't know why. But it bleached color from the sky and faded all the cars, reminding him of a photograph that had been overexposed. He blinked several times and narrowed his eyes even more, blurring it all to a color that almost resembled white.

And snapped them open again when he realized the road was empty. It happened that way sometimes; a traffic light in town and one up at Seaside stopped it all for just a moment, and in that moment all movement ceased on Summer Road as well. The lingerers were gone, no bicycles or motorbikes, and it was as if winter had returned and all the tourists had gone home.

Except for the heat.

The telephone rang.

"All right, all right," he muttered. It was probably his father wanting to know if he was having fun, or his mother reminding him to lock the doors when he left.

He picked up the receiver.

A robin slammed into the window.

THREE

ow this, thought Mike as he slid into a corner
booth at the Summerview Diner, is the way God
meant weather to be—cool, a fair breeze from
above, and tinted oval windows to tame the sunlight and
save his eyes. It was only a matter of time before the man
who invented air conditioning was going to be made a
saint.

He had practically run all the way from the house after
talking with Tony, ignoring the heat until it almost
slammed him to the pavement. Now he was paying for trying to prove he could still do it, and he took his pulse,
deliberately slowed his breathing, and with a low grunt
banished the throbbing in his hip. Then he yawned and
picked up a two-foot, laminated menu, glancing down the
page without seeing a single item because after all these

years he couldn't remember Tony's father ever changing a thing; and besides, all he had ever wanted was a hot dog, all the trimmings, and a large glass of chocolate milk.

But it was something to do now, something to kill time until he had to go to the beach. There was no sense looking around; he already knew what the place looked like because that had never changed either—eight high-backed booths on either side of the entrance, a counter so long it was split in the middle for the waitresses to pass through, walls darkly stained to resemble the sea and draped with fishing nets, lanterns hanging from the ceiling, and restrooms marked with a fisherman and a mermaid.

If he tried hard enough, he could even probably remember how many holes there were in the acoustical tiles above the lanterns.

His mother said it was tacky, but she'd never tasted the food; his father said it was an eyesore because of the neon waves on the roof; and most of his friends came here because Sal Riccaro never yelled when they ran short of cash.

The menu dropped to the table.

He cupped his chin in a palm and stared out the window.

Despite the fact that it was only a few minutes past noon, the diner was nearly empty, and the few customers at the counter and the other booths weren't exactly giving his eavesdropping skills a workout. In fact, their conversations were so quiet, he felt like he was in church, and when he shifted his silverware to one side and the fork clanged against the knife, he winced and looked around as though someone else was guilty.

Weird, he thought, and looked back at Summer Road, at the shops under striped awnings clustered on the other side—a drugstore, several clothing and shoe stores that would close the moment Labor Day was over, and the neon-marked side entrance to the Sand 'N Surf Motel whose front was around the corner. The road itself was four lanes wide for the seven blocks of the business district, and he wondered what had happened to the plan that would have put trees and benches on center islands.

He leaned forward, to look up to the next block, sat back and looked down a block.

Nothing different.

Nothing changed.

It was like watching a movie for the seven hundredth time, hoping that this time you would see something new.

But over there, same as always, was Stump Harragan, heading north and carrying money bags to the bank on the next block, his white shirt blinding even behind the tinted glass, his Bermuda shorts baggy, and his argyle kneesocks sagging close to his ankles; Prayerful Mary, a red-faced stout woman in a violet muumuu, reaching into a wire trash can, her straw hat flopping, the spangled heels of her cowboy boots flashing as she bent over; little kids racing on skateboards, bigger kids cruising in convertibles, once in a while a shirtless and shoeless guy parading past on a bike with a girl clinging to his back. He straightened for a moment when he thought he saw Devin's Jeep, but when it slowed for the corner light, he realized he was wrong, and he slumped again and sighed.

"You want something?"

His eyes moved, not his head.

"Hi, Charlene," he said to the waitress, Tony's cousin from up north who was making his life hell.

"You want something or not?"

"Hot dog," he answered quickly, because he knew that wasn't what she wanted to hear. For some reason she spent every summer with the Riccaros, working days at the diner and walking the boards most of the night, carrying some stuffed animal or other in her arm while she smiled at every guy whose clothes cost more than her wages.

She smiled at him often enough too, and he didn't need Kelly's bitching to tell him what she was thinking, even though he knew what she saw—a tall kid without much shape, with sunbleached mousy hair cut too short for the times, and a nose that wrenched to the left where it had been broken two years ago in a fight he'd had with one of his cousins. Not even a bully, for god's sake; not even in a football game. A cousin who had made one crack too many about the way he walked.

"Hot dog, huh?" she said, scribbling the order on her pad. "Anything else, Doc?" A smile from a mouth gleaming with too much lipstick, eyes with too much makeup; a calico uniform too snug for the weight she carried, and an expression that was less leering than it was wistful. "Dessert?"

He shook his head. "Chocolate milk."

"Bad for your skin," she said, touching a finger to his cheek. "Men need clear skin, you know what I mean? Turns a woman off, you don't got clear skin."

"My skin's fine," he said, abruptly nervous. "It's my stomach that needs help now."

"Sure thing, Doc. You're first on my list." And she touched his cheek again, winked, and strolled away, making sure she took her time in case he was watching.

He squirmed and looked up at the sky, down at the pavement, back to the menu to read every word.

Julie hadn't been like that, he thought; she didn't even ask him about his limp, and when he finally told her, she didn't say she was sorry. Broken hips happen, was all she'd said, and sometimes they don't heal right, that happens too. He hadn't been offended; she was only telling him it was no big deal to her so why should it be to him.

And it wasn't.

His walk, when he moved slow, seemed only a mild swagger unless closely watched; the only time it was blatant was when he tried to run too fast or take too long a stride. His left hand drifted down to his hip and touched it, prodded it, felt nothing except the way the bone seemed somehow too large, not quite where it belonged. Then he snapped the hand away and scowled at the table. No big deal, he reminded himself; it's no big deal, so knock it off, forget it.

He shifted again, absently arranging the silverware in front of him, the paper place mat, the glass of water, all of it just so. As if he were in surgery, readying the instruments that would prevent yet another child from suffering his affliction.

And as he did, he remembered something else Julie had said, one of the last things she'd ever told him before she went out on the pier.

"Mike," she said, "your being a doctor is the dumbest thing you ever thought of in your life."

He stared at her, knowing full well his mouth was wide open and his hands were curling into fists. "What the hell do you mean by that?" he demanded.

He had been walking home from the beach, thinking about July ending, leaving only August before the end of life on this planet as he knew it. He had just passed the recessed, pebbled entrance to the Sand 'N Surf Motel when she came out, swinging an oversize straw bag in her right hand. A bathing suit halter provided a top for her skirt, and her hair was tied back in a hasty, tangled ponytail. Sunglasses too large for her face. No makeup. There were creases on her legs, the kind a sheet makes when it's lain on too long.

He almost looked away, pretending not to know her in case she was embarrassed, but she fell immediately in beside him and asked him to take her to lunch.

"I'm supposed to meet Kelly," he said, glancing over his shoulder in hopes of seeing the guy.

"She can wait, Doc. We have to talk."

He would have argued, Kelly was going to scream at him for being late again, but Julie had already taken hold of his arm and was leading him across the street. Not to the Summerview. Instead, they headed two blocks south to the Hamburger Onion, a strictly summer place with too many tables crowded into too small a room, and only ceiling fans to shift the stale air. None of his friends ever ate there unless the diner was crowded.

A table near the kitchen door was empty, and she bulled her way through those waiting at the take-out counter in back, dropped the bag onto the floor, and waited for him, hands cupped under her chin, sunglasses pushed up on her head.

He was nervous as he joined her. He didn't want Kelly to know he was with another woman, and he couldn't help remembering the hints Tony had dropped, about what had happened one night back in April. Nor could he help it when she shifted her elbows closer and his gaze kept drifting toward the rise of her tanned breasts.

Kelly would kill him if she saw because he wasn't being too cool about the looking, but more than once he'd wondered if she'd rather have him blind—if, the wondering continued, she'd rather have him at all.

"So," he said with a forced smile. "What?"

"You ever go to church?"

He sat back abruptly in the tiny wooden chair. "Huh?"

"I asked if you ever went to church, Mike." She wasn't smiling; neither were her eyes.

He didn't know what to say and was altogether too effusive when the waitress came to take their order. When she told him there were no hot dogs, didn't he read the menu in the window? he settled for a soda, while Julie ordered a special.

"Time's up," she said when they were alone.

"I guess," he finally answered. "Sometimes. It isn't a big thing with the Nathans, you know?"

Without taking her eyes from him, she fumbled a pack of cigarettes from her bag. "Lousy habit," she said, lighting one and blowing the smoke over his head. "Doctors should never smoke, Doc. It's bad image stuff, you know what I mean?"

"I don't," he said, trying to figure out what was going on.

"Good. It'll kill you."

He grinned, let it fade, watched her stub out the cigarette and promptly light another. Then she turned to the wall and made a show of examining the faded print of a bullfighter taped over the table. "It's a bitch," she muttered.

"What is?"

"Church, among other things." She looked straight at him then. "It's a guilt trip, that's all. Do this or that'll happen; do that, or you're damned. It's a bitch, Doc, you'd better believe it."

He should have known it—she was drunk, probably still drunk from the night before, from whatever party she'd been to. Or maybe she'd been with a guy who didn't treat her right, but she loved him anyway and couldn't make up her mind whether to leave him or not. Then what about Tony? She had been with him, and she didn't love him—at least that's what Tony said—so maybe she's just learned she has a terrible disease and she's trying to find out if there's a heaven or not.

"Figure it out?" she said with a half-smile, pushing her untouched plate away.

"I . . . no." He hated it when she read his mind; it was the same with Kelly.

"You want to be a doctor, right?"

"Sure."

"You want to make sure no one else ends up like you."

It wasn't said in malice; he nodded solemnly.

"Mike, your being a doctor is the dumbest thing you ever thought of in your life."

"What the hell do you mean by that?"

She lit another cigarette; the other still burned in the tin ashtray. A ribbon of smoke got into her eye, and she damned it as she wiped away a tear with the back of her hand.

"You just want to go to school," she said at last. "Doctors take a long time, longer than most. I've seen it before, you know. All you want to do is hide."

He stood, fists pressed against his thighs. "What the hell do you know about me?" he demanded, lowering his voice when he felt people staring. "You can't even stay in school yourself, so where do you get off, huh?"

"That's easy," she said, looking back at the bullfighter. "I'm just as scared as you are. Only with me, it's dying."

The hot dog was great, the chocolate milk just right, and he leaned back and belched softly, something he read that the Germans or someone did to show their appreciation for a really great meal. Then he grinned at Charlene, who was loitering by the counter's near end. She grimaced at him and held her nose, waving a hand in front of her face.

Obviously she didn't know about the Germans. And just as obviously she was going to come on to him again if he didn't get his ass in gear and get out to the beach for some rays before Devin took that picture.

He wondered if he would miss her, watched her turn sideways and arch her back in a slow stretch. A little on the hefty side maybe, but really not so bad. It might even be fun, he decided, to call her bluff just once before he left, and take her out. Maybe she's really secretly rich. God, maybe with her clothes off she's the woman of my dreams.

Right, he thought; and I'm a goddamn stud.

He picked up his glass and caught the last drop on his tongue.

Tony was going to New England.

He put the glass down.

He was going to California.

And Kelly . . . Kelly was going to the same university as he; but once she saw what the rest of the world was like,

44

he was going to lose her. He knew it. High school sweet-hearts didn't stand a chance when someone turned on the lights.

And to make it worse, so worse he couldn't think about it without wanting to throw up, he didn't have just four years and then pick up a diploma and join the world; hell, no. He, smartass Michael Bernard Nathan, was going to be a doctor. And not just a plain doctor in a small hick town in the country either—he was going to be a surgeon. A zillion bucks and a new Cadillac a year while she got sick of waiting and went off with some bum who looked good on a surfboard.

doctors take a long time longer than most

He frowned and turned his fork over and over in his hand—if she was so scared of dying, why had she been on the pier?

Oh Jesus, he thought; maybe somebody killed her.

"You look like hell."

With a startled gasp he shoved back in his seat, a palm clamped over his heart, his throat closed tightly. "Christ, Charlene, don't ever do that, huh? You could give a guy a heart attack, you know it?"

Charlene gathered up his plate and glass and leaned over, grinning, letting him see she'd undone her top two buttons. "I guess you'd need mouth-to-mouth, right?"

"That's for drowning," he said weakly, not knowing where to look.

"Same thing in my book, Doc. Besides, it couldn't hurt, right?"

She left when a customer called impatiently from the other side of the diner, and he closed his eyes, took several deep breaths. He'd seen Kelly in a hundred bathing suits that showed him more than that, but god, this was some-how different—the image of faintly freckled breasts large enough to smother him, the scent of fresh talc, that god-

45

damn look in her eyes, made him glad the diner wasn't busy. There was no way he'd be able to stand now without embarrassing himself to death.

The heat, he decided with a glance outside; it's all this damn heat. It's doing weird things to your mind, man, dumb things, knock it off, you jerk, before you get your ass in trouble. Besides, she's practically old, older even than Julie, though he remembered seeing an article someplace that said that older women liked younger men because they had more stamina or something.

He blinked.

He leaned over and looked down the aisle, hoping to catch a look without Charlene catching him.

And Salvatore Riccaro slapped him lightly on the back of his head.

"You messing around with my waitresses, son?" the man said, scowling.

Mike immediately shook his head at the burly, white-aproned man. "No sir, Mr. Riccaro. I wouldn't do that."

Riccaro glided a finger along his thick greying mustache, then traced a pale scar that slipped along his cheek, shaped like a lightning bolt. "You sure, son?" His eyebrows were almost comically dense, and he raised one to echo the question while his hand came to rest on the table.

"Me?" He pointed down the aisle. "With her?"

"Hey, what's the matter with Miss Iano?" Riccaro snapped, both eyebrows up now, the mustache fairly twitching. "You got something against my family? You figure she's from up north, she's a slob or something, huh?"

Mike swallowed hard, praying suddenly for a tidal wave, an earthquake, even Tony.

Riccaro glared at him, brow lowered now and eyes squinting, and reached into a trouser pocket and pulled out a five-dollar bill. "You pay the check, son?"

"Sure I did!"

The bill was slapped into Mike's hand.

"No."

Mike stared at the money.

And Riccaro finally smiled. "You don't pay nothing in here from now until you get outta my life, you understand, boy? Now get the hell outta here before I call Charlene over and tell her you want to marry her."

Mike grinned but didn't say a word. A look of thanks, and he was out of the booth and hurrying down the aisle, pausing at the register long enough to scoop a handful of mints into his pocket before pushing out into the tiny lobby where there were two empty newspaper dispensers, and two video games that had been out of order since July. A look to the righthand door, and he chose the left one instead, slipping on his sunglasses as he took the three steps to the sidewalk and checked his watch.

And the notion came again: maybe somebody killed her. If that's right, he'd better say something to the guys. Maybe . . . maybe even Devin.

Kelly, though, probably couldn't care less; even at the funeral last weekend, she hadn't dropped a tear, had even managed to look bored. They had fought about it that night, in fact. He accused her of being heartless; she told him to shut up, what did he know, he'd probably fucked her.

She'd never said that word all the years he had known her, much less accused him of being unfaithful.

When she said it again, he'd walked out the door.

A tap on the window over his head.

He looked up, and Charlene was leaning into an empty booth; she was sticking out her tongue and laughing.

He saluted her, blew her a kiss, and walked on.

Not so bad a day after all, he decided, in spite of Julie's ghost; by the time the sun set, he would probably have every woman in town panting after his body.

And maybe, if he was going to lose Kelly anyway, he might as well do it in style.

FOUR

KELLY jumped and yelped, "Hey, watch it, mister!" to the bald, sunburned man on the other side of the counter. He ducked his head in apology, tried a smile she finally returned, and halfheartedly threw his last two darts at the balloons tacked to the scarred, chipped wall behind her. They missed, didn't even come close, and he ducked his head again, as though he'd committed some sort of sin. The other dart, his first throw, she retrieved from the shelf of stuffed animals on her left, out of the stomach of a panda with a ribbon tied around its neck.

It had almost caught her ear.

The man moved on.

"Win it all at Balloon Heaven!" she cried. "Three throws for a quarter."

Awkwardly she shifted on the high wood stool her boss

had provided and watched the faces, the outfits, the tourists flow past. Birds in tropical plumage, and all the colors bleached by the glare of the sun; even the tans seemed pale, and the shadows darker for it.

And the noise, somehow fragile, somehow false—the grind and roar of the rides on Harragan's Pier, the music and pitches from the stands, the talk, the chatter, the shrieks, the laughter. A river of constant sound far more shallow than it seemed.

"Win it all here! Best chance on the boards!"

God, she thought, I'll go to hell for sure.

Her stomach rumbled loudly and she patted it silent with a resigned sigh. She was hungry, practically starving, but Jimmy had taken away her lunch hour in exchange for the afternoon off. It was a pain, but she had no choice, not if she wanted that picture done right. Besides, he wasn't such a bad guy for a summer boss; at least he didn't keep trying to cop a feel or look down her blouse or anything like that, not like some of the others she'd worked for, especially at night.

"Hey, you two," she called with a practiced smile, picking out a young couple walking with a kid between them. She held up three darts. "Break a balloon, win a prize. It's easy, no kidding. Two bits a try."

The woman smiled, the man ignored her, the kid was too busy with a wobbly tower of cotton candy.

Fifty balloons of varied sizes and colors ranged along the concession stand's back wall, none of them completely filled, none of the darts very sharp. Break one, win a ticket; break two, pick a small doll; break three and take your choice from the yard-high, kid-high animals that looked over her shoulder with blind glass eyes.

A fan under the counter blew on her bare legs.

Her hair was pulled back in a loose ponytail, her bangs held away from her forehead by a pair of bobby pins, her T-shirt snug enough at Jimmy's mock-leering orders to attract the younger guys who spent more time flirting than aiming, more quarters than they wanted.

"Win an elephant! Three tries for a quarter!"

The stand next door was a wheel of fortune, machine-gun clattering every few minutes as fast as the shill could talk; on the other side, the right, the softball in a peach basket game, but the balls were slightly lumpy and the baskets were tilted just so.

She sipped from a warm can of diet cola and called to a trio of elderly women in straw hats and straw handbags.

The wheel of fortune clattered.

A softball bounced over the counter to the boards.

From her spot in the corner she could see down to the next block, to the Ferris wheel turning slowly, the open cages slowly rocking.

She wished Jimmy would let her have a radio, but he claimed it would distract her.

"See, the deal is, little girl," he had told her back in June, "you gotta be ready, right? All the time you gotta be ready for the people, they're the ones that pay your salary. Heavy metal, that sort of crap, that isn't ready, that's loud. We don't want loud, right? Right. We don't want to force the people over, we want them to want to come on their own, get it? You force them, they get bitchy, they don't spend the bucks. So all I want from you, darlin', is a pretty face, a pretty smile, and a wink for the little kids so they don't think they're being cheated."

Right, she thought sourly, absently stabbing the darts into the counter's side to dull them further, just like he'd taught her. Right.

"Win a teddy bear! Three tries for a quarter!"

The sun flared off the water, rose shimmering from the boards, and she touched at the sunglasses rocked high on her head: lotion and sweat and pizza and beer.

"Only wear 'em when you gotta," Jimmy had told her. "They gotta see your eyes. Mystery they can get at the fun house, got it? You, they want to see your eyes so they don't think you're laughing, if you know what I mean."

She covered a yawn with one hand.

"Win a genuine velvet lion! Three tries for a quarter!"

Julie had told her once that she had worked the boardwalk for five summers straight, doing everything from the ducking stool on Harragan's to waiting tables at the bars, and she'd laughed a bit sadly when she wondered aloud how much fun she had missed despite the money saved.

Kelly asked her if it had been worth it.

Julie said, "Damned if I know, Kell. I'm still figuring out why I'm still alive."

And ever since the fire, Kelly couldn't stop herself from wondering if her hatred for the woman had contributed to her death.

Jeez, she thought, a guilty glance around, that's awfully strong, don't you think? Hatred had nothing to do with the way Julie died. Nothing.

Four young soldiers in short-sleeved khaki, from Fort Dix, sauntered up, rolled their quarters at her, and tried their luck. They didn't talk. They only threw the darts. One at a time, each man in turn, until the last one was nudged by his friend just as he let go, and the dart landed on the counter, not an inch from her thumb.

"Hey!" she said, snatching the hand away.

The soldier laughed, his buddies slapped his back, and they moved on down to the wheel of fortune.

Kelly looked at the dart, at the frayed plastic feathers, and took a deep breath as she glanced out at the horizon. With the way her luck had been running lately, there was probably a prize-winning hurricane brewing there, just waiting for her, the worst in a decade. First she nearly loses an ear, then nearly gets punctured. She should have accepted Mike's invitation to have breakfast with him someplace instead of going straight home after waking again at dawn.

It had been there, at the house on Cockleshell Lane, that she'd seen the start of a truly bad day.

Her father was still out on the road, stuck someplace in North Carolina with his briefcase and samples, her mother was still in bed suffering a party the night before, and her sister was god knew where with god knew who doing she damned well knew what and was probably still at it.

Then, when she'd started out for work, the car had over-heated before she'd even gotten out of the driveway and she had to walk; some idiot in an overloaded station wagon had almost run her down outside the Summerview Diner; and when she finally got here, ten minutes late, already sweating and praying for a shower, Jimmy Opal had left the keys with the softball guy and a scribbled note that told her he'd be gone for the day, and though the afternoon was still hers, she couldn't leave until her replacement showed up, a girl whose name she didn't even know.

There was a blister forming on her left heel.

And counting the four soldiers, she'd had less than a dozen customers since starting up at ten.

Not even Mike had showed his face, and it was already past noon.

"Hello, are you there?"

She started, catching her hand before it traveled to her throat, and had to lean away slightly to focus on the bearded face that poked around the partition separating her stand from the wheel's.

"Oh, hi, Frankie," she said, smiling wanly, letting it fade.

"Hi yourself."

A yawn surprised her, but she didn't bother lifting her hand.

"Bored, huh?" His beard, like his hair, was light and cropped short, and all of it matched the unpleasant thatch of chest hair he exposed with a tight Hawaiian shirt opened to his belt. He was in his late twenties or early thirties; she had stopped guessing when he had started taking his breaks the same time as hers.

"Tell me."

"You wanna get married? I got the honeymoon suite at the Maya just for tonight."

She giggled in spite of herself; the Maya was painted purple and not known for its family appeal. "I'm underage, Frankie."

"I'm overage, so what?"

She looked away, at the drifting crowd.

"Better yet, why don't we trade," he said, his lips barely moving to help cover a lisp and to keep an unlit cigarillo from falling out. "I think I've made a whole buck, maybe two, since I opened. At this rate I couldn't sell a blind man if I gave him the numbers."

She pulled the dart from the counter, held it up, and sighted along its squat body. "You cheat, that's why."

"Who, me?" His eyebrows lifted. "I run an honest wheel, lady. Honest."

A doubtful look; he shrugged, shifted, and shook his head at the people who didn't look back.

"To tell you the truth, cross my heart and hope to die, I think it's the invasion of the zombies, Kelly. Television zombies. I bet I'd make a million if I added commercials to the pitch."

A little girl pushing a doll in a toy carriage stepped up to the counter. She held a quarter in her left fist and she stared at the balloons.

"Hey, kid," Frankie stage-whispered. "You'd do a lot better over here. I got candy, not stupid anteaters."

Kelly pointed; he vanished.

The wheel clattered to his pitch, but no one looked over.

I can't stand this much longer, she told herself then. It was truly a seriously bad day when a guy like Frankie Junston could make her smile instead of making her skin crawl.

The little girl slowly put the quarter down, and Kelly leaned over and smiled.

"Go for the red ones, honey," she said quietly, pointing the fatter ones out. "They break easier. But don't tell my boss, okay? He'll skin me alive."

The girl picked up the first dart, leaned over and said something to her doll, straightened, and threw. The balloon broke, and she didn't smile.

"We have a winner, folks!" Kelly called out automatically, holding up a striped ticket. "Two more and it's the grand prize, right here at Balloon Heaven!"

The second balloon broke, and Kelly applauded and laughed. She wished Jimmy was here because he hated to lose his stock, especially to kids, and she did everything she could to make sure they won.

The third dart missed.

"A winner, we got another winner!" she called, applauding louder and whistling. Then she slid off the stool and leaned over the counter. "Okay, honey, you can have any one of those dolls over there, okay? Just pick one and it's yours. How about the one in the wedding dress, the white one? It looks just like you, don't you think?"

The little girl walked away, pushing the carriage before her.

Kelly couldn't move for a moment, and by the time she'd swung onto the counter to look for the girl, the crowd had hidden her as if she hadn't been there at all.

"I'll be damned," she said, sitting on the edge and swinging her legs. It was the first time that had ever happened, and she wasn't sure what to do. She wanted to chase after her and give her the prize, but she didn't dare leave the stand unattended. If she did, that's for sure when Jimmy would show up and fire her on the spot.

The pay stunk, less than minimum wage since he had his people working slightly less than full time. But she needed it, every dime, because without it there'd be no college in the fall. The scholarship she'd won was small, and if she wanted to eat, she had to add to her savings. Her mother wouldn't do it, not even when she was sober, and her father . . . she grunted his face away and stared instead at the Ferris wheel at Harragan's, watching it swing up, swing away, cages rocking over the surf.

And suddenly thought of Devin and felt herself blushing. And just as quickly felt someone watching.

A waist-high, triple metal railing ranged along the far edge of the boardwalk, breaking only for the steps that led down to the beach. In front of it, and bolted to the boards, were long wooden benches whose slotted backs could be shifted so those resting could watch either the beach or the strollers. She usually saw mothers there, massaging their feet and feeding the toddlers, and guys trying to decide which moves should be made on which girls passing by.

Now a man sat alone, opposite Balloon Heaven. She couldn't tell if he was really staring at her or not because the crowd kept interfering, letting her see him for only a brief second at a time. But she could feel him—just sitting, not moving, here when the flow parted, gone when it closed.

Behind dark lenses that reflected nothing but dark.

It wouldn't be the first time she'd been the object of such attention, though it had taken her an entire season to get used to the fact that some men just liked to watch, without mayhem on their minds. But it didn't stop her from working up a good case of nerves, and she even considered asking Frankie if he would talk to the guy, ask him to turn the other way or move on down the boards, out of her sight.

The crowd closed; he was gone.

She leaned over to see if Mike was talking to Stump down at the pier.

The crowd parted; he was gone.

The bench was empty.

"Can I try, Kelly?"

"God!" she said loudly, nearly falling off the counter. She looked down and saw Angie Riccaro gazing innocently back, her hair damp and stringing to her shoulders, leaving glistening beads of water that shimmered when she moved.

Angie pointed at the darts.

"You're nuts," Kelly said without moving. "It's all a gyp, don't you know that by now? God, doesn't your brother tell you anything?"

"I don't care, I wanna try."

"Angie, you're wasting your money."

"So?"

She shrugged, swung her legs around with a feigned groan, and hopped to the floor. "You with Tony or what?" Picking up the darts, the points hot to burning. She stared at the crowd. "I thought he was working today."

Angie placed her quarter firmly on the counter, waited until Kelly had dropped it in the cash box, then held her first dart close to her cheek, the tip of her tongue poking between her lips. "He's mowing the lawn and goofing off. Mrs. Kueller brought me down. She's over there, trying to make out with the lifeguard."

Kelly nodded without speaking. There was something about Angie she didn't trust, something sneaky, the way she looked at people just a bit sideways, measuring them, deciding how far she could go before trouble. Like the way she'd hung around those first couple of nights after Julie's death, playing with her toy horses, then blabbing to her parents that the big kids were going to the dark pier, to find out why Julie had been the only one there the day it burned down.

The dart missed and bounced off the wall.

"Nuts."

Mr. Riccaro had stormed into the rec room and laid down the law to all of them. *She was stupid,* he'd said, furious at them, disgusted at Julie. *No one deserves to die, don't get me wrong, but she was stupid being there. You all know it, so drop it. Now.*

Angie pouted and glared at the balloons.

"Try again, you can still win a doll."

"A doll? Who wants a stupid doll?" Angie said with a sneer. "I want a poster." She scanned the shelves of prizes and sneered again. "So how come you don't have any posters, huh?"

"Ask the boss."

"Everybody else on the boardwalk has posters, y'know. I got posters all over my walls. I'm gonna start on the ceiling next, if my mother'll let me."

Kelly wasn't surprised, though she suspected it would be the girl's father who made the decision. From everything she'd seen, Mr. Riccaro would jump off the roof dressed like Superman if his daughter begged him hard enough. Her own father hadn't been home on her last birthday, and though he had called from St. Louis and talked to her for an hour, somehow, when she blew out the candles, it wasn't the same.

"I like cowboys best," the little girl said, testing her throw and aim without letting go. "Lots of guns and things, and horses. Lots of horses."

Kelly looked over her head at the faces that never once glanced in her direction.

"I'm gonna marry a cowboy when I grow up."

Then she threw her second dart and broke a balloon.

"A winner! We got another winner! Always a winner at Opal's Balloon Heaven!"

"You sound like a jerk," Angie said, giggling.

"It's the rule," she told her. "You break a balloon, I gotta shout."

Angie cocked a hip and closed one eye. "Suppose I lose?"

"You're out a quarter."

"It's a gyp."

Kelly shrugged. "That's not my problem. I already told you, remember? Throw, kid."

"Mrs. Kueller lets me swim without my tube, you know that?"

Kelly smiled: *that's nice.*

Angie lined up her shot again, her lower lip turned over, her tongue sticking out. She took a breath and held it, narrowed her eyes and stared at the balloons. Then she lowered her arm and looked over her shoulder. Kelly followed her gaze and saw nothing out of the ordinary or anyone she knew. When Angie didn't look back, she realized that the crowd had somehow slowed down. The rushed strolling was gone, the chatter was more quiet, which made the music and the rumble-roar from the rides all the more grating.

The fan blew on her legs; a headache lurked behind her eyes. She felt a sudden chill and rubbed her arm, for no reason at all thinking about Tony's dream. "You gonna stand there all day or what?"

Angie turned and threw in a single swift move, and Kelly gasped when she felt a stabbing at her shoulder.

"For god's sake, Angie!"

But Angie was gone.

And the dart dangled from her shoulder, its shadow running blood.

FIVE

I AM an idiot, thought Devin as he stood naked in the kitchen with hands firmly on his hips and wondered what in god's name he could put in his stomach that wouldn't taste like straw and gag him. He yawned. His jaw cracked. He snarled at the sink and at the cupboards above it. The alarm had wakened him just after eight, and he had promptly rolled over, slapped it off, and had fallen back to sleep.

Now it was near twelve-thirty, and he still felt as if he hadn't slept at all.

The noise outside didn't help—overlapping shouts and shrieks of games announced that he wasn't the only one still home; so, apparently, were all his summer neighbors and all their screaming children. They must have decided to have lunch here instead of at the beach for some goddamned reason, and the kids were taking out their disappointment on him.

He hoped they drowned the next time they went swimming.

"I do not deserve this, you know," he complained to the house as he postponed a decision by stumbling into the small bathroom, the tiles cold and gritty on his soles. He shouted when the shower gave him only cold water; he glared helplessly when the sink's faucet spent more time gurgling than running; and afterward he nodded a *why the hell not?* when he opened the refrigerator and wrinkled his nose at the stench of sour milk. For three days he'd been telling himself it was high time to clean out the old, go shopping for the new, and generally get his act together before ptomaine left him lying on the floor, the body not to be found until winter. But like calling Viceroy back, there was always something else to do, something more important; going to the market never felt as if it counted.

With a grimace he poured the milk down the drain and told himself he'd have to wait for his food, fitting punishment for his sloth, then dressed, combed his hair, and stood away from the bathroom mirror. Head tilted, chin up, searching for a hint of wattle or jowl, for the grey hairs and the bald spots, for the wrinkles that were already there in fine lines about his eyes and the corners of his mouth.

Too much sun, too much wind. A woman he'd known once remarked that the result made him look rugged, especially in autumn when everything but his shirts were worn-out denim and slightly ragged.

"Rugged," he said aloud, testing the word and watching his face. "Rugged."

Then he stuck his tongue out at the reflection and walked into the front room, where he opened the draperies and turned away from the sun.

It was afternoon already, the first time in months he had unintentionally overslept, and he was beginning to think maybe Gayle was right—his body knew him better than he did, and it was going to give him the rest he needed whether he wanted it or not. In fact, he admitted as he fetched the newspaper from the stoop, he did feel okay. Not half-bad at all, thanks to the cold shower.

He glanced at the headlines, saw nothing that interested him, and tossed the paper onto the couch. Sunlight warmed the room; the sound of distant surf rose and subsided, and with a deep breath that cleared his lungs of last night's smoke and sleeping, he decided, without argument or trace of guilt, to take the day off. The whole day, not just the part he'd slept through—every last minute and second of it. And that meant no cameras, no framing shots, no nothing. Today he was going to be a tourist.

He stretched and forced a yawn.

A brief moment, then, when something nudged the decision, a glimmering of something he was supposed to do. Something . . . then he looked at the phone machine.

"Tourist," he muttered; the glimmering was gone. "Who are you kidding, pal?"

No, not a tourist.

Today he was going to find out who had played at being a ghost.

And despite the distaste of memory, that too somehow buoyed his spirits, sending him into the bedroom for scuffed, untooled boots to keep the sand away from his feet, jeans that fit better than anything tailored, and a bright shirt with long sleeves he folded neatly to his biceps. A pair of sunglasses. A pack of cigarettes and a lighter. Wallet and keys.

At the door he automatically reached for the camera bag, realized what he was doing and stood for a moment, staring at it, frowning when that *something* he should be doing wouldn't give him a name. It'll come, he told himself then, and opened the door, nodding contentedly at the salt air and a steady strong breeze that made his eyes flutter closed as he took a series of deep breaths. White clouds lazy in the sky. A dragonfly poised at the top of the dunes.

Gulls gliding and hovering. The block finally quiet, touched with peace.

Indecision made him rub his palms together while he tried to figure out just how to play detective. Easier said than done. Talking to the kids would be a waste of time; he was certain neither Tony nor Kelly had done it, and even this was beyond the pale of one of Mike's outrageous pranks. What, then?

He stared at the newspaper.

Maybe it wouldn't hurt to have a word with Marty Kilmer, the only policeman on the local force who was an Oceantide native. It sounded right; he really didn't know. But probably there wasn't a thing the man could do for him. Still, he might be able to point him in the right direction, if there was a direction to follow at all.

Forgoing the Jeep because he still felt somewhat stiff from being in bed so long, he hurried to the corner and strolled up to Summer Road. When the breeze shifted, he could hear music from the boardwalk, racing engines, the voices of bathers in concert with the sea.

A police car siren, shrill and oddly out of place.

Half-expecting the cruiser to come shrieking up behind him, he headed north—slowly, in deference to the heat—peering in the cluttered shop windows and wondering as always what in hell people actually did with all the junk on display, junk that carried prices that would shame a city merchant. Wobbly ashtrays of polished seashells, tea towels with embroidered sailing ships, sailing ships in bottles, brown girls in grass skirts, woven straw hats, salt water taffy, toy lobsters and bathtub fish, glasses and mugs and plates and cups with scenes of an idyllic beach Jersey never had in its life.

He supposed most of it ended up in closets, in boxes stored in attics or basements, dragged out on moving day and weighed against the memories the sight of them sparked.

Like his earlier photographs, he decided, the ones he

used as yardsticks to measure his progress—they were necessary only when he told himself they were. The rest of the time they were gladly forgotten.

My, he thought with a briefly raised eyebrow, your mind is simply crawling with profundities today, Mr. Graham. You think you're going to need a shovel anytime soon?

He grinned and walked on, dodging pedestrians who paid him no heed, idly watching the traffic moving past the shops. As he passed the Summerview Diner and spotted Sal through one of the oval windows, his stomach lurched; but before he could head for the steps and the cool air inside, he promised himself food later. A carrot while he hunted, a reward for doing whatever had to be done.

At last, his head bowed and shoulders slumped under the drag of the sun, he came abreast of a block-long swath of well-kept lawn edged with whitewashed stones, and centered with a flagpole. The town hall. Single story in front, two stories behind, its fresh brick facade incongruous among the older clapboard buildings around it.

A sprinkler sprayed a tenuous rainbow over the grass, and he watched it for a while, and a pair of sparrows taking a bath, before turning into a narrow, shrub-lined walk that led to a wide doorway at the building's rear corner, the entrance to the police station.

But the closer he drew to the white, *Police*-marked globe jutting from the wall above the door, the more foolish he began to feel. Kilmer, a decidedly unimaginative man, was going to laugh him back onto the street for complaining about a mysterious message on an answering machine.

Jesus Christ, Dev, have you lost your effing mind?

And the more he thought about it, the slower he walked, his hands slapping his thighs. Less than five yards from the entrance, he stopped. It was, after all, only a voice. Realistically, nothing more than an unpleasant jolt at the end of a less than successful day. Coming at a time when he was tired, somewhat anxious, perhaps even overly receptive to anything that even faintly smelled unusual.

It was nothing more than a voice.

Only a voice that just happened to be hers.

The decision to leave was just about made when a patrol car abruptly raced out of the back parking lot, siren blaring as it bumped onto the street and swung south. He watched it for a moment, and started when a hand dropped hard on his shoulder.

"Turning yourself in, Graham?"

Devin barely moved. "You got a murderer on the loose?" he replied with a nod toward the speeding cruiser.

"Beats me," said Marty Kilmer. "I don't know what's going on, I just work here. Wouldn't surprise me, though. Not this week."

Devin gave the taller man a quick smile and wondered how his latest publicity campaign was faring—an attempt to get everyone to call him Martin now that he'd made sergeant. He suspected it wasn't working; despite the man's height and heft, his face was too young, his hair still too carrot-top bright. Martin was too sober; Marty was just right.

"So what's the matter, Dev? Don't tell me you've lost a dog or something."

Another patrol car passed them, engine racing, spinning lights dying, heading for its slot near the door. It parked with a jerk and bob, and two patrolmen yanked two men from the back seat and hustled them none too gently inside.

"A crime wave," Devin said lightly.

Kilmer only swept off his hard-peaked hat and wiped his brow with a grey-sleeved forearm. "I'll tell you something, Dev," he said solemnly, squinting up at the sky. "Just between you and me and the gatepost, the last two or three days have been a bitch around here, and I don't know if it's just coming on Labor Day or what. People are getting themselves mugged, robbed, pushed around by punks, you name it, and the chief's on our asses from dawn to quitting time. Christ, the whole place's falling apart, y'know? Next

64

thing you know, we're gonna be like all the other towns on the shore, for god's sake. Jesus, I should've been a priest. At least my mother'd be happy."

Devin commiserated with a grunt, trying not to smile because the man sounded like he'd been enforcing the town's laws sixty years instead of being only twenty-nine. At the same time, however, he was positive now that his own problem wasn't worth the trouble. Again he started to turn around, but Kilmer stopped him with a puzzled look.

"So, you got a beef or what? Your cameras gone? Your place trashed?"

He shrugged. "No, but . . . ," and he gestured toward the door, which swung open as if he'd willed it, and another patrol pair ran for their vehicle.

"Hey, look, it can't be any weirder than what I've seen lately. Even old Mary's acting off the wall, and that's saying something, you know what I mean? Do you believe, and I ain't shitting you, Dev, do you believe some idiot that runs a couple of concessions on the boards, a guy named Opal, Jesus Christ, he claims some of the other guys are using unfair business practices to keep him from earning a decent living." Kilmer dusted at his tight-fitting grey shirt. "Shit, Dev, I don't even know what the hell that's supposed to mean."

"Ghosts," Devin said then, trying not to sound as though he were accepting a dare.

Kilmer slapped on his hat, adjusted it carefully, and stared. "Ghosts?"

Oh lord, Devin thought, I should have stayed in bed.

"Well, not ghosts exactly. Only sort of."

The policeman hitched his gunbelt and stared again.

Quickly, and knowing how incredibly like an old maid he was sounding, he explained about the voice, reminded him about Julie Etler's death and burial when Kilmer frowned his ignorance of the name, and wondered aloud if there was anything he could do about it. He, Devin, that is; he had

65

already figured out that the police couldn't do a thing. Especially not with all this other stuff going on.

"Well, you're right there," Kilmer agreed without much regret. "If I were you, I'd pass it off as a sick joke and leave it at that."

"Yeah. I guess." And winced when his stomach growled loudly.

The policeman laughed loudly and slapped his shoulder. "First thing, pal, you'd better get yourself something to eat before you keel over and I have to scrape you up. Second thing, let me know if it happens again. It ain't obscene calls, nothing like that, so we can't bother the phone company, but maybe we can think of something, okay?"

There was nothing else to say. Devin nodded, shook the man's hand, and walked off, knowing he'd accomplished nothing, yet feeling better for having tried.

Then he noticed that his shadow, slipping to his left off the curb, seemed dimmer, less defined, virtually vanished in the grass. He checked the sky for rain clouds or fair weather puffs, saw nothing, and looked down a second time. The shadow was the same. And there was a weakness to the day's light he hadn't noticed before, a vague blurring of definition that gave him a brief moment of vertigo before his stomach growled again and he knew it had to be hunger deceiving his vision. A decent meal would cure him, and after that he'd stop in at Gayle's shop and let her soothe his rugged brow, bolster his ego, and perhaps even let him know that he was taking the message too seriously. As unnerving as it had been, he certainly couldn't believe it was really Julie Etler.

Not even when he brought to mind the picture he had taken.

A long block from the town hall, he was distracted by a group of children in bathing suits, gathered in a ragged circle just around the corner to watch a bearded teenaged boy painstakingly drawing a picture of a sea gull with powdered chalk on the pavement. At the top of the already com-

66

pleted, simple white frame, there was a shoe box that held a few silver coins, a few one-dollar bills.

While it wasn't great art and would vanish in the next rain, he was impressed, and when the boy glanced up to see who belonged to the new shadow, Devin nodded his appreciation, received a grateful nod in return. Among the kids there were a few giggling comments that the wings were too large, the eyes crossed, but the shirtless artist only joked back, teasing, growling, feinting a punch at a chubby kid's tummy.

It was so normal, and at the same time so special, that Devin reached for his camera, and muttered a silent *damn* when he remembered where it was.

That figures, he thought; it happens every time.

Then the sputtering of a motorcycle made him look down the street, to a huge chrome-and-black machine smoking toward him under the spotted shade of the trees lining the curb. The driver was small, barefooted, and his helmet had a black visor that made him appear headless.

Neither the kids nor the artist paid it any attention.

Devin looked away as well, leaning forward to see over a kneeling girl, while his left hand fumbled in his pocket for some change to leave behind.

He almost didn't acknowledge the altered sound of the engine until its sudden, uneven racing turned his head just as the driver rose in his seat, jumped the bike over the curb, and came straight toward them.

There was no time for anything but a hoarse yelled warning before he shoved frantically at every child he could reach to get them out of the way, at the same time spinning around to face the bike without knowing what to do.

The visor reflected nothing, dead black without form, and as Devin braced himself with arms outspread, the motorcycle swerved at the last possible moment and leapt back into the street—the unmistakable sound of the driver's laughter almost lost in the engine's roar.

Immediately, a crowd of onlookers surrounded the now

crying children, trying to soothe them while a few thanked him for his quick reflexes, a few more giving belated futile chase that ended half a block later. One man hurried back toward the police station, but Devin, once assured none of the kids was hurt, pushed his way clear and walked as slowly as he could down the street, toward the diner.

His hands were shaking, his throat was dry, and as much as he told himself that it was only some beer-drunk on a suicidal tear, he couldn't shake the notion that the bike had been aimed at him.

SIX

T HE lobby of the Oceantide Savings and Loan was cool, almost ludicrously cold, and the mosaic tiles of its floor were damp and dangerously slippery from a recent cleaning. Yet Stump Harragan was determined to take as much advantage as he could of the comfort the building offered before he had to step back out into the heat and get himself on the pier. The money he had brought—the previous night's receipts hardly worth the counting—had been duly counted and deposited, each of the tellers had been duly flirted with, and he had spent an unexpectedly disappointing fifteen minutes jawing with bank manager Samuel Planter, who didn't dare not take the time because Stump wasn't just one of the bank's best customers—Harragan also knew the stiff-jawed, pompous man as Dumbo Planter, from back in the bad days when the two of them had been pretenders to the throne of chief Southside terror, over in Philadelphia.

It was a fact not generally known along the Jersey shore, and Stump enjoyed the squirming torment he knew he was causing. To his way of thinking, the chicken-scrawny pea-brain had it coming. It was all well and good that badass Dumbo had dragged himself out of the gutter and into the rarefied realm of the black middle class, complete with weekly trimmed beard, Ivy League accent, and a three-piece tailored suit that hid the foreign beer he guzzled every night. A feat surely to be proud of, all things considered, and considering their common roots. But the man had a tendency to let things slip his mind, and Stump figured it was his duty to play conscience whenever he was in the mood.

The trouble today was the mood was there, but the jibes, the innuendo, the gentle reminders had come out like whining, and for the first time in ages, Planter had bested him, and was smug about it without repentance.

It was surely a bad sign, and Stump rolled his shoulders to shed a ghostly chill of impending distress, stepping aside when a rouge-cheeked matron in paisley passed him, her gaze letting him know that she knew a bum when she saw one.

Shit and damn, he thought; shit and damn.

Nothing for it now; he had no choice but to feed a vice every doctor in his life from Georgia to Jersey had told him was lethal, no potential about it—he pulled a half-smoked black cigar from his shirt pocket, glanced at the discreet no-smoking sign on the fake marble pillar he was leaning against, and fished a scratched tin lighter from his shorts. The guard at the entrance watched him carefully, and Stump made a show of flipping back the lid and thumbing the wheel before noticing with shocked widened eyes the admonition above his head. His best martyr's expression saddened his face, and he walked heavily to the door, where the guard tipped his hat politely and pushed at the revolving door to give him room to leave.

"Thank you, sir," Stump said with a slight bow. "Appreciate the kindness."

"Stuff it, Harragan," the man whispered as he smiled. "You still owe me twenty bucks."

Stump's abrupt laugh was loud and high, and he stepped out to the street with a snap of his fingers, a wink to the sky. Maybe it won't be such a bad day after all; the fat bastard cheats at cards and expects to be paid. Waiting was good for what ails the soul. And Chuck Geller's soul was definitely ailing, even a quack could see that from a dead mile away. The bloated, fat-nosed man was the damnedest turn-around bigot he'd ever known, and he'd definitely pay up, sooner or later, just to keep the chump coming back for more.

Meanwhile, he figured the anticipation would do the man a whole world of good.

Unfortunately, anticipating the mood of the crowds this past week hadn't been doing him a bit of good at all. Not at all. It was going to hell on a handrail around here, and he couldn't figure it out. Most of the rides were half empty, there weren't nearly the right screams from the big wheel, and first thing this morning he'd discovered three of his cables nearly chewed through. Had he switched on the power before checking, the pier would have gone up like the Fourth of July.

Shit and damn.

The biggest weekend of the season coming up, including Memorial Day, and folks were suddenly behaving like they were poorer than Georgia clay.

For a second he was even tempted to abandon his plans for tonight, plans that had thus far taken him miles along a road he had previously thought too dark to travel. The way things were now, though, he'd probably end up killing him-

71

self, and wouldn't Geller have a laugh at that, the white prick.

Shit. And damn.

None of it was working, he thought glumly as he turned the corner; shit and damn, I oughta retire. And he thought nothing more when a motorcycle barreled past him on the sidewalk, slamming him into the wall.

"Son of a bitch, what the hell now, Jesus wept," Chuck Geller muttered angrily, banging through the bank's revolving door when he saw the sleek motorcycle jump the curb on its rear tire and disappear around the corner where Harragan had gone. God damn, if it ain't one thing, it's another.

One hand was hard on his gun, the other holding onto his hat, and he moved as fast as his shifting weight would take him, part of him knowing he shouldn't be leaving his post, the rest of him not giving a damn because wouldn't you know it, there was the old black sitting on the pavement, legs out, eyes closed, hands limp on the concrete.

"Christ in heaven," he said softly when he knelt and saw the blood on the wall. With his luck, the cotton-head would be dead. "Hey, Stump, you okay?"

The motorcycle was gone, the stench of its exhaust heavy in the heat.

The old man didn't move.

A shadow covered Geller then, and he snapped, "Get a damned doctor, will ya?" over his shoulder. It was time to play the game, make himself look good.

"What's going on here, Mr. Geller? Why did you leave your post?"

"You blind, buddy? The man's been hurt. Get a doctor before he croaks, huh?"

The shadow didn't move, and exasperation puffed him to his feet, where he came face to face with that asshole Planter, whose expression of concern seemed more like a pout. The bank manager stared down at Harragan, looked up and down the street, and Geller finally shoved him away impatiently and returned inside. Several of the tellers were watching him anxiously, and he told the nearest one to call the police, told the one beside her to get hold of a doctor.

That, he figured with a nod, ought to cover his ass with the cops.

Planter came in behind him, wiping his palms fastidiously with a handkerchief, lips puckered in distaste. "He's coming around," he said, and walked away toward his office.

"What?" Geller stared after him, took a step forward and immediately turned it into an about-face before he did something stupid. Harragan or no Harragan, this was no time to be slugging a boss. Especially a black one. Back home the jackass wouldn't have gotten off the farm; here, on the other hand, he had to treat him like he was normal.

Damn; and three days to go before his vacation began.

Voices outside took him back through the door, and he used his best official voice to part his way through a group of quietly chattering women standing around the fallen man.

Harragan moaned softly then and opened his eyes. "Jesus," he said.

"Closer to it than you know, you lucky bastard. You okay?" He watched while Harragan put a steady hand against the back of his head and pulled it away to stare at a thin line of blood across the pale palm. "Man, you could've gotten killed, you know? You could've been squashed."

"Where's the bike?"

Geller helped him to his feet, trying not to grunt because Stump weighed a hell of a lot more than he looked. "Gone. I don't know where. And where the hell do you think you're going?"

Harragan looked at him as if he had three heads. "Work. I got a pier to run."

The women protested, expecting him to keep the jerk around until medical assistance arrived. But he only waved

73

the old black on in disgust, telling him loudly that he'd be sorry for leaving, he'd probably drop in his tracks before he reached the beach.

One of the women gasped.

Harragan waved back without turning around.

Jackass, he thought, bulling his way back through the crowd. Stupid old bastard. Hasn't got a brain in his goddamned head, walking away like that. But it wasn't his concern. The old nigger had cheated him out of twenty bucks, not for the first time, and right now he didn't give a damn if the deadbeat walked right into the ocean, straight across to goddamn France.

Stupid bastard.

You come right down to it, they were all of them stupid, and he wouldn't give a plugged nickel for the whole lot of them, parading around like they owned the whole damned world, daring you to look at them crossways so they could sue your ass off and laugh all the way to the bank. Stupid bastards.

Still scowling, he took up his position just inside the door and shrugged when one of the tellers glanced a question in his direction. Then he looked over his shoulder, through the tinted window, and saw the cruiser pull up, heard an ambulance right behind it.

Aw shit, he thought when that fuzzhead Kilmer crawled out, doffed his cap, and began talking to one of them dumbass, blue-haired old women, who immediately pointed a beringed finger at him; aw shit.

Planter came back out of his office.

Harragan's gonna pay for this, Geller decided, and considered making the bleeding-heart cop come to him, but Planter was in his doorway staring, clearly giving him an order. So he adjusted his uniform and went outside again, marched over to Kilmer and waited, almost at attention, until he was noticed. The women backed away.

And just as he had the first of what he figured were several pretty decent excuses for letting the old bastard go, he heard the motorcycle whine out on Summer Road, the agonizing shriek of brakes, metal colliding with metal. Kilmer raced past him, the attendants right behind. He hesitated, looking first to the bank window where Planter was standing, then to the street where traffic was already piling up.

The hell, he decided, and went inside; it was too hot to watch. He'd read about it in the paper.

Smoke from a burning engine choked Kilmer into coughing, and he fumbled a handkerchief from his hip pocket while he tried to assess the damage, reconstruct the accident for his later report, the one he would take his own sweet time writing, back in the air-conditioned station.

God, he was hurting.

If he had a choice now, he could probably cut off his head and not miss the damned thing.

A van with its slanted blunt nose bashed in and smoking stood sideways across Summer Road's northbound lanes; ahead of it was a chrome-sidepiped pickup slewed in the opposite direction, and behind it a milk delivery truck leaking radiator fluid onto the tarmac, its driver sitting on the street and holding his head.

The sudden rush of a fire extinguisher across the van's front forced him back a stumbling step, and glass crunched loudly beneath his feet.

Christ, he had a headache! The same damned one he'd had since getting up this morning. At first he thought it was a hangover, fitting retribution for the free drinks he'd picked up along the boards, and he hadn't felt quite right by the time he'd gotten off his second shift and had fallen into bed. But when it persisted, and worsened as the sun climbed, he knew the headache itself was back, no hangover to blame. It wasn't sharp, and it wasn't dull; it was just *there,* and he hadn't been able to string together two decent thoughts all day. Now he had to put up with this. It was better, by half a shot, than Devin Graham's blather about ghosts, but Christ, he just wanted to go home.

A woman sobbed loudly and two trembling children stood beside the wreckage of their van, thumbs firmly in their mouths, their father standing behind them with his hands kneading their shoulders. The man looked to Kilmer, angry and frightened, and Kilmer could only look back, blinking away the pain that burned behind his eyes.

Please, he pleaded; just let me think.

On second thought, he decided, maybe those stupid ghosts weren't so bad after all. They at least helped him forget the pain for a while.

A siren hurt his ears, and he winced at the orders of the attendants who were peering under the van at the driver of the motorcycle. The bike itself had been flipped into the bed of the pickup.

A cruiser arrived, and the traffic patrol's station wagon.

Dust bit into his right eye, and he cursed at it, rubbed it angrily, and shook his head when someone asked if he was hurt, took another step back and lowered his head.

He knew he was supposed to do something. He was a sergeant after all, in charge of this and that and whatever else the chief didn't want to be bothered with, so he ought to be taking charge here as well, making sure statements were taken, the injured brought to the hospital, witnesses rounded up before they drifted away.

He knew all that, and still he couldn't move.

Not even when the body of the cyclist was finally dragged into sight, and he could see the crushed helmet, and the dark running down the shattered visor.

On the near corner, in front of the bank, Prayerful Mary was mindful of her duty, though she was certain that Officer Kilmer wouldn't see it her way. He seldom did; he usually claimed she was bothering the tourists. Not that what he thought mattered; it had to be done. God's work was God's work, and no two ways about it, no looking for escape.

It was painful sometimes, sorrowful other times, but like the man said, you can't run from your shadow.

76

After scratching around the eye patch, lifting it and rubbing at her eye, she cleared her throat, composed herself, and placed a hand over her chest. Oblivious to the onlookers gathering at the curb, she raised her voice in a hymn, shivering in the sudden cold that drifted down from the sun.

On the boardwalk, Kelly inhaled sharply when she tried to move her stiff shoulder, swearing at the four-eyed goof at the first aid station who'd practically wrapped her arm up like a mummy's. Scumbag. Acting like a TV doctor on those shows her mother watched while she lay on the couch and drank what she called her wake-me-up cocktail. He'd wanted to give her a tetanus shot too, but she'd refused when she saw the way he handled the needle, promising with crossed fingers to see a doctor as soon she got off work.

The goof hadn't minded, had even tried to cop a feel under pretext of a clumsy examination, and she'd come this close to slapping the glasses from his fat nose and screaming rape. It would have served him right. His goddamn nails weren't even clean.

"Balloon Heaven!" she cried. "Win it all at Opal's Balloon Heaven."

She hissed, and probed the bandage, and wiped a line of sweat from under her bangs.

In her right hand she brandished a dart, and wondered with a giggle if Tony would mind if she shoved it through Angie's ass, so the kid's brains would leak all over the beach.

"Balloon Heaven!" she called.

And in spite of Jimmy's orders, she turned on a portable radio; the sirens were driving her crazy.

On the beach below Harragan's Pier, Mike strolled through the crowds, doing his best not to stare at the women half-naked and posturing as he watched, making sure his chest was out, his leg muscles tight. He felt like a general reviewing his troops, and for a moment he imagined what it would be like to pin medals on those chests. A flash of Kelly's

77

probable reaction to the fantasy didn't faze him; she was back there and he was out here, and it was wonderful.

Then he saw Mrs. Kueller lying on a blanket, her already tanned skin gleaming, running sweat, looking soft and warm. Tony's sister was playing with some other brats at the edge of the surf. When he stopped, shading his eyes and pretending to search for someone he knew just over the woman's head, she lifted herself up on her elbows and gave him a nod and a smile.

"Hi," he said.

"Hello, Mike."

"Hot."

"Sure is."

He shifted from foot to foot before lifting a hand and moving on, looking back once to see her watching him, her left hand brushing sand from the top of her breast.

"I've got some fresh lemonade here," she said, just loud enough for him to hear and pointing to a Thermos bottle poking out of a straw handbag. "You're welcome to some if you want. You look like you could use some."

He almost went back.

But when her hand settled lightly on her stomach, rose and fell with her breathing, he grinned stupidly and waved again, and didn't look around although he knew she was still there, still staring.

For some reason, it made him feel cold. And for some reason, he suddenly wished he was already gone.

Tony left the house at a dead run.

The telephone was still ringing, but when he'd picked it up before, no one was there.

Static crackling and popping, the sound of a distant fire.

SEVEN

THE food aromas along Summer Road were strong, and Devin's stomach increased its complaining as he walked, squinting despite the sunglasses at the glare bouncing off windows, rising in waves from the pavement. There were fumes from the traffic as hunters of the sun sought a place to park. By the time he reached the diner he was starving, and he closed his eyes in a brief *thank you* when the air conditioning blessed him.

Fans in slow motion turned below the ceiling. Utensils clattered, cups clattered on saucers. A thin man in white brushed a mop across the tiled floor.

He stood by the cash register for a moment, taking off his glasses and waiting for his vision to adjust. As he did, he looked around, smiling absently at Charlene, lifting an eyebrow in silent greeting to Sal Riccaro behind the counter.

No one here seemed to have heard or noticed the accident outside, and when he had turned around at the noise, not really caring about anything but getting food and being cool, he had only seen what he thought was a fender-bender between a van and a delivery truck, and Marty standing off to one side, rubbing his temples, while Prayerful Mary sang a solemn hymn in front of the bank entrance.

Then he heard footsteps and quiet voices behind him, and saw a family of four climbing the diner steps to the outer door. A shrug to himself, and he moved quickly down the aisle to the empty booth, grabbed a menu from a pile on the counter, and sat. Before he could even check the special of the day, however, Charlene was by him with pad and pencil, one hip cocked.

"You," she declared, pencil pointing, eyebrow raised, "look pretty bad today, if you don't mind me saying."

So much for rugged and wind-tossed, he thought.

"Y'know, Mike Nathan just left," she said, touching a tongue to the pencil's point. "Now there's a guy who always looks good no matter what, don't you think? Must be all that exercise he gets or something. What comes of wanting to be a doctor. I guess, going away to college, you gotta look good for all those coeds and stuff."

"Save it, Charlene," he said with a polite smile. "Just bring me a soda, a well-done burger with everything but tomatoes, plus some french fries. And silence."

She cocked her other hip and raised a thickly penciled eyebrow. "Jeez, you hung over or what?"

"Neither," he protested. "I'm feeling pretty good, as a matter of fact."

"Sure you are." She looked down the length of the diner, then leaned over and winked. "What was her name, Devin? Anybody I know?"

He narrowed his eyes. "Food, Charlene," he said, tapping a finger against her pad. "Remember?"

She straightened, snapped her gum at him, and did her best to swing her hips as she wound around the counter's end, tearing the order from the pad. "You're no fun anymore, Graham, you know that?" she called over her shoulder. "You must be getting old or something."

Her voice was loud, too loud, but no one looked around. And he didn't answer. Charlene Iano was Sal's second cousin, and she worked here during the summers because, Riccaro had once told him, her mother was positive that sooner or later she was going to meet the man who would take her away from home, and with luck never bring her back. He doubted it. Even when she wasn't working, she seemed to have forgotten than the coarse, over-madeup look had died a natural death more than a decade ago. And he'd long ago stopped wondering what she'd look like with her face scrubbed clean and her hair brushed for a change.

At least once a week she managed to drop more than a subtle hint that she'd like him to show her the sights after dark.

He wondered with a quick smile how Mike had handled her flirting. Tony would blush and bluff it out; Mike, he guessed, would just blush.

While he waited, then, he looked out the tinted window, at the traffic, the pedestrians, and frowned, suddenly feeling as if he had turned a familiar corner into a street he didn't know. A street that didn't belong.

But there was nothing he could put his finger on, not a single tangible sign he could hold in his hand and examine. The faces were the same, the outfits, the rush to the beach. His frown deepened, finally blaming the effect on the idiot who'd nearly run him and the children down. And he only grunted displeasure when Charlene nudged him with an elbow as she served him his lunch.

"Well, excuse me for living," she said.

He ignored her.

And he ate, watching the other diners sweep through their meals, picking out the locals from those on vacation by the way they lingered over coffee, quietly joked with Sal and the waitresses, and called insults to the cook who never showed his face in the serving window to answer back.

Something different.

He didn't know.

Maybe it was the voice last night, and the voice he thought he had heard after the machine had been turned off. He supposed he should have played the message back before leaving the house to see Kilmer; he supposed that there was a good chance he had misunderstood. He had been, after all, damned tired, and feeling sorry for himself, and missing Gayle, all at the same time.

Maybe; maybe not.

But he had talked to the police as he'd promised himself he would, and now . . he didn't know. He didn't feel quite right.

He ate without tasting, and only waved when Sal spotted him and mouthed his name. He shook his head in apology. He didn't feel like talking. He wanted to eat, then walk; nothing more. Put food in his stomach to keep him going until dinner, and walk. And he was mildly surprised when he recalled that this would be his day. Maybe that's what was so different—he really wasn't working.

A shrug without moving.

The empty plate pushed away, the check picked up and paid at the register by the door. Paula wasn't there; a new girl who didn't know him only smiled because she had to, and handed him his change. He smiled back because he wanted to, and went outside again, wincing at the contrast, silently grunting at the heat, then turning left and moving on.

The accident had been cleared away.

Shadows of clouds rippled and stole across the street as the sky slowly lost its color; the breeze that followed failed to bring relief, pulsing instead like a laboring, dying heart, like a slow slap in the face.

Devin touched his forehead, then looked at himself in the window of a drugstore. He was sweating. On a day no worse than any other, and better than those in the middle of July, he was sweating as if he had been running since dawn, and when his knees began to weaken, he moved to the corner of the building and leaned against it.

I'm sick, he thought then in disbelief; Jesus, I'm sick.

And as soon as he thought it, the feeling passed, his face was dry, and when he stood on his own, one arm slightly out in case he lost his balance, nothing happened.

Blaming it on the hamburger, he hurried down the block to a small shop between a real estate office and a grocery. A quick touch to his hair, a palm smoothed over his chest, and he stepped inside and took his sunglasses off again.

It was a newsstand, only one of two in the entire town, and as always was never filled, and never completely empty. There were no rush hours here. Customers came in for newspapers from the nearby motels, for paperback books to read on the beach, for postcards, candy, magazines, cigarettes, dozens of the odds and ends that filled purses and pockets and were never brought from home.

It smelled like tobacco, like chocolate, like the candles on the shelf right next to the door.

He loved it.

There was no music, no radio, no tapes, no video games and their sound effects, no arcade games with their infernal bells and shrill sirens. Not exactly a place for browsing, but customers browsed anyway—for the peace, for the stillness, and for the smile of the woman seated on a stool behind the counter at the back.

She grinned when she saw him.

With a broad wink he moved to a rack of paperback books while she waited on an old man who couldn't seem to decide between a briar and a corncob pipe. He was being silently difficult and would probably waste another ten minutes before leaving without a decision. Devin didn't mind. It gave him a chance to look at her again without her

83

telling him not to stare—at the sweep of her hair brushed straight back from her high forehead, at the sweep of what he called her aristocratic English nose, at the figure not fashionably thin but one she herself said was lush and no cracks please, I'm a lady.

The old man left; she had sold him both pipes.

"I got your message," he said, stepping to the end of the counter and leaning against it.

"How late?" she asked without looking at him.

"After three, I think."

She shook her head. "You're a jerk, Devin."

"I guess."

There was a simple gold chain around her neck, no rings on her fingers, no watch on her wrist. Her white shirt was open two buttons down, and her shorts were loose enough to let the air circulate when she walked.

"Do you ever think about getting any sleep?"

"I slept to almost noon today."

"Swell, Graham. I'll give you a medal."

They listened to the silence.

"Well, as long as you were up that late, did you get anything good?"

"Nope. Just a lecture from Stump, that's all."

She looked at him sideways. "He only wants the best for you, you know."

"He wants me to get laid."

"Like I said."

He couldn't meet her sudden, direct stare. That was the one thing he knew he would never get used to—her frankness. All his life he had fantasized about women throwing themselves at him, whispering every wonderfully forbidden word into his ear, doing every wonderful forbidden thing to every part of his body. But it was fantasy; that's what he'd been taught by parents who had emigrated when both were in their teens.

Fantasy, at least, until Gayle had come along.

She put a finger lightly to his chin. "A penny," she said softly.

He smiled. "Nothing much. Reliving my glorious past, that's all."

"Oh really?" Suddenly she put her hands behind her back and lifted her chest and one eyebrow. "You wanna tell me all about it, sailor?"

"Jesus!" he said, and turned away, though not before he'd taken a good look.

She laughed and hugged him from behind. "You're something else, Graham, you know that?"

"What does that make you, Cross?"

"Don't ask."

With her cheek gentle against his back he felt at once comforted and uncomfortable. He was trying, he told himself; he really was honest to god trying, but there were times when outrageous didn't come close to describing the way she acted whenever they were alone.

His eyes closed briefly, and a smile came and went. He had no idea yet if he loved her, even after knowing her for several years, even after seeing other women as well, but as long as the fascination lasted, he knew he couldn't leave.

Her arms slipped away when a sunburned couple came in, arguing softly and cutting themselves off when they realized they weren't alone. Devin picked up a candy bar, tore open the wrapping and began to nibble, and found himself intrigued by the way they moved around the tiny shop. Picking up things. Putting them back down. Flipping through books and magazines. Staring blindly into small mirrors. Finally before leaving, as if embarrassed, buying cigarettes and gum they clearly didn't want. Without a word. Only brief smiles for Gayle when she handed over the change.

"Boy," he said.

"What?"

"Didn't you see that?" He pointed at the door.

"Sure. By the end of the day they're going to have sun-burns that'll keep them inside for a week."

"No, I didn't mean that. Didn't you see it? They were so quiet, you know?"

She closed one eye and shrugged. "So?"

"I don't know."

"Devin," she said, "are you all right? You seem kind of quiet yourself."

"Yeah, sure, I'm okay," he answered quickly, not wanting her to fuss. "It's just . . . I don't know. I really don't." Then he looked at his watch for something to do and slapped the top of the register. "Oh hell!"

"Now what?" she said as he started for the door.

"I'm an idiot!"

"I know that. So what?"

"It's the kids. Something's been bugging me all day, and I just remembered I'm supposed to do their portraits this afternoon. On the beach. In twenty minutes."

He had the door open when she called his name, and when he looked back one hand was buried in her hair.

"The kids," she said, her tone deliberately neutral.

"Right. I promised."

She sighed. Loudly. "What about dinner?"

He looked to the street, back to her and lifted a hand, and blinked when she started to laugh. "No, dope, we didn't have a date. I'm asking for one."

"Oh. Well, sure. Yes. Fine. I'll . . . Jesus, I'm going to have to go back for the stupid camera."

"I'll pick you up," she said with a shake of her head. "Seven o'clock, and you'd better be there, Graham, or I'm coming after you."

He blew her a kiss—an apology and a vague promise—and hurried onto the pavement, checked his watch again and began a slow trot. He was going to be late, but he didn't think the kids would mind, not really; knowing them as he did, they'd be too busy anyway, playing and getting themselves ready to leave for college. And one of these days, if all went well, Gayle was finally going to understand why they interested him so much. It was something he couldn't tell her, not in words; she was simply going to have to see.

A pause when he realized he hadn't told her about the voice, and he almost turned back. But the day was too bright, and he decided it would be better if he learned something first before mentioning anything to Gayle. If he had only speculation, he knew what she'd say: *you're working too hard, Devin, you're working too damned hard.*

Maybe he was, but he wasn't getting anywhere with the camera, at least not far enough to please him.

A sudden dash across the street before he reached the next corner, holding his breath in case the cyclist returned for another go; an all-out sprint for a block before the heat slowed him down and he felt himself panting, less from the sun than his own poor condition.

And as he swung into the turn that would take him down the street to his block, he spotted something lying still beside an overturned garbage can, in a pile of trash scattered along the gutter. He slowed because there were a handful of people standing beside it. Quietly. Staring. The breeze passing over them and not touching them at all.

As he passed, he glanced down, and stopped.

It was the mongrel he'd seen rooting in the garbage the night before. It was dead, dried blood tracing its ribs, the outline of its muzzle.

No one moved.

He tapped a portly man on the shoulder. "Did anyone call the police?"

And they all walked away.

EIGHT

THE dune rose above them as they sat on the sand,
Kelly in the center with her hair loose and blowing.
There were others on the beach, scattered along islands of blankets and umbrellas, and a few in the water,
riding the waves on rubber rafts and huge inner tubes; but
there were no games in progress, no races, no beach balls,
and no one on the wet shelf, building a castle for the tide to
besiege.

Tony shifted impatiently, raking a hand through his hair,
sneering at Mike, who had taken off his shirt and had
thrust his chest out, flexed his biceps, squared his chin.

But it was wrong, all wrong, they looked as if they were
sitting at the foot of a prison wall just before lockup. With
frustration puffing his cheeks, Devin slowly lowered the
camera and squinted hard enough to force a tear, trying to

command the scene he wanted to come to focus in his mind. Then he moved them around until their backs were to the water. Smiling at them. Nodding to them. Framing them through the viewfinder and shaking his head without moving.

Wrong; it was all wrong.

Damned if he knew why.

"Hey," Mike shouted, "y'know I only got less than fifty years before I retire."

He suggested they kneel with Kelly standing behind them; he wondered how they'd look lying prone on the wet sand, waves covering their feet, palms framing their faces; standing in a column, Tony in front, Mike and Kelly leaning out to either side; sitting; running three abreast; leaping for the sky; squatting on their heels.

"If I'm gonna be myself," Tony complained, "I'm gonna need Angie around to strangle."

"Not nice," Kelly said.

"Big deal," he grumbled.

None of the other people watched them; the lifeguards wore pith helmets and looked asleep on their stands.

Mike trying to hold each of them on an arm, a circus balancing act that had them laughing and tumbling within seconds; Kelly unnervingly seductive, with the boys begging at her feet; Tony wrestling Mike with Kelly as fierce referee; the trio in a huddle, Devin lying on his back to catch their faces, a halo beneath the sky.

"You guys promised me ice cream," Kelly said with a pout, pointing to her bandaged shoulder and glaring mockingly at Tony.

One at a time.

Against the sea, the dunes and houses, against the hazed northern horizon.

A surfboard slipped in on a wave, spun slowly and caught, and spun slowly again.

Then Kelly with the dark pier crouching a hundred yards at her back, and Devin lowered the camera in stages, let it hang from its strap as he gazed over her shoulder until at last she turned around.

"Devin, are you all right?" Tony asked, coming to stand beside him, watching him watch the pier. "You look bummed, y'know?"

"Tell me about it," he said quietly.

The dark pier was too dark, the rest of the world too light, as if the pilings were thieves of everything that had color.

He lowered himself to the sand, capped the lens, and pulled off the strap. "This is really dumb," he apologized when they dropped down around him. "I nearly kill myself getting here on time, you guys are hanging around sweating to death, and I guess I left my so-called artistic genius in the closet." He smiled wearily and shrugged. "Sorry, guys. I didn't think it'd be this much trouble."

"No problem," Tony said.

"You sure you're a pro?" Mike asked with a grin that made his broken nose seem much larger.

"Of course I am," he answered close to anger, and pulled in his chin when he saw the boy flinch. "Sorry again, Mike." A weak shrug. "I guess that's what we big folk call a touchy subject these days."

"Why?" Kelly said. "I've seen the magazines and stuff. I thought you were famous or something."

"Not quite."

"But all those pictures—"

"Are just pictures," he interrupted, and saw the confusion in her eyes. He cleared his throat, looked around, followed the glide of a gull over the hump of a breaker. "A photograph isn't the same as a picture. I want a photograph of you all."

Mike scratched his head. "Man, when you're gloomed, you don't make any sense at all."

Devin pulled up his knees and wrapped his hands around them. "Actually, I am. Making sense, that is."

"You wanna bet?"

He nodded. "It's easy, actually. See, Tony here, for example, has that instant thing, and that takes pictures. They used to call them snapshots. Back in the Stone Age, when I was a boy." He gathered the bag between his legs and held it close to him, one-handed. "Lots of other people, they have cameras like me, and all they get are pictures too."

"So?" Mike said, his tone announcing boredom.

But suddenly Devin didn't care. Someone had to understand, and if Gayle didn't, or wouldn't, maybe one of these kids would. It wouldn't pay the bills, and it wouldn't guarantee him a gallery showing, but here, in the sun, it suddenly mattered.

With a look that demanded they at least give him a hearing, he leaned over and stabbed at the sand. "A photograph isn't like a graduation picture or a snapshot. It's like a painting when it's done right, something you see in a museum."

"Oh, art," Mike grumbled.

"Right," he said, resisting a silent command to be properly modest. "Well, something like that. But instead of creating with oils or acrylics or water colors or whatever, somebody who takes real photographs creates with light and shadow, with colors, with his eye. It's not a *re*-creation of what he looks at. He captures it." He tapped his forehead, hard. "I see something in here, like today, and I try to get what I see on film. A feeling as well as an image, if you see what I mean. Without the feeling, all you have is a picture. It may look pretty, or impressive, but it's still only a picture."

His hand slapped his knee. "The point is, I don't want to take pictures. I want to . . ." His hand where it lay began to tremble, and he bunched it to a fist that pulled back across his thigh.

The point was, he no longer thought he could actually do it.

He felt them staring, heard them breathing, and fought with the temptation to apologize a third time.

"You're lucky," Riccaro said quietly. "At least you know what you want."

He glanced up quickly, but Tony was already looking away, and he couldn't help thinking that he'd lost something then, something he ought to have been able to remember.

"Okay," he said, abruptly sitting up and clapping his hands. "I blew it today. You just tell me when, and we'll try it again."

Mike squinted at the sun. "No hurry. We got all summer."

"No," Kelly said. "A week. Less."

Devin watched them, saw Tony's expression harden, saw Mike's become distant, and without thinking he said, "I'm going to see Maureen Etler this afternoon."

They stared at him in mute amazement, which soon shifted to guilt, and he realized that none of them had been to see Julie's mother since the funeral on Sunday. And as soon as he suspected they were accusing him of a subtle scolding, he hastened to explain that he wanted to find out if Mrs. Etler had been bothered by any calls like the one he'd had the day before, asking about the picture.

"Picture? What picture?" Tony demanded. "What are you talking about?"

He pulled the camera bag closer and tapped on it in broken rhythm, half listening to the shouts of a gang of kids charging into the water, half listening to the wind that began to sough off the dunes. There was no attempt at description; he told them they would have to see it, if they wanted, but it was a photograph, accidentally taken, of Julie in the midst of the conflagration.

Kelly bit her lip, and Mike slipped his arm around her.

Then, with less reluctance, he told them about the message someone had left on his machine. "It's a damned poor excuse for a joke," he said sternly, just in case it was one of them. "And if it was someone trying to give me a scare, they did a damned good job at the time. I even talked to the cops."

None of them smiled, none looked abashed.

A gust lifted sand, and he turned his face toward the water.

"Can I go with you?" Tony asked.

"I guess," he said, though he wasn't sure it was a good idea, and looked down at the bag to watch his finger, still tapping. "Anybody else?"

Mike almost shook his head, then nodded when Kelly did, and Devin decided that now was as good a time as any.

He stood, slapping the sand from his jeans, and looked at the pier again, at the ribs of the roof, some snapped, most standing. And when he saw them following his gaze, he didn't feel quite so bad. They were wondering too. They needed to know why.

The single-level house was on a tree-lined, dead-end street—the last home on a block whose blacktop hadn't been repaired in a number of years. Beyond it was a tangle of rigid reeds and brittle weeds that separated it and the others from the shore of the bay. The house was swirled stucco and Spanish tile, with a picket fence that wanted paint; the narrow porch and front windows were hidden behind a screen of untrimmed yew and untrained ivy on a trellis, the ground in the yard showing through in ragged patches.

Devin turned the Jeep around to face the center of town and switched off the engine. He had never liked this street; it had always been too quiet even with people on the pavement. Not the kind of silence that came on his own block when the neighbors were calm at twilight and he could sit on the stoop and watch the rise of the moon; nor was it the silence of past midnight, tranquillity that filtered through the cool of the night's breeze.

Here, even in the middle of the day, it was as if all the houses were deserted, and all the toys seen in the yards had been placed there just for show.

The Etlers, mother and daughter, had once lived across

the state in Trenton, had moved to the shore eight years before, when the father died and left them nothing but this and a few dollars of insurance. Maureen was a secretary for one of the attorneys in town; Julie had attended Princeton until, this spring, she'd dropped out of her senior year.

"I don't think anyone's home," Kelly whispered.

"How can you tell?" Tony said, grabbing the top of the windshield and pulling himself up.

Devin watched the house, his hands still on the wheel, thinking that any minute Maureen would come to the screen door, see them and wave them all in.

Shadows slipped across the sidewalk when the breeze blew again.

"Well, I guess telepathy doesn't work," he said lightly and slid out of his seat, told the others with a look to stay where they were, and pushed open the gate. The hinges creaked. Ivy fluttered. A pebble skittered away from the heel of his boot.

After knocking on the doorframe, he glanced down the length of the porch, over the railing to the empty lot. Things lived in there; he'd often heard them at night, saw their progress as the reeds bent contrary to the wind. He had never seen anything and assumed they were prowling cats, but Julie told him it was her place to go, to dredge up the occasional nightmare when her life got too dull. He'd laughed. She hadn't smiled.

He knocked again, looked back to the kids and shrugged.

"Hello the house!" he called, shading his eyes and peering through the baggy screen. The front room was empty as far as he could tell, and the dimly spreading light from the kitchen window in back made it impossible to see anything there. The bedrooms, he knew, were off the living room to the left. "Hey, Maureen, it's Devin!"

The crunch of footsteps on the grass, and Tony hurried past. "I'll try the back," he said, and Devin nodded.

Suddenly it occurred to him that Maureen was probably

at work. She had said she'd be taking time off, but it was possible that the house, small as it was, had grown too large, the memories too strong. A husband and a daughter in less than two years. He was surprised she had even stayed; he'd almost assumed she would want to sell and move on.

"Nothing," Tony said, vaulting over the railing. "Bet she's at work."

"I just thought of that," he said sheepishly, and they headed back up the walk. But he couldn't shake the feeling that he ought to see her now, before it was too late. He had no idea what "too late" meant, though he suspected it had more than a little to do with his conscience and the picture.

The key turned in the ignition, the Jeep pulled away from the curb, and he drove to Summer Road and turned right, drove another block and parked in front of a new brick building set deep on its lot. The windows were tinted, the sign on the lush grass without ostentation. He stared at it for several moments, feeling the others watching him. Then he suggested that they might want to wait outside, the mixture of shame and relief in their expressions so blatant that he was hard put not to laugh. They knew they had to do the right thing, but it didn't have to be now.

His grin died the moment he stepped over the threshold, into a cool lobby whose otherwise glossy image was pleasantly offset by high-standing plants in redwood tubs along the walls. Behind a modular desk sat a receptionist, who nodded a polite greeting when he tucked his sunglasses into a shirt pocket and stepped up to her, and nodded again when he asked her if Maureen was still in the office. Then, as she picked up a telephone and pressed a clear button, she directed him through a door behind her, into a small waiting room carefully and comfortably furnished in dark leather and subdued brass. Oils on the wall. Open blinds on the window. A wall-to-wall carpet thick enough to sink in.

He felt a bit awkward, dressed the way he was, and was

still standing when a door opened in the righthand wall, and Maureen Etler walked in.

"Devin, it's good to see you," she said without extending her hand.

"Hello, Maureen."

"What can I do for you?"

He smiled at the sight of her, and at the same time felt a touch of oddly cool sorrow. She was the woman her daughter would most likely have grown into—a tall and slender, self-assured woman with features just shy of chiseled that softened with a laugh and just as quickly sharpened with a scowl. Right now her face was nearly blank, and he gestured toward one of the two leather chairs.

"I wanted to see how you were doing," he said as he sat and crossed his legs.

"Fine," she told him. She remained by the door. Almost rigid, nearly formal.

He watched her and was puzzled. Her hands were clasped in front of her, her suit was severe, and her hair, once long and tumbled, was now pulled back behind her neck and gathered into an austere bun that narrowed her face and made her eyes seem too large.

Hiding, he decided, keeping a lid on her grief and refusing to share it.

His hands gripped the armrests. "Are you all right?"

"Devin, you know I have work to do," she said flatly. "I appreciate your coming, I really do, but . . ." A gesture, more a twitch of her head. "I don't have a lot of time."

Before he could bat aside his astonishment, she turned to leave, and he could only blurt, "It's about Julie."

Her hand grasped the doorknob; she looked over her shoulder and waited.

Damn, he thought, not really knowing what he expected but knowing this wasn't it.

A push got him to his feet, but he didn't approach her. He had a feeling, one that made him turn quickly to stand behind the chair, that if he touched her now, even in friendship, she would scratch his eyes out. "Last night someone left a message on my answering machine," he said, instantly realizing that no matter how he told it, it was going to come out all wrong. "She pretended it was Julie."

Maureen simply stared.

One hand traced a row of brass studs across the top of the chair, the other pushed through the hair that curled over his ear. "It made me mad, naturally. And when I thought about it again this morning, I thought of you right away. I was worried. I wondered if you were being harassed too. Getting these stupid messages, I mean, or maybe someone was hanging around the house. Bothering you. Being . . ."

A telephone burred in the lobby.

"Julie is dead."

"For god's sake, I know that. I was there, remember?"

"This isn't funny, Devin."

"C'mon, Maureen," he said angrily. "You think I want to joke about something like this?" He grabbed the chair and shook his head, once. "Look, there's an idiot out there who thinks she's being cute, and I don't appreciate it one bit. It's . . . it's sick, and I just wanted to see if you were being bothered too."

Still looking over her shoulder, Maureen closed her eyes, opened them, and slightly lifted her chin. "My daughter is dead, Devin. I am alone." Her eyes narrowed and her lips lost their color. "I am alone, and I want to stay that way. Do you understand? I want to stay that way."

He reached out toward her as he stepped away from the chair. "Maureen, I can understand why you feel this way, but don't you think—"

"She committed suicide."

Whatever he'd planned to say came out as a grunt instead, and he nearly dropped back into his seat again. "What?" A whisper, a demand.

On one of the half-dozen dates they had had, before Julie went off to college, Maureen had told him her husband had slashed his wrists in the bathtub; her daughter found him five hours later.

Maureen, though she said nothing, seemed unwilling to leave, instead watched his reaction without blinking, without moving.

"Maureen," he said at last, thinking of the picture in the darkroom, "that isn't . . . it's not true."

The smile startled and repelled him—a parting of her lips, nothing more. "Like father, like daughter," she told him quietly, her teeth exposed as the smile widened. "She went out there to die, Devin. She knew it would happen."

"Surely not," he protested. "She never said—"

Maureen stared him to silence. "Oh, but she did, Devin. A hundred times a day, and no one was listening. Not me, not you, not any of her friends." A long hissing sigh while the smile faded, the lips closed. "She wasn't looking for help, you know. She just wanted us to know."

And she left, closing the door softly behind her.

Impulse had him across the room in two steps before he veered with an oath and stalked out to the lobby, through the door, to stand on the walk. His eyes stung in the sunlight. He could see nothing but white, and within it figures drifting without outline or form.

He walked carefully to the pavement, shuffling his feet to stay off the grass he couldn't see. Blinking until the glare retreated, blinking again when he put on his sunglasses and found himself looking down at Prayerful Mary. She was frowning up at him from beneath the floppy brim of her straw hat, one eye dimmed by cataracts, the other hidden behind a patch he knew she didn't need.

"You near ran me down, boy," she said, lips gleaming with saliva. "You run an old lady down?"

On most days he would have talked with her, listened to her stories of her fairy-tale past and her magic sparkling boots, and at the end would have given her some money, enough for a meal at the diner because he knew she didn't drink.

Today he only stared until she moved on. "Forgive him, Lord," she prayed at the top of a painfully rasping voice. "Let me tell you how he is so's forgiveness come his way."

He was at the Jeep in a stride, at the wheel before he realized the kids were still waiting, and making a point of not looking at him as if he were crazy.

A decision made. "Listen," he said as he turned the ignition key, "can you guys spare me a few minutes?"

There was a momentary silence while the traffic hissed by.

Then: "I don't know," Mike told him solemnly. "I have to learn to start charging by the hour. No discounts for friends, not even you."

"Dinner?" He remembered Gayle. "Tomorrow?"

"Done."

"Great. Tony's treat."

And he laughed as Riccaro protested loudly, swinging first to him, then back to the others while the Jeep spat gravel from beneath its wheels and took the side streets to Devin's house. By the time they reached it, they were red-faced from laughing; by the time they tumbled through the door and onto the couch, they were gasping.

Grief, he thought as he waited for them to sober; it's got to be grief. Julie didn't kill herself. She couldn't have—the fire wasn't arson.

When the kids had finally settled enough to give him their attention, he sat on the edge of the cocktail table and placed the answering machine in his lap. "Listen," was all he said, and they leaned forward, ready.

Mr. Graham, I want my picture—it filled the room and killed the sun and made Kelly clamp a hand to her mouth.

He replayed it several times, ignoring the girl's loss of color and Tony's enraged glare. And when he'd had enough himself, he looked at them, expectant.

"Why does she call you Mister?" Kelly finally asked.

He put the machine aside and folded his hands between

his knees. "It was a private joke. I, being the old man, demanded a certain respect, or so she said."

"Sure," said Mike, and crossed his eyes.

"But it's her, or a damned good imitation."

Tony stood and walked to the window, fingers jammed into his hip pockets. "What did Mrs. Etler say?"

"Not much," he answered, not certain the lie was wise. Yet there was no question of telling them what Maureen had said, not when he didn't believe it himself. "She just wants to be left alone for a while. That's understandable. I told her we'd be around if she needed something." Another lie; he didn't care.

"I saw her last night," Tony whispered.

"What?"

"At the beach. I saw Julie."

"It was a stupid dream," Mike snapped.

Devin waited for the explanation; and when it came, he didn't laugh, though clearly Mike wanted him to, and just as clearly was annoyed when he didn't.

"Oh, c'mon," Mike said. "You gonna tell me you believe in ghosts?"

"It wasn't a ghost," Tony said. "It was her."

"She's dead!" Mike told him. "Jesus Christ, Riccaro, she's dead, for god's sake!"

Devin pushed away from the table and walked into the kitchen, listening to the argument that exploded behind him. Kelly wasn't part of it. But when he opened the refrigerator just for something to do, he saw her through the backless bookcase, rubbing her shoulder just above the bandage.

Finally, with a gesture of disgust at Riccaro's back, Mike stomped over, slumped into a chair, and softly banged a fist on the table. "There's no talking to him when he gets weird like that," he said, less in anger than frustration. "God, there's no talking to him."

"It's only been a week," Devin reminded him.

"I know that."

"So . . ."

"Oh, Jesus, you believe in ghosts too?"

"Just the memory kind, Mike. Just the memory kind." He took a seat himself and pushed it back until it touched the wall. "She meant a lot to him."

"Right, sure," he said, making it clear that Julie had no monopoly on affection. "So he was special?"

"Maybe he cared a bit more than we did."

"Bull."

"He saw the ghost."

Nathan shook his head and thought a moment before shrugging. "So I was right. It was a dream."

"It doesn't matter one way or the other. Dreaming or not, last night he saw her, and he believes she was real."

"What about your machine? Do you believe that's her?"

He looked at the boy for a long, thoughtful second before standing. "I want to show you all something," he said loudly.

Tony didn't move from the window; Kelly only looked over the back of the couch and timidly shook her head.

He opened the darkroom door and waved Mike in ahead of him. On the righthand wall were metal shelves that held his paper, his cases, his notebooks and texts, bottles of chemicals in and out of their boxes; on the floor near the door were propped sections of wood and chrome frames; against the rear wall, two low filing cabinets; along the lefthand wall, a long table upon which his printing and developing equipment was ranged.

There was a wall phone by the door.

Mike stared at it all, saying nothing as Devin walked to the back and opened a bottom file drawer, took out a folder and let it fall open. He looked up, and Mike joined him, swallowing once before looking at what Devin pointed to with a crooked finger.

It was a curious picture—the top half filled with frozen smoke and skeletal beams and white tongues of flame that made the photograph seem torn; the bottom half was much brighter—people racing toward the camera, backing toward the camera, standing in the sand with hands up to protect their faces from the shards of wood and glass that hovered over them like insects.

But in the center, in the center of the pier, was a large gap in the wall, and in the center of that a stick figure standing, arms slightly wide, head back, hair blowing in the stormwind born in the fire.

Mike leaned closer and pulled quickly away, swallowing as he looked everywhere in the small room except at Devin. "How do you know it's her?"

He picked up a magnifying glass from the table and handed it to him. "And she was the only one found. Not even a trace of anyone else."

Reluctantly, Mike looked, then handed the glass back and left without a word, head down, one hand in a hip pocket. Devin heard the three talking quietly a few seconds later, and as he turned to put the folder back in its place, he stopped, and held the glass over the figure standing untouched by the flames.

Though the magnification made the face somewhat grainy, and though the features were slightly blurred because of distance and the heat, there was no doubt that it was Julie Etler.

And there was no doubt that she was laughing.

NINE

I T was dumb, sitting like a lump on the couch and staring out the window with the setting sun in his face. It was dumb, it wasn't getting him anywhere, but he didn't feel like moving, and hadn't moved since the kids had left him. Silently. Eyes touched with memory, faces touched with shadow. They'd said nothing to him when he finally came out of the darkroom, and said nothing upon their leaving, though Mike had granted him a tentative wave as the door closed behind him.

He stood at the window and watched them pass the house without looking in, slipped his hands in his hip pockets and watched the neighborhood fill for supper, and empty again as he finally sat down, this time to watch the afternoon clouds sail out of the west and blind the sun, let it see, and blind it again.

She was laughing.

she committed suicide

She was laughing.

A knock on the door.

Something was wrong, and he nearly laughed aloud at the understatement. Crazy. It was crazy. Either the photograph lied or Maureen had lied or something was wrong that he couldn't put a name to, something that raised ghosts and used telephones and put a laugh on the face of a girl burning to death.

He was strongly tempted to call Maureen, to ask if he could come over, just for a talk, a chat, find out why she'd turned so quickly to stone.

Crazy.

Another knock, a bit harder.

Something . . . wrong.

A third knock made him blink and shift, but he was forestalled by the sight of a gull that swung into the street and hovered over the curb. It was neatly framed by the window, staring in at him, watching him, drifting side to side as the wind came in gusts and sand scrabbled across the yard to claw at the house. At the pane.

The door swung open and he turned his head, saw Gayle step in with a muffled oath and slam the door behind her. When she noticed him on the couch, she scowled, lips working; when she saw him more clearly, the scowl shaded into concern and she dropped her purse on the table, sat beside him and slipped the fingers of her right hand into his hair.

He breathed deeply and smelled her, the Gayle smell of salt air and candle wax, sunlight and skin, and he tried to imagine her taking her own life. Gas. A razor. Driving off the bridge into the bay. Sleeping pills. Drowning.

Fire.

He shuddered and put his arm around her, held her close, and shook his head slowly.

The gull was still there. Floating.

"She didn't do it," he said at last, the sun dropping behind the houses across the street, the glare gone, the clouds still coming, endlessly drawn by the wake of the wind.

Gayle didn't ask who. She shifted closer, her silence gently prodding, and he spoke in a voice that sounded too old to be his; not looking at her, not looking at the gull, seeing only his reflection in the glass, fragments of himself growing together as the light dimmed and the houses across the way remained dark and empty.

He told her about Julie, about her father, about her mother, about the extraordinary claim Maureen had made in the office that afternoon. And he told her that he knew the woman was wrong (clearing his throat), she had to be wrong because Julie was too young and had too much to live for (clearing his throat) despite the cliché; that it made no difference to him about the sins of the father because he had known her too well and knew she had only been lost, not suicidal; that even if it were true, conceding a great deal but conceding nevertheless, she hadn't destroyed the pier just to destroy herself.

Clearing his throat because a thorn was stuck there.

"How do you know?" Gayle asked.

"It wasn't arson."

He turned his head, holding his breath, and she was staring without commitment.

"Marty Kilmer," he explained. "It was in the papers. He said it wasn't arson."

"Then how?"

He shrugged. "I don't know." He was pleased to hear her voice because he knew about her as well. She had never cared for Julie because Julie was too young, and too pretty, and too free too much of the time. "I don't know. Far as I can tell, the investigation's closed."

"Then I don't understand why this whole thing bothers you so much," she admitted with a helpless lift of a shoulder, taking her fingers from his hair and brushing them over his chest. "I can see why the kids are upset, though.

She's close to their own age, and they think they're going to live forever. This came as a shock, the way it always does to kids that age."

"Tony was in love with her."

Her lips parted in a smile that made him feel as if she were patting his head. "That much would have been obvious to a perfect stranger, m'dear. He couldn't keep his eyes off her. But it doesn't explain you." Her hand stopped. "Shoot me for asking, but did you love her too?"

"No," he said truthfully, not having to think. "She was just a friend. No, not *just* a friend. She was a friend, and she wanted to take lessons in photography."

"You didn't charge her, did you."

He gave her the answer with a look, and she smiled again.

"All right," she said. "A friend. But even so . . . why are you so sure she didn't do what her mother said?"

Slowly, not sure if it were lead or fear in his limbs, he pulled away, stood, and gazed out the window, to the hovering gull, rising, falling, once in a while flexing its wings.

Watching.

"Wait here a minute," he said. "I want to show you a picture."

Mary didn't want to be discouraged. Singing the praises of the saints and the Lord to half-naked heathens hardly worked anymore, but it was her burden gladly taken, and she had to do it, because the day she stopped singing was the day it would all come down around her and bury her like she was nothing more than a pebble in the tide.

On the boardwalk she sang to cover the sounds of evil in the bars, and on the streets she sang to cover the sounds of the cars; tonight, however, she stood at the rubbled entrance to the dark pier and raised her hands over her head, grabbed the straw hat before it toppled, and contented herself with one hand, it was just as good as the other.

There weren't so many people down this end, hardly any at all, because the last few concessions weren't anything different than the ones that came before, and there was no other reason to come this far, now that the pier was closed. But there were enough. Poking around the blackened wood, trying to see through to the other side, once in a while turning to look at her with questions in their laughing eyes.

She stood until her arm grew tired, and a gust off the ocean unsettled hat and wig. As she adjusted them, a policeman walked up to her just as the sun took the last light, shaking his woolly head and doffing his cap.

"Mary," he said wearily, "how many times do I have to tell you not to bother the people?"

"Ain't bothering no one that I can see," she answered, staring up at him, wondering for the hundredth time how God could have let Himself make a man so tall. "Just doing what I has to, that's all."

He scratched through hair the color of fire and shook his head again. "You can't stay," he told her gently. "You'll have to move on."

She straightened, her heavy bosom barely making a dent in the muumuu's folds. "I got a right."

"Well, that's true enough," he said, nodding his agreement. "But these other people have rights too." He winked at her. "One of them being not having to listen to you preach at them when they're just here to have a good time."

"Good times are over," she told him solemnly.

Puzzled, he cocked his head. "What?"

"I said, the good times are over. All you got to do is look around, you know that well as me."

He sighed and made a noise like snapping gum. "Good lord, Mary, have you turned into one of those end-of-the-world folk now? You carrying placards and stuff? Repent, and all that stuff?"

She thought about it seriously, and decided she didn't

know, and decided too that this cocksure young man probably wouldn't understand until it was too late. Yet she couldn't just let him walk away; it wouldn't be right. She had a duty. She had a duty to all God's children, even the police.

"Look around," she said, nodding sagely. "Look around and say these folk are having good times."

He didn't. He only replaced his cap and put his hands on his hips, thumbs hooked in his belt. "Mary, I've had a splitting headache all day and my feet are killing me. Do me that one favor and move on, all right?"

She shook her head.

"Damnit, Mary!"

Mary blinked her milky eye and stamped a booted foot. "Marty Kilmer, you gonna run me in?"

He laughed, clearly annoyed that he did. "For god's sake, Mary."

"Exactly," she said with a single sharp stab of her finger in the air. "It's for His sake I'm doing this, and don't you forget it! You think I want to do this when I could be riding the wheel or quenching my thirst with a good cold beer or sitting out on the beach and getting me a tan? You think I'm doing this for fun? You think I really like this?"

There was a crowd now, albeit a small one, and she whipped off the hat and slapped it against her leg. Sometimes Marty Kilmer just didn't understand, though God knew she'd known him since his hair wasn't fluffed all stupid like that and he was still raising all kinds of hell back in school. She had thought that by now he'd know what she was doing.

Her eye closed. And opened.

Kilmer took gentle hold of her arm. "Don't start," he said quietly. "C'mon, Mary, give me a break."

So she sang.

Tapping her foot, slapping her free hand against her hip, nodding to the crowd who clapped along with her.

She had a good voice, one of the best she'd ever heard,

and she knew all the words to all the hymns in every hymnal she'd ever seen. She never did the slow ones, though, because they only made people grin and talk about her behind their hands; but the fast ones got them listening, got them moving, got them sometimes even singing along with her, especially when they realized she wasn't going to pass the hat.

She sang, and Marty Kilmer only lifted his shoulders in a surrendering shrug and moved out of her way, leaning against one of the stands and keeping his eye on those who listened.

She sang until the wind blew, and something moved on the pier.

Stump held on to the guard rail as the Ferris wheel took him up, the open cage swaying and creaking as if it were going to drop the moment he let go.

You are not going to die, he told himself fiercely; you are not going to die 'cause you know you're in good hands.

Then the kid working the ride stopped it at the top, just as he'd been ordered.

You are not going to die 'cause you got the power back, and this time it ain't leaving.

The other passengers squealed and pointed and called down to their friends in showers of mock terror and laughter, but Stump kept his gaze straight ahead, paying no attention to the cramping in his fingers or the way his feet pressed against the floor as though he were trodding on the brakes of a car about to plummet off a cliff.

He faced the eastern horizon, the melding of black air and black water, and swallowed until the dryness in his throat forced him to stop.

Not gonna die.

Not gonna fall.

There was spritely music below, blending into noise from which a fragment of melody occasionally escaped, a note or two that prompted a lyric, a title that prompted a fleeting image of the past.

He sat there, staring, doing his best to keep his mind blanked until sweat masked his face and dripped stinging into his eyes. Then he held his breath, raised a rigid arm, and the wheel moved again.

A soft sibilant moan as the night sky retreated, the boardwalk rising to block the sea, and he staggered out of the car and leaned against the railing, not giving a damn if he was grinning to split his cheeks. He had cause. He had done it again. He had ridden to the top and he hadn't panicked once.

"How long?" he asked the curious attendant, who was holding a stopwatch up to the light.

"Two minutes, ten, Mr. Harragan," was the answer.

Stump nodded sharply and slapped the boy's arm, thrust a trembling hand into his pocket and pulled out a brand new, ten-dollar bill.

"Hey, thanks, Mr. Harragan!"

"Don't matter," Stump said, his legs functioning again. "Tomorrow we try for three."

As he hobbled away, massaging his left thigh, he felt the kid watching him with a mixture of wonder and confusion. He didn't care. Let the kid think he was drunk or on some kind of drugs. He didn't care at all. Tonight he had taken yet another step forward in reconquering height, and by this time next year he was positive he'd be able to get back what he'd lost.

And as soon as it was done, the very second it happened, he was going to get Devin to take his picture. In the car. At the top. Standing, and waving his arms. Laughing. King of the goddamn world, and he was going to hang that goddamn picture in his living room, right over the mantel.

Jesus Christ, in a few years he might even get back in an airplane!

The very notion of flying again made him a bit dizzy, and he dropped into one of the benches scattered along the pier, used mainly by fathers whose patience was fraying and by mothers whose feet were near to falling off. He gripped his knees. He sniffed. He watched three children ride round and round on a boat ride that usually held fifteen.

Damn, but he couldn't wait to tell Mary what he'd done.

Gayle paced from the kitchen to the front door while Devin watched her from the couch, trying to decipher the frown, then the smile, then the frown on her face. In her left hand was the picture, and her right hand worked the top button of her blouse—open, closed, open, closed, until she lowered the arm and began to pick at nothing on her shorts.

"You're beautiful," he said to her suddenly.

She stopped and looked down at him. "Devin, this is sort of frightening, you know it?" A finger tapped the picture, and when she realized what she was doing, she dropped it on the cocktail table and backed away from it a step. "She must have . . ." She shook her head. "It must have been the fire. It made her crazy. It's the only answer."

"Okay," he said. "But even if I grant you that—and I'm not sure that I do—the question remains—what was she doing there in the first place?"

Gayle measured the room again before perching on the couch's back. "No, sorry, you're wrong. The question is, Devin, why does it matter so much? I mean, you don't think she was murdered or something like that, do you?"

"No, of course not."

"Well then?"

Feeling like a fool, he spread his hands helplessly, telling her in the gesture that what he felt he couldn't put into words, at the same time realizing that his failure was a condemnation. She wouldn't accept it; she wasn't from Missouri, but she had to be shown.

She snapped on a lamp and the pane turned black, hazed like frost around the edges from the glow of a streetlamp.

"I'm hungry," she announced abruptly, shoving his feet off the coffee table and sitting in front of him, hands clamped to his knees. "It's past seven, in case you haven't noticed, and this is supposed to be a date."

He stared at her. "But—"

"Later," she ordered, quietly but sternly. "We'll talk about it later."

There was no use arguing. Each knew the other too well, and he surrendered by sitting up, leaning over, and accepting a kiss to seal the bargain. A long kiss. Barely felt, and felt well.

"Let me change my shirt," he said.

"What? You want to go naked?" Her eyes widened in feigned shock.

"You want me to?" he asked, stepping away from the couch before she could grab him.

"What I want, in case you're interested, is something to eat. And," she called as he turned into his room, "I don't want diner, you hear me, Graham? I don't want grease. I want restaurant. I want tourist. I want overpriced."

After pulling off his boots, he stripped off shirt and jeans and stood before his closet. Not a hell of a lot of choice, but she'd seen it all anyway, in every possible combination, none of which approached even the middle heights of fashion; so he grabbed a white shirt, grey slacks, and a pair of shoes that wanted buffing. When he returned to the living room, she was standing in front of a large picture that hung over the sideboard—the rim of the Ferris wheel and one cage, against the sun rising above a jagged bank of clouds.

"You know," she said while he sat and slipped into his shoes, "there are days when this is really beautiful, and days when it depresses the hell out of me."

"And today?"

She glanced over her shoulder before looking back and tilting her head side to side. "I don't know. I just don't know."

He opened the door to check the night air, frowning

quickly at the chill, wondering what was going on that August nights were suddenly too much like late September. The guys on the boardwalk weren't going to like it—people wearing windbreakers didn't eat much ice cream and didn't like standing around for the wheel of fortune to bring them stuffed lions. They walked to keep warm, and even the little kids didn't take the rides very much.

"Damn," he said, "I'm going to need a jacket." He closed the door and turned. "You're going to freeze in those shorts."

"Never," she answered, walked over to her purse and pulled out a square of pastel cloth. Flapped it open with a flourish. "Voilà! Instant chic."

When she zipped open her shorts and braced herself against the table to step out of them, he said, "Instant lust, you mean."

"That's dessert, Graham, and don't you forget it."

He laughed, watched her slip into the skirt, run a brush through her hair, and when she was done, he took her in his arms and held her just a moment. Seeing her eyes take his temperature. Seeing the skin of her brow. Seeing her lips before they touched his cheek and pulled away.

"Hungry," she said.

He fetched a sport jacket from his room, picked up his keys, and said, "The Jeep awaits, madame," as he opened the door.

"Only if you put the top up."

"Steak?"

She groaned. "Jesus, when did adventure become your middle name?"

"Steak," he insisted.

"Deal."

He left the light on, pulled the draperies across the window, and locked the door behind him.

"Hey, Devin?" she whispered.

He looked up, smiling, and saw the gull soar away, black in the nightwind, looking like a bat.

"What you need," said Stump to the policeman slumped wearily on the bench, "is some high-powered medicine what I brought back with me from the Orient that time I was there with my sister, rest her soul."

Kilmer stared while he pressed his temple with the heel of one hand.

"I mean it," Stump insisted. "That headache, it ain't going nowhere without my good stuff."

"So what kind of medicine is that, Harragan? Some kind of bug juice or something?"

The black man grinned with discolored teeth that made Kilmer's stomach churn. "You kidding? Bug juice?" His laugh was amiable enough, but his eyes remained open and they weren't laughing at all.

Kilmer squeezed his eyes shut again, his brow in folds, and he gasped when he felt something crawl across his nape. His free hand slapped at it, and he twisted around, looking at his empty palm, trying to pick out of the dancing air whatever had flown into him and stabbed him.

Then he sagged, one arm draped over the bench's back.

Jesus, he thought; Jesus God, it's a tumor or something. In the brain, eating me alive.

Something cool pressed lightly against his right hand. He looked; it was a glass filled with a clear liquid.

"Bug juice," Stump intoned, and this time his eyes were laughing.

"Shit it is."

"Officer Kilmer, sir, you mean you don't trust me after all these years?"

His answering smile came unbidden, and with an exaggeration of caution he brought the glass to his lips and sniffed. "Jesus, Harragan, Jesus." Then he sipped, widened his eyes at the gentle flame that coursed into his belly and rose again, much tamer. "What is it?"

"You really want to know?" the hunched black man asked.

"I'm on duty, you know," he said sternly. "Maybe you're trying to get me in trouble."

Stump shrugged and walked away when one of his workers called him for some help.

Kilmer stared at the glass, at the liquid, and couldn't deny that his headache had eased. It couldn't hurt, he decided, and anyone who was watching would think he was having a glass of water. It couldn't hurt. He drank it. And he didn't feel a thing.

They were gone. All of them who sang and all of them who just stared, including high-and-mighty Marty Kilmer who had given her a mild warning stare before ambling away, one hand on the butt of his fancy cop's gun. All of them weaving into the weaving crowds of heathens who hardly looked in her direction.

Mary sighed, and slapped on her hat.

Too long, she decided. She had taken too long, sung too many songs, got carried away by the pure glory in her voice. It always happened, and every promise she'd made to pay more heed to the audience was always broken when the power took her and the notes and words took over.

A ringless black-nailed finger rubbed under her eye, up to her temple, and when she turned toward the concession stands immediately to her right, ready to challenge any of the shills who didn't like her music, her eye widened when she saw they were all closed.

She didn't blame them. Anybody that had to sit and look at the dark pier all day, all night, day after day, probably got the screaming jitters. Too bad they didn't remember how the old days were.

Even now it seemed massive, despite the layers of plywood nailed over the posts that held up the ornate arch marking the entrance, despite the one sheet that hung slightly open, just like a door.

Massive, in a way those dinosaur bone things were when she'd taken a bus to New York to see the museums.

With a slow whistling sigh, she remembered a time when the pier was open, and inside was a vast glittering hall with tiny shops and games on either side, and a mirror-polished floor leading to the back where there were three sets of polished double doors at the top of a flight of twelve broad stairs. She'd gone through them once, when she was a girl, and discovered to her delight an auditorium suspended over the water. A concert it was if memory wasn't lying, and beneath the strings and the horns, the woodwinds and percussion, was the constant rolling sea if she listened hard enough.

It didn't hold many people, not more than two or three hundred at most, and she seemed to recall that it was filled every night, sometimes with folks from as far away as Philadelphia: orchestras and vaudeville, folk singers and comedians, animal acts, auctions, charity balls and dances when the seats were torn out and the pier began to die.

When times changed, the pier had changed, and before it had closed down, the auditorium had been converted into one gigantic fun house. She'd never gone in; she had heard the shouts and screams.

Her gaze shifted, and she followed the rise of the barrier wood to the twin-peaked filigree arch that had once held dancing lights; she peered through the gap to the ticket booth in the center, and the jagged-mouth glass front that had survived the fire.

What do you say, Lord? she thought; ain't doing no good just standing here like a lump.

A furtive glance down the boardwalk for signs of bigshot Kilmer and his stupid haircut—but there was nothing but people strolling, children running, barkers and shills competing with the music, night waiting above them, above the haze of the lights that were oddly muted, oddly wan, taking health from every face and replacing it with wax.

And the wind from the west, funneling onto the boards—it was chilly, almost cold, and if she hadn't know the month, she would have sworn it was autumn, late autumn when all the leaves and flowers had already died. The muumuu flapped against her legs, she had to hold the hat with one hand, and with a tap of one heel she decided there was no sense walking the beach tonight for treasure. She wouldn't find anything because she wouldn't be able to take the cold.

Warmth was what she needed, but it was too early yet to go home. It was empty there. Too empty. Besides, there wasn't anything but repeats on the television tonight. No sense watching them; she'd seen them a hundred times, knew every one of them by heart.

Wood creaked.

A plywood sheet, when she looked, torn loose and hanging.

Lots of music in those days, she thought as she debated; wouldn't hurt to bring it back.

Another scan for Marty Kilmer, and in spite of her girth she was at the breach and squeezed through before anyone could see her. At least she didn't think anyone did, and she doubted anyone would follow. Most of them, and she had seen plenty of them down there on the sand during the day, were waiting for the pier to collapse. Watching as if they were witnesses to an accident, only this time they knew ahead of time and would have held picnics if they could.

Heathen; they were all heathen, and she didn't know why she bothered.

Because God loves them anyway, she answered, and drew herself up, shook her head, and tapped the heel of a boot while she wondered what to do next.

"My," she said calmly. "Well, Mary, will you have a look at that." Reaching a stained hand behind her to be sure the exit hadn't closed.

The hall was still there, but nearly unrecognizable under fallen beams and mounds of rubble; the stores were gone, the games of chance, the little ice cream parlor down in the middle on the left. The gaudy paint that had her squinting, nightmare colors, blackened and peeled.

She could barely see a thing because the light from the stars through the great holes in the glass-square ceiling and the light from the boardwalk through the gaps in the walls didn't pass through. Brilliant white outside, like solid fog, like cloud; black inside, like midnight on moonless nights, like sleep without dreams.

Lord, she thought, it's *empty* in here.

"Lord," she whispered, and didn't like the sound.

Fearfully she began to hum the first hymn she could think of, forgetting its name, fumbling for the right notes that taunted out of reach, her heel tapping faster, her left hand grabbing a fistful of cloth.

A boneyard. It looked like a boneyard where giants came to die.

Oh Lord, this isn't the place for Mary. This isn't the place at all.

Bones all black and brittle, shining in their own right without benefit of light.

And something else.

Something that had never been here before.

"Oh," she said softly.

She could feel it in the way her lips went numb with a cold that was deeper than the wind that forced it in through the cracks; she could feel it in the way her tapping heel made no sound, and the hymn she had to sing wouldn't leave her dry throat no matter how often she cleared it; she could feel it in the swing of the doors at the far end of the hall, not knowing how she could see them, knowing only they were opening to a greater blackness beyond.

Ash stirred.

A canted beam shifted.

With her right hand she flipped up her patch, but nothing was any clearer though she rubbed the eye and stared.

The fun house doors opening.

The dark turning grey.

The sound of wings.

The sound of claws.

And a sudden explosion of stench that whirled through the debris, some of it she knew and some of it she didn't, but all of it bringing acid to her mouth, slamming her into a post, watering her eyes, dribbling saliva down her chin, had her scrabbling with her nails for the edge of the board. Weeping. Whimpering. Tearing a gash in her upper arm. Lifting the hat from her head and sailing it through the roof.

Something in here that smelled like death.

Banging with her fists.

Kicking with her boots.

Something in here whispering to her.

Finally cracking the plywood and setting herself free.

She stumbled onto the boardwalk, panting, head hanging, then feeling a shadow at her back that set her running with a cry—away from the boardwalk until she was level with the sand, then onto the beach and north. Not looking behind, not caring about the hat, not caring about the waves that roiled about her ankles and scoured the sparkles from her heels.

She fell when she couldn't lift another leg; she rolled onto her back when she couldn't breathe in the hiss of foam and water around her face; she looked at the night sky and felt the fire in her arm and wondered if she'd be able to get to a doctor before she died.

She didn't care.

Deserving to die was all she could think of.

It was fit punishment for her sin . . . because she hadn't prayed.

Not for one minute, not for one second, did she utter a single prayer when something came to find her in the grave of The House of Night.

TEN

THEY hadn't made love.

Gayle stared dully at the receipts she'd been trying to tally since opening the shop, poking at them with a finger, chewing the end of her pencil.

They hadn't made love.

"Damn," she whispered, and scooped the papers into a drawer hidden in the base of the register.

The seduction she had planned had been abandoned midway through the tasteless meal, when the distance in Devin's eyes belied the conversation and the smiles and the occasional reach across the table to brush a finger over the back of her hand. She had even tried to get him talking about Ken Viceroy's job offer—a chance to work for a prestigious magazine dedicated to subsidizing and publicizing photographic art. Viceroy, in exchange for the right to publish first, would send him anywhere he wanted to go, as long as when he returned, he returned with visions, not snapshots.

When that hadn't worked, when he'd responded only vaguely, she became indignant and had been ready to stomp out with head high and ego in tow; then there was hurt and self-pity, which had lasted until they were riding home.

On the low bridge that spanned the bay, black water below and starless night above, she had seen Oceantide— dark where there should have been lights in cottage windows, no headlamps moving on the streets, barely a glow from the boardwalk despite the fact that it was Friday—a band of dark that stretched almost to the oceanside in spite of the streetlamps' burning, as if it were December and all the tourists gone. Only a fan of hazy white marked the length of the boardwalk.

A questioning look to his profile made sickly by the dashboard glow, and she was startled, almost shocked, by the fatigue there, and hurt shifted to concern. He'd been working so hard, so goddamned hard, and she knew he felt he was drowning. Something was missing from his work, something mislaid, and the more he searched for it, the more lost he became. The harder he tried. Frustration, then, and the weariness of despair.

The reason why he was afraid to call Ken and tell him he'd take the job.

He had kissed her on her doorstep, an apology for his failure to rise to the occasion, and she'd slept not at all, thinking about the picture he had showed her, about the stories he told her—Tony's ghost, the answering machine.

A dapper old man sauntered into the shop, doffed his cap to her with a slight courtly bow, and stared at the newspapers on the window shelf before shrugging and leaving.

Gayle lifted an eyebrow.

Then she reached for the telephone on a shelf beneath the counter, changed her mind and decided to wait until

Devin called her. But she wasn't going to wait long. She would give him until midafternoon before she took steps herself to nudge him back on the track.

Whatever was going on—if anything was at all outside Devin's own suspicions—it was Julie's fault. Her expression hardened for a moment, features more harridan, the prettiness gone. She'd always thought Etler was a self-centered, undisciplined brat. It was too bad she was dead, god knew, and horrid the way she had died, but Gayle couldn't for the life of her understand why something so apparently cut-and-dry had gotten Devin into such an uncharacteristic state.

It didn't make sense.

Unless he had lied, and they had in fact become lovers for a time.

"Bull," she told the register. She would have known it. His idea of a poker face was to turn his back and change the subject.

The worst part of it was, it was disrupting his work.

The worst part of it was, she was probably in love with him and jealous that a dead woman could command so much of his time.

A lopsided smile finally broke her facade. "Well, which is it, jerk?"

Both, she admitted.

And if solving Julie's death would get him back to his camera, it was clear she'd have to butt in whether he liked it or not. The kids, with college snapping at their heels, were running around like chickens with their heads cut off, working solely on feelings and letting them stir confusion. If they were going to do it right, they had to have a plan. One step at a time, until they reached the end.

"My god," she said to the register, "you're beginning to sound like them now."

But there was Oceantide last night. And the gull. And the picture.

"So do it, Gayle, do it."

A relieved exhalation. If she had to, she would even close the shop. Hardly anyone had come in today anyway, and she didn't need the money. Most everyone in town knew she was a major partner in a string of successful real estate offices from here to Cape May, and the income from that had never let her starve.

She hated selling houses; candy was more her style.

Another customer popped in, nodding and smiling gratefully for the air conditioning's blessing, and bought a postcard without speaking, bumping into the rack as he left, fluttering several cards to the floor. She groaned, picked them up, was slipping them into place when she saw Prayerful Mary staring through the window. A wave, a smile, but the woman didn't respond. She shrugged and turned her back, turned again and hurried to the door as the woman walked away.

"I'll be," she muttered, standing beneath the striped awning and shading her eyes against the sun. It was the first time in years she'd seen Mary Heims without her hat, short hair like wire, thinning and dull grey. Nor did the woman have her bag. And when she looked down, she realized Mary was barefoot; the spangled boots were gone.

"Mary!"

Mary didn't turn, nor did any of the pedestrians pay her any mind.

Gayle took an uncertain step forward—"Mary!"—raised a hand to beckon—"Mary, hey!"—and slumped in puzzlement when the woman turned the corner without stopping. Her right hand slipped absently into her hair to scratch her scalp; her squint against the light became a frown. Another first—Mary hadn't tossed her so much as a single verse from a loud-voiced prayer; that, more than the missing hat and boots, worried her enough to send her back to the shop to call Devin in spite of her promise.

No one answered, and the answering machine was off.

The airconditioner sputtered.

"Don't you dare," she commanded, and blinked rapidly

in embarrassment when she realized Tony Riccaro was standing at the counter, right in front of her. He wore a white shirt and good trousers, and there was a spot of dried blood on his jaw where he'd cut himself shaving.

"You talk to it a lot?" Tony said, smiling easily, looking at the unit over the door.

"When I have to," she said, and nodded at his clothes. "Very nice. You looking for a job?"

He pointed vaguely behind him. "My mother's taking me to the mall. I gotta get clothes for college, she says."

"College? College?" And she slapped her cheek in feigned scolding for her forgetfulness. "But of course! How foolish of me to forget! You're going to be a famous Olympic wrestler and I'm going to watch you on TV, right?"

He ducked his head, and a curl of dark hair fell over his brow. "I don't know. Maybe."

"You're excited, I'll bet. I guess it's only a couple of days, huh."

He shrugged.

And suddenly, watching him squirm and wondering why Kelly stayed with that goofball Nathan when she could have this one, she had an idea.

"Tony, when are you coming back? From shopping, I mean."

"I don't know. After supper, late, I guess." He allowed her a grin. "She takes longer than God to make up her mind."

She laughed, louder when she saw his face, because she'd gone shopping with Paula once and had sworn never to do it again. "Okay, do me a favor. Talk to Mike and Kelly, I'll take care of Devin, and first thing tomorrow, all of you meet me here. Damn, no, Frances is working nights again. It'll have to be later. At your father's place because someone's gonna buy me lunch, okay?"

"Why?" he asked.

"Julie," she said, and barely suppressed a wince at the way his eyes narrowed. "I know all about it," she said

* 124

more gently. "Devin told me last night. And I want to help, really. You guys, if you'll forgive me, are so involved right now, you can't see the forest for the trees. Maybe a fresh eye will do you some good."

There was doubt in his eyes, and gratitude.

"Good. Then beat it before your mother kills you."

"But Miss Cross, Devin—"

"I said I'd take care of him, didn't I? You just be sure the rest are at the diner."

He opened his mouth, perhaps to protest, but she came around the counter and took his arm lightly, led him to the door and opened it.

"Go forth," she said, giving him a gentle push. "Go forth and make your mother happy."

The airconditioner sputtered and switched off.

The door closed with a hiss.

He saw the expression on her face as she glared at the unit, and walked quickly away. He was supposed to meet his mother at the diner, but the impulse to see Gayle Cross had been suddenly too strong.

Now he was sorry he'd given in.

What she had said almost made him feel better. Something was going to be done at last. Something was going to happen. But the moment passed when he wondered if she really did care if anything was done or not. For her, Julie evidently didn't matter as much as Devin did.

Well, so what? he demanded silently as he trotted across the street; what does it matter what she thinks if we can find out what's wrong?

He didn't know.

He only felt that it mattered very much.

"Tomorrow," he reminded himself. "That's tomorrow."

Today was something else—the last Friday at home, and he had to go all the way to the stupid county mall just to watch his mother frown at his choices, argue when he insisted, and finally walk away with a *do what you want* disgusted wave that told everyone in the store what an ingrate he was. That's the way all their buying trips ended, yet when his father had suggested simply giving him the money and letting him go on his own, she had disagreed: "Honestly, Sal, the boy'll just spend it all on jeans. How's that going to look—wearing nothing but jeans and T-shirts when he's supposed to be in college?"

Right, Mom, he thought as he approached the diner. So how come you can't decide what I'm going to do with my life?

He kicked at the steps in disgust and jerked his head around when he heard the shriek of brakes, the unmistakable crunch of bumper meeting bumper.

A man in a pale linen suit was climbing out of a car whose rear end had been smacked by a station wagon. The woman driving it was opening her door, and the two of them were glaring at Prayerful Mary, who was just stepping onto the curb, ignoring the voices raised behind her. Instead she seemed about to walk right into the diner wall, swerving at the last moment to grab Tony's arm.

"Death," she whispered, and cocked her head so that her cheek almost touched her shoulder. "You know any prayers to save you from death?"

Not knowing what to do, he could only shake his head and try to free himself without yanking.

"Too bad, boy," she said. "I don't know them either."

Her hand dropped.

A siren called.

She brushed a palm over her bosom and wandered away, shuffling, head down, the tangles of her hair bobbing like weakened springs.

He glanced toward the accident and saw the man gesticulating to a short-sleeved policeman, every so often pointing at Mary and looking to the woman driver for corroboration. When they all stared in his direction, he hastened into the diner and spotted Charlene in one of the booths, watching the scene on Summer Road while she snapped her chewing gum.

His mother was waiting at the end of the counter, dressed in summer white, her short blonde hair freshly curled, her face in profile like a woman ten years younger.

Shaking off the touch of Mary on his arm, he moved silently down the aisle, signaling to his father not to tell her he was there.

He covered her eyes with his hands. "Guess who?"

Her hands touched his for the briefest of moments. "A tall, dark, millionaire stranger who's going to take me away from all this. Preferably to the desert."

"You got it," he said, slipping onto the stool beside her.

And when she looked at him, he had to look away. They were there again, the tears, always hiding behind her smiles, crouching behind her words. *My baby*, they would say, and he'd feel like crying himself.

Then his father came over and, ignoring a stern look from Paula, handed him a few bills. "When she's done making you look like Joe College, buy yourself something decent."

"Sal!" she said.

"Gotta work, hon," he told her and hurried away.

Tony didn't count the money; he folded it into his pocket, braced his elbows on the counter, and nodded when Charlene asked if he wanted something to drink.

"We're going to be late," his mother warned.

"I'll be quick, Mom," he said. "It's hot out there. I'm dying."

Sal wandered by, flicking the coffee urns with a towel, rearranging stacks of cups and plates that didn't need it. Tony watched him, perplexed at his aimlessness, before looking down the length of the counter. There was no one else there. And no one in the booths. It was lunch hour, the start of summer's last weekend, and the place was empty except for family.

"The casinos must be having a sale or something," his father said with a painful smile, passing yet again. "End of the summer clearance, something like that."

"Right," he said, quickly draining the glass Charlene gave him. Suddenly he wanted to be gone, out of the diner, out of town. He wanted to be in a place where there were people, lots of them, who weren't acting as if they were walking in their sleep.

"Let's go, Mom," he said, standing. A nod to his father, and he went outside to wait, bowing his head against the heat, telling himself this wouldn't be as painful as he feared.

Lying to himself; it was one more nail in the coffin, one more shove to send him out of the house.

There was no sign now of the accident, and he walked down the block to his mother's car, groaning when he saw the closed windows. An oven. It was going to be an oven in there. The glass was nearly white with the glare, the tires looked as if they were melting. He turned to scowl in the diner's direction, turned back and sighed. A goddamned oven.

He tried the handles; the doors were locked.

With resigned hands on his hips, he stared at the intersection, watching without seeing the traffic slip by, feeling a runnel of sticky perspiration make its way from his temple. He wiped it away with a sleeve, checked to see if his mother was coming, and eased himself down onto the fender to wait. She'd snap at him for it—*scratches, Tony, scratches*—but it was better than standing.

And it gave him another chance to consider what Miss Cross had said. Something was bothering her, that much was clear, but he doubted she believed he'd seen Julie on the beach. His gaze lowered to the pavement. Maybe she'd seen something herself. Maybe she'd heard the voice on the machine.

"Tony."

His head snapped up, and he barely stopped himself from lunging at Mike, who was standing in front of him.

"Sorry again," Mike said, hands up, smiling. "It's getting to be a habit."

128

Tony looked down again, fingers half in his pockets.

"Talked to Miss Cross," Mike told him.

He nodded.

"You going?"

"Why not?"

He could feel Mike shrug, and was too hot to care. Where the hell was his mother? Did she want him to fry?

The silence, weighted by the heat.

The heat, turning everything lifeless white.

"Well," Mike said, somewhat reluctantly, "gotta go. Kelly's waiting."

Tony looked up without raising his head. "Okay."

Mike smiled, touched Tony's shoulder in farewell, and moved on, cutting across Summer Road through a break in the traffic, trying not to run. His hip was killing him. From the moment he'd gotten out of bed, there'd been a tiny knife working at the bone, just painful enough to feel when he was standing still, slipping into the background when he was moving.

It scared him.

He hadn't felt anything like this since the first few days after it had been broken, and he hadn't said a word to anyone because he didn't want X-rays to find anything wrong. Not now. Not when he was about to join the world.

Swerving past the main entrance to the Surf 'N Wind, he was reminded of the day he had met Julie there, and that reminded him of last night. The picture. Julie laughing. All the way home and into his dreams; mouth open, teeth gleaming, eyes reflecting the fire around her.

Laughing as if she didn't believe she would die, as if it were one of his backfiring jokes.

It had gotten to Riccaro too, he could tell. The guy looked like he hadn't slept in a week, and Mike didn't think anything Miss Cross could do was going to help. He didn't even think he'd go in the morning. Time was too short. There was packing to do, plane tickets to confirm

. . . and plans for one last Michael Nathan special so Oceantide wouldn't forget him while he was gone.

He grinned and rubbed his palms together.

It was going to have to be a good one, not just sneaking around scaring kids half to death. It was going to have to be special. Unique. With his indelible stamp upon it—without getting him into trouble.

There was a glimmering somewhere back in his skull, and as he took the wooden incline up to the boardwalk, he teased it a little to see if he could find out what it looked like. And when he couldn't, he shrugged; it would come. In time it would come, and then not even Kelly would laugh at him again.

He hesitated for a moment at the entrance to Harragan's Pier before climbing up on a bench, with a curse for his hip, and looking over the slow-moving crowd up to Balloon Heaven. And smiled. There she was, sitting on her stool, hair matted around her face, holding a dart in one hand. Beautiful. Looking a little tired, though, just like Tony. Her mouth moving as she called out her spiel.

"Son, this ain't no parachute jump, case you hadn't noticed while you're watching all them girls."

He turned around and jumped off the bench with a proper guilty expression.

Stump shook his head. "You trying to kill yourself?"

"Just looking, that's all," he said.

The black man snorted at the mind of a teenager, took out a handkerchief and blew his nose. "You going soon?"

"Couple of days," he said, dropping onto the bench.

The rattle of wheels on iron tracks; the pop of a balloon and the cry of a child.

"Well, you get that pack of yours together," Stump said as he walked away, "and you come down before you go. On the house, you understand? All night 'til I close."

Mike smiled his thanks, but the man's back was turned, and he jumped up again and headed for Kelly. This might be it, he thought; this might be the plan.

A dozen steps later he heard the faint cry of someone screaming. His head swiveled to find the sound, a hand above his eyes, and he saw a small clump of people down by the last lifeguard stand, the one nearest the dark pier. They were milling at water's edge, and he was able to make out the lifeguard in the ocean, carrying a flotation cone. There was no one in the water that he could see, but the swells were high, and the people were pointing, and he went up on his toes as if the extra inch would let him see better.

The lifeguard bobbed and slid down the far side of a wave.

Another pair from the center stand was pushing the lifeboat into the water, one scrambling in and picking up the oars.

A whistle blew, and someone was yelling with a bull-horn.

When a hand took his elbow, he didn't move; the touch was too familiar.

"Can you see anything?" Kelly asked.

"Nope. They might've gone under already."

Kelly shuddered. "God, I hope not."

His hand drifted to her back and scratched it lightly, absently, until the sunlight on the water grew too much and he looked away.

The whistle blew again.

The lifeboat rode the waves.

"C'mon, Kell," he said quietly, "we can read about it in the paper. You left the cash box, Jimmy'll shoot you." He led her back to the stand and helped her over the counter. "Can I have a freebie?"

"Sure," she said, handing him a dart. "That's about the only way I'm going to get a customer today."

"Tell me about it, darling," Frankie said from the wheel of fortune. "Hey, Nathan."

Mike only nodded. He didn't like Junston, especially the

way he smiled—it reminded him too much of the way a doctor smiled just before he jabbed in the needle.

A distant shout.

The bearded man leapt cleanly over his counter and trotted to the railing. Mike watched him and turned around, aimed the dart and threw it.

It missed.

Kelly was fanning herself vigorously with a magazine, and he told her what Gayle Cross had told him an hour or so ago. She didn't answer. He lined up another shot, missed again. Then he slumped against the counter and put his hands into his pockets.

"So what do you think?" he asked over his shoulder.

"I think," Kelly said, "it's silly."

"What?"

"It's silly."

"But how can you say that?"

"You asked, I told you." The magazine moved even faster. "She's dead, for crying out loud, isn't she? Are the cops worried? Is her mother making noise? This is dumb, Mike. We've got better things to do, don't you think? Don't you think we've got more important things to worry about?"

"But the machine—"

"A practical joke, what else?"

"Well, Miss Cross thinks—"

"I don't care, okay? I have to sit out here all damn day doing practically nothing, I have to go home and get ready to go, I have to watch you making eyes at every skirt on the boardwalk—"

"Hey!" he said, finally turning all the way.

Her face was flushed and drenched with sweat. "It's true, and you can't deny it."

"Well, for god's sake," he snapped, "I'm not blind, am I? I mean, can't I even look?"

"It's not the looking I care about," she snapped back, "it's the thinking behind the looking!"

"Well, Jesus, we're not married, you know."

"And not likely to be either," she said, slamming the magazine on the counter and snatching up a handful of darts. "Do you know, really know how long it takes to be a doctor? Do you have any clue at all what it's going to be like?"

He blinked in confusion. He had no idea what was going on, and people were looking at them, at him, because he was arguing with a stupid girl selling chances at breaking balloons. He threw up his hands, slapped his legs, and started to walk away. Then he made an about-face and marched back.

"For crying out loud, what did I say?" he asked her, voice deeper than normal, tension raising the muscles in his neck. "What did I say, huh?"

"Nothing," she answered flatly, staring past him toward the beach.

"Then what was that crack about being a doctor?"

"It wasn't a crack, Michael. It was a statement of fact."

Again he couldn't find the words; again he started to walk away, and came back.

"Kelly—"

"Death," a voice said behind him.

He whirled, anger giving him a fist he held cocked and ready. "Oh, for Christ's sake," he said in disgust when Prayerful Mary stepped so close she forced him against the counter, the heat of her, the smell of her, averting his face.

"Death," the woman repeated, and opened her mouth in a grotesque smile, her eye fixed on a point above his shoulder. "You talking about death?"

"No!" he said, anger abruptly gone. He looked to Kelly, who was only staring.

"You better," the old woman said, still smiling, rocking her head side to side as she took a step back. "You better. 'Cause I know, boy, I know."

A siren at the far end of the beach; no one passing the stand moved any faster.

Mike struggled to find a smile. "Hey, look, I don't know what you're talking about. I mean . . ."

Mary took a deep breath so slowly he thought she would fall over. Her face lifted to the sky. Her arms hung limply at her sides. "*I* know," she said, a child with a secret. "*I* know."

Frustrated, and without the faintest idea how to get rid of her, he said to Kelly, "I'll see you later. We have to talk, I guess."

"Death," Mary said.

"There's nothing to talk about," Kelly answered, still refusing to meet his gaze. "And don't expect me at your stupid meeting tomorrow. I have a job, unlike some other people I could name."

"Oh . . . Jesus!" he yelled, and stomped away, colliding with Junston just as the man made to climb back over his counter. "Look where you're going, huh?" he yelled. "A guy can't even walk around here anymore."

"Grief, what's the matter with him?" Junston asked.

"I'm sure I don't know, or even care." Kelly snatched up the magazine and began flipping the pages. She saw nothing. She felt nothing in her hands. When she saw what she was doing, she threw it across the booth and winced at a twinge in her shoulder, where Angie's dart had pierced it.

She wanted to cry.

She wanted to roll down the shutter and run after Mike, to tell him she was sorry, that she didn't mean anything she said, that she'd do anything if he'd only forgive her.

She wanted to ask Mary why the hell she wasn't locked up in an asylum someplace, but the woman was gone, a gap where she had stood that none of the crowd passed through.

An hour, she noted as she checked her watch; one more hour and she could go. Jimmy would take the night shift; and then she could leave, find herself a nice dark corner and have a good cry.

The siren wailed, high and low.

She didn't bother to look; it was too far away, and she could only hope that whoever had been in the water was all right.

A cyclist swept past, tiny bell ringing.

"Balloon Heaven!" she called listlessly. "Three for a quarter only at Balloon Heaven!"

Making an ass of herself, she decided, taking a sip of warm cola in a can made warmer by the sweat on her hands. All day, ruining her last summer home, making an ass of herself while Mike wanders around, undressing the women, flirting, not giving a damn that some people have to work to earn their money, some people don't have parents who don't have to worry about bills. He was going to be in for a shock when he found out just how hard it was in medical school; no dumb jokes, no stupid plans, no time for anything but corpses to cut up and pictures of people's insides.

No time for her.

She frowned, trying not to remember the last time she had spoken to Julie, five days before the fire. Thinking maybe it would have been different if it hadn't been so damned hot.

"Christ, I'm going to fry," Julie said, wearing a bathing suit that was practically invisible. She ignored the looks and the whistles, winked at Kelly instead and told her she ought to wet down the T-shirt a little, give the guys another reason to come over and spend their money.

Kelly blushed, hating herself for doing it, hating Julie for suddenly breaking into a laugh.

"Hey, doesn't Mike like it, seeing you that way?"

She turned to straighten the stuffed lions. "I don't know. I never asked."

This time Julie's laugh was more like a cackle. "Jesus, you sure are sure about him, aren't you?"

She didn't answer with anything more than a brusque nod.

"You watch too many movies, you know that, Kelly? It's like you spend half your life in a theater."

"What do you mean?"

"You watch too many happy endings. Boy and girl go off to college together, study together, fuck around a little, graduate together, and live happily ever after. That about it?"

"No," she said sullenly, leaving the animals alone. "That's not it at all. I'm not stupid, Julie."

"Oh yes you are," Julie had said with a smug smile. "He's a good-looking guy, your Mike is. You think those California girls aren't going to try to get into his pants?"

Kelly had looked at her then, eyes half-closed in suspicion. "You interested or something?"

Julie turned a dart over in her hands. "Maybe."

"Well, don't be."

"Oh my. Is that a threat?"

Her temper rose near to breaking. "Just stay away from Michael, okay? Just leave him alone."

Julie leaned forward on her forearms and dropped the dart to the floor, looked up and said, "Kelly, if I want him, I'll have him. If he wants me, he can have me. And believe me, kid, there isn't a goddamned thing you can do about it."

Kelly lifted a hand to slap her, pulled it down and gripped the counter's edge. "Don't be too sure," she answered, her voice tight enough to hurt.

Julie leaned away, eyes wide, mouth open, then gave her a wink as she started to walk away. Before she slipped into the crowd, however, she looked back and said, "You want to bet, Kelly? You want to bet he's really yours?"

She had shrugged, not really caring.

But she hadn't forgotten, because suddenly, that night, and every night thereafter, she'd wondered what it would be like to be touched by another man. To smell another man's breath. To feel another man inside her. She wondered if Mike was thinking the same about different women, and by the end of the third night she'd become convinced that he was.

Happy endings.

She felt like a little kid, and like a goddamned fool.

Which was exactly what she didn't need right now. Right now she needed peace, time to think, time to get herself together because in less than two weeks she was leaving home—with Mike right behind her.

Oh Christ, she thought in sudden panic; oh Jesus, what the hell have I done?

A young man, obviously drunk and just as obviously not giving a damn, clapped his hands to get her attention, handed her a five-dollar bill and loudly demanded all the darts. She handed them over and found something to do that required she bend down below the level of the counter. There was no smile when she was proved right—with a grunt he threw all of them at once, most of them showering harmlessly onto her back.

"Beat it," she said when she straightened.

"Hey, I got more chances," he complained, swaying, face contorting.

He tried scrambling over the counter, but she placed a palm firmly against his chest and shoved as hard as she could. He sprawled, yelled, rolled onto his hands and knees and staggered to his feet.

She waited for him to try again.

He sniffed and adjusted his collar. "Bitch," he muttered, and strolled away, weaving toward the railing, stiffening suddenly and collapsing on a bench.

Kelly stared at him.

"It's the heat," Junston offered, calling from his side of the wall. "Fourth or fifth one I've seen today. All that water out there, and they're dropping like flies."

The man lay on his stomach, shirt hiked out of his shorts, one sandal hanging.

"Maybe I should call the cops or something," she said.

"Forget it, darlin'. They'll only hassle you."

"But if he's sick . . ."

Two elderly women stopped by the bench. One leaned over and touched the man's neck, the other hurried away.

"Good Samaritans," Junston said with a laugh. "Wait long enough and you find a good Samaritan."

A loose, mouse-eared balloon rose from the beach.

Kelly couldn't stop watching the woman bustle around the fallen drunk, stretching him out, taking off her hat and placing it over his face. Then she perched beside him and chaffed his wrists.

A lifeguard blew his whistle.

A dark figure stepped in front of Kelly, and she blinked and leaned away, and blushed when she saw Devin, cameras around his neck, a western hat shading his face, pastel shirt darkly damp against his chest.

"Ran into Mike," he said, nodding to his right. "He said you were crazy, so I decided to come around and throw cold water on you or something."

Her smile was self-conscious.

"You okay?"

"Oh, sure," she said without conviction, bending over to pick up the darts the drunk had thrown. "No sweat." When she stood again, hair webbed over her face, she heard the double click of a shutter and the whir of a camera's motor. "Hey," and she looked for Devin, saw him at the far end, lifted a forearm to knock the hair away from her eyes, and he took another picture.

"I'm going to call it 'Slave Labor,'" he said with a grin. "You want a copy?"

The tears then, working like acid in her eyes, and she turned her back on him. "Don't," she said. "I don't like that."

Blinking at the stuffed animals ranged above her, asking herself what the matter was, why someone couldn't even take her picture without her taking his head off.

She pulled up the bottom of her T-shirt and wiped her

eyes, smoothed the top down and took a deep breath. "Sorry," she said.

"No problem. My fault, I should have asked."

A timid smile. "Am I going to be famous?"

His expression froze for just a second before folding and creasing into a broad smile. "Just like all my other models, Kell. You're just the prettiest, though."

She wanted him to stop it, now, and wanted him to go on, and felt the tears again when he picked up a dart she'd missed and tossed it underhand at the wall.

A balloon broke.

He laughed with his head back. "Y'know, that's the first thing I've done right today, and I don't know how I did it." The laughs came in spurts, as if he were choking. "Do I get a prize?"

She wanted to say *me* so badly her chest began to hurt, but she shook her head instead, and he gave her a clown's sigh. "Well, maybe next time."

Again her mouth opened to say something else, and again the words scratched her throat without forming; and before she could think of something to keep him from going, Jimmy Opal came up with a brunette on his arm who made Kelly feel as if her figure was no better than Angie Riccaro's.

"Time," the little man said, crooked teeth constantly showing. "Check the loot box, my girl, and let yourself free."

She was startled, not realizing the time, and sputtered when Devin told her he'd see her tomorrow, and reached over and touched her arm with a finger. "No kidding," he said, holding up one camera. "If it works, you'll be the first to see it."

Then he moved on, dodging women with strollers, toddlers determined to slam into his knees, weaving through the crowd and barely noting a bare-headed man sitting limply on the boards, another man beside him, mopping his face with a wet cloth. He'd already seen enough of that for one day, and after checking a half-dozen places where thermometers were posted, had given up trying to understand why it was happening.

It was hot, but only summer hot; no more humid than one could expect at the shore; and nobody seemed engaged in any activity more strenuous than trying to find shade. He felt like an idiot with the cowboy hat on, but after he'd seen his fourth or fifth victim of heatstroke, he'd decided he'd better not take any chances.

When he had stopped at Gayle's store to apologize for his inattention the night before, she had thought the hat hilarious and kissed him so many times he felt himself blushing. Then she'd told him about the next morning, and he'd left the shop at once grateful to her for not trying to laugh his uneasiness away, and wondering if perhaps she'd been right from the start—that he was, in fact, making too much of all this and ought better to be spending his time working at his living.

He couldn't decide, and spent the rest of the day ducking into keno parlors, Skee-Ball halls, arcades, and caverns where pokereno was played. Mainly for the cool air, sometimes to take a picture, finally taking to the beach when a woman toppled from her stool in a bingo parlor, sighing as she fell, her head hitting the floor with a thud that turned his stomach.

Now he was going to take some daylight shots of The House of Night. Stark against the sky. Brutally dark above the sea. It had come to him while he'd been talking with Stump, about nothing, about everything, and had found himself staring over the heads of the bathers at the dark pier.

He wasn't going to try to go in. The outside only, from the sand and the boardwalk and maybe from beneath.

The crowd grew sparse.

Families were dragging umbrellas and children off the sand toward supper.

Clouds, some weighted with grey at the bottom, hovered

over the water as the breeze changed direction. No feeling of rain yet, but the air seemed cooler, and a balloon bobbed and darted above the boards in the breeze, before it was thrust over the buildings and vanished toward the bay.

And the closer he came to the fire-ravaged pier, the slower he walked, remembering a time when he'd strolled into the fun house, out over the water, taking pictures of himself in the distorting mirrors, cursing when a floor gave way and he tobogganed to the next level. He'd decided then that fun houses were for kids who had a better sense of humor.

Closer, then, and slower. Searching for angles, for frames, letting his eyes do the lens's work while his mind was on hold; letting his instincts do the work while his imagination did the goading.

Curved and twisted roof supports; panes of tinted glass still miraculously in place; ragged gaps in the walls that didn't match gaps on the other side; the black of it not reflecting the white of the sun, the rippling of the water, the colors of those who remained on the beach for that last touch of tan.

And Prayerful Mary standing in front of the entrance, minus hat and boots.

He was fifty yards away before he brought the camera to his eye, shaking his head without moving when he couldn't see enough of the pier to set the scene, pressing against a narrow wall that separated two stands, hunching over and waiting for a skateboarder to pass.

Sing, Mary, he told her silently, moving forward, still crouching; sing for me, love, and I'll buy you the best dinner on the shore.

The shutter snapped, the motor whirred, and he angled to the middle of the boardwalk; shutter and motor; leaning against the railing, just Mary and the pier's corner; shutter; motor; back to the center where he stopped when the woman dropped heavily to her knees as if she'd been clubbed from behind.

"Hey," he said softly and started to run.

She pitched forward onto her hands, her head low and trembling, and the wind slapped at a sheet of plywood as if it were a door loose on its hinges.

"Hey, Mary!" he called, and pushed a man aside, kicked a tennis ball out of the way, and found himself in the clear with nearly forty feet still to go. "Mary, hang on!"

Too big, he thought; she's too big for this kind of weather, for her age. A heart attack. Exhaustion. He tried to pick first-aid procedures out of his mind, couldn't find them, ran harder just as she fell prone, arms out before her, fingers reaching for the plywood.

Slinging the camera around his neck, he dropped beside her—"Take it easy, Mary, take it easy; it's only Devin"— and took hold of her shoulder. She was trembling, quaking, and he averted his face when sand and dust clouded over them from the pier. "Take it easy, you'll be all right." He looked back down the boardwalk, yelled for someone to get a cop or call an ambulance, and tried to roll the woman onto her back.

She didn't move.

The wind blew.

He used both hands to take hold of the shoulder and, with an effort that made him grunt, finally had her faceup.

Her patch was gone, both eyes tightly closed, her chest rising and falling, one bare heel drumming against the boards. The face was pale, lips without color, her double chin coated with sand clinging to sweat.

"Mary . . . Jesus, I don't—"

Her left hand snapped over her stomach and grabbed onto his wrist, and he gasped at the pain and tried to pry the hand loose.

"Mary, don't, it's Devin! For god's sake, please, let me—"

The eyes opened.

"Death," she said, groaning.

But he couldn't tell her she was wrong; he couldn't tell her help was coming.

"No prayers," she said. "I know. *I* know."

Her head tilted back then, as if she were trying to look at The House of Night, neck straining, heel thumping, her hand whipping away to claw at the air.

But he couldn't tell, because one eye was pure white, and the other solid red.

And the flesh of her cheeks was peeling off and turning black.

ELEVEN

I N time there was Marty Kilmer, flushed from running, panting heavily as he slipped a gentle arm around Devin's shoulder and eased him away from Mary's body, glancing at but saying nothing about the shirt over the dead woman's face. A few questions Devin heard as if through sporadic radio static, a few monosyllabic responses while he backed away and held his camera close to his bare chest.

The breeze was cooler.

He couldn't look away.

The lights somehow brighter.

He couldn't look away from Mary and the dirt-black of her soles.

The curious began drifting to the boardwalk's north end as the sirens returned, and a rescue-squad van sped up on a ramp and stopped with lights spinning. A heavyset attendant set his equipment down beside the dead woman, lifted the shirt, and turned away with a harsh inhalation; his partner looked as well, and the two of them stared at Devin before opening the van's back and taking out a stretcher.

There was no attempt at resuscitation.

Devin's teeth were chattering.

Voices low and questioning, and he wrenched his head toward the dunes when he felt people watching him as much as they watched the attendants do their job.

He didn't think. He couldn't think. And his fingers bound themselves with the strap of the camera, a reaction he didn't notice until his fingers began to tingle. When he freed them, he flexed them to start circulation again, ignoring the jabs of pain when a gust of wind fluttered the hem of the muumuu and made it seem as if Mary were trying to rise.

No one else noticed.

Devin closed his eyes.

Soon after, three more patrolmen arrived in a squad car, and within seconds, forestalling questions with a grunt and a look, Kilmer had them in a line to keep the onlookers away. Then he walked over to Devin and with him watched the ambulance swallow the stretcher.

"Do I have to go?" Devin asked as the van backed away toward the ramp and the street. "With them, I mean."

Kilmer shook his head. "Not unless you're a relative."

"No."

Kilmer nodded, and nodded for him to stay where he was while he walked over to the dark pier and looked at the gap in the plywood barrier. He stepped closer and peered in, and jerked back with a grimace and a wave of a hand in front of his face. He spat and shook his head, and glanced up at the twin arches that barely caught the boardwalk's light.

Don't think, Devin told himself; don't think.

When the policeman returned, expression professionally blank, Devin pressed his arms tight to his sides and forced himself to shudder, to shake off the cold inside and out, to stop his teeth from clacking together. A slow breath. He puffed his cheeks and blew softly.

Then Kilmer asked, "What happened?" and Devin didn't know.

Stump disdained a last-minute, desperate prayer and raised both hands over his head. He trembled so violently he feared he would topple. But the trembling soon calmed. The night air dried his palms. He clapped his hands once, knowing he was grinning like a madman, or a dead man, and not giving a damn. The first time; this was the first time in years he'd stopped counting that he had been able to let go of the safety bar without biting his tongue, swallowing a scream, and he wished Devin was here to take that picture, so he could prove to the world that he wasn't too old a dog to learn a great new trick.

Dumbo Planter's ego-puncturing be damned, *this* was a true triumph.

When he spotted the gathering crowd at the far end of the boardwalk, he lowered his arms slowly. Lights whirling. A siren. Squinting in the night breeze, he forgot where he was and leaned to his left, trying to see more clearly, to make sense of sight and sound. When the car tilted and creaked, he gasped, looked straight down, and saw with widening eyes the tiny people standing quietly in line below him, the tops of their heads, nothing else, and he almost lost every drop and bite of his dinner.

Sonofabitch, he thought, grabbing the bar again and swallowing the night air; sonofabitch, you ain't gonna get to be an old man this way, you stupid shit.

His eyes remained closed while he regulated his breathing; his eyes opened when the siren sounded again. A fight, he figured, or a mugging, some idiot drunks getting out of hand—something stupid that seemed to fit right in nowadays, and glad he was that none of those creeps tried to mess around on his pier. They knew better. Only one lesson, and they knew better than to mess around with a white-haired black man who could toss any one of them over the side with one hand.

They knew better.

So did he; he was pressing his luck.

He nodded.

The wheel turned.

When the cage reached the bottom, he got off with a strut and grin, and handed the kid a ten-dollar bill, waved away his delighted thanks, and sauntered off denying the quaking weakness in his legs. It hadn't been three minutes—shy four eternal seconds—but it was still a milestone he would tell Mary or the cop as soon as they came around and the Friday crowd wound down. Meantime, he'd treat himself to a bit of that bug juice he'd given Kilmer last night.

It wouldn't cure the terror that lingered in his gut, but it would tame it a little, sure as hell.

In time there was a T-shirt borrowed from Kilmer's locker in the police station basement, a worn padded chair in a tiny office, pale walls, and the harsh sounds of typewriters and a dispatcher and someone shouting to someone else to get to a fight at a bar on Summer Road.

Devin watched the stark metal desk and Kilmer seated behind it, knowing it wasn't Marty's, vaguely remembering a rumple-suited man telling them they could use it until the report was finished, but don't take all night for crying out loud.

"I'm not sure," he said, as Kilmer poised a pen over a lined sheet of paper.

The world was returning as he allowed his senses room to breathe again—the smell of coffee, and plastic, and an airconditioner that worked only just a bit harder than the warmth in the building. A damp warmth, muggy, as if the insulated windows had found July again and trapped it. Though Kilmer was taller and larger than he, the T-shirt felt as if it were strangling him, and he kept tugging at the neckline to give himself some air.

"You didn't see anyone hit her?"

Devin shook his head.

"She just fell?"

"Right."

Kilmer lit a cigarette and immediately stubbed it out, immediately lit another one and glared at it before putting it to his lips.

Again Devin explained what he thought he remembered—leaving Kelly with a promise, following Mary with his camera and seeing her standing and falling, then kneeling beside her as she started to die. The sound of her heel on the boards. The sound of the ocean. Telling a man he'd known for several years that he hadn't the slightest idea what had driven her down. Kilmer only shrugged, rubbed a finger under his nose, and muttered about a doctor, and asked him yet again who might have tossed acid into her face.

Devin shook his head.

"Maybe from the pier," Kilmer suggested with only the slightest hint of hope. "From that hole. She was facing it, right?"

"Yes. And maybe. But what kind of acid would take that long? Maybe not as much time passed as I thought, but surely I would have noticed something, don't you think?"

Kilmer shrugged again: *i'm a cop, pal, and you take pictures, who the hell knows?*

Devin shifted, pulled his legs in and crossed them at the ankles. "What did they find in the pier?"

Kilmer looked startled. "What?"

"In the pier," he repeated. "Did your men find anything in the pier?"

"No," the policeman said. "Junk, that's all, crap I wish they'd clean up before someone breaks his neck." He rolled his eyes toward the ceiling. "Shit. Sorry."

148

Devin said nothing. Kilmer was lying; no one had searched The House of Night since the day after the fire.

Kilmer cleared his throat roughly. "You know her long?"

"Everyone knew her," he said.

Spangled boots and huge straw hat, a grating voice that somehow seemed clear when the hymns began. Prayerful Mary. Mary Louise Heims to those who went back that far and could remember how her once-wealthy father had been mayor of the town for almost a decade, how her mother had drowned during a boat race off the South Carolina coast, how Mary had been married to someone no one remembered, and no one knew what had happened to the husband or if there'd been any children.

"Maybe," suggested Kilmer, "there was someone under the boards. When she fell—face down, right?—he threw something in her face."

"Just then?" Devin said, skepticism a scowl. "What was he doing, just waiting for someone to keel over? Besides, the wood wasn't burned, only Mary."

"You're a sicko, you don't act like other people." But the man's tone didn't believe any of it either.

Devin held the camera in his lap, turning it over, wrapping and rewrapping it in the thin black strap.

"Don't suppose you got a picture of him," Kilmer asked then, pointing the pen at the camera.

"There wasn't a him," he insisted, and said nothing more when he remembered Julie and the fire.

Impatiently, Kilmer tapped the pen on the form he was trying to fill out and sighed loudly, explosively. "Didn't see her hat either, huh?"

Devin frowned. "What?"

"Her hat. You know, that thing she always wore? It wasn't there. Did you see what happened to it?"

"No," he snapped. "I didn't see any stupid hat. And I

don't know where her boots are, and I sure as hell didn't take that stupid patch."

"Okay, Dev, take it easy, just asking."

The telephone rang.

The policeman hesitated before answering, looked at Devin once, and scribbled something on the paper. When he hung up with a disgusted roll of his eyes, Devin stood. "Do I have to stay?" He knew the official word was in, and the smell of coffee was making him sick.

"No," Stump said weakly.

Samuel Planter, in snug polo shirt and tailored shorts, nodded solemnly, though without much sympathy. "I just heard it up there," a hand with an unlit cigar gesturing vaguely toward the dark pier. "Heart attack, I guess. Laureen and I were taking the air when we heard it."

Stump shook his head in dismay and eased himself slowly onto a bench. "I can't believe it. Heart attack? Christ, her heart was better than mine, damnit." Said without heat. Staring at his tennis shoes streaked with grime and oil.

Planter sniffed, and stroked his jaw as he surveyed the Friday night riders with cultivated amusement. "You having a thing with that white lady, Harragan? You know what's under that thing she wore?"

Stump looked up. "Shut up, Dumbo. I'm mourning."

Planter laughed and threw the cigar down to the beach. "Crazy old man and a loony old woman. Jesus, Stumpie, Laureen's gonna love it. You got to come over to the house when you can, tell her all about it."

"On a cold day, Dumbo."

The man walked away, laughing loudly and shaking his head, stopped under the clowns and looked over his shoulder. Laughed louder, threw up his hands, and vanished into the crowd.

Stump didn't move.

The Ferris wheel creaked.

In time there was a shaky signature on a typed version of his statement, a friendly clap on the shoulder, a murmured thanks for his help, and Devin was outside at last, blinking, shivering once, thinking stupidly that he had to walk all the way home because he hadn't brought the Jeep.

Two blocks south and he stopped, half turned, and kept on going. Maybe he should have stuck around a bit longer, or at least asked about—what? Heart failure? Murder? Accident? Maybe he should have waited to learn something more about the poor woman. He knew nothing of medicine, but enough to understand that whatever had happened to the fat woman's face and eyes probably wouldn't be determined for a while yet.

He stopped again.

If at all.

Mary had no family; there was no one to demand answers, and Kilmer didn't look as if he cared one way or the other and certainly not much beyond official boundaries.

He held the camera snug against his hip, and with a click of his tongue against the roof of his mouth, he knew how he'd be spending the rest of the night.

First, however, he had to tell Gayle what he was going to do, and he quickened his pace, hoping to catch her still at work. But by the time he reached the shop, the night clerk was already on duty, and with an unconcerned shrug she supposed when he asked that Gayle had gone straight home. She hadn't left any messages. When Devin asked to use the telephone, Frances Kueller answered, "Why not? It's not my dime."

Awkwardly, he reached over the counter and pulled the phone to him, ignoring the fact that the woman didn't move out of his way; if anything, she was daring him to brush against her. Tonight, like most nights he could recall this summer, she was dressed as if she were going to a party—a cool summer dress scooped low in front, no back at all, and her hair done so well it almost looked natural.

He had heard a hundred rumors about her—mostly from Gayle, a smirking whisper or two from Stump—and once in a while, when things weren't right and he didn't feel like talking, he'd been tempted to find out if what they said was true, if Fran wasn't tied to marriage as much as her husband thought.

But not tonight.

In spite of the fact that she rested her elbows on top of the register and watched him, unblinking, cheeks coyly in her palms. Humming softly to herself, lips pursed, a manicured finger tapping her temple. Making sure the dress showed him as much as he wanted, without showing a thing.

He dialed Gayle's number and turned to face the street, wrinkling his nose at Fran's perfume; he wrinkled it again into an exasperated sneer when an answering machine clicked on and gave its message.

"Sorry, Gayle, but we'll have to forget tomorrow morning," he said when it was time. "Mary's dead, and I think someone killed her. I'm working tonight, and tomorrow I'm going to the hospital to see what happened. You tell the kids."

"Mary?" Mrs. Kueller said, straightening, a hand at her throat. "You mean that woman in the whatdoyoucallit? That awful dress and the hat? She's dead?"

He nodded.

"Oh, dear."

"I know," he said, telling himself to leave.

She fussed with some papers, arms close at her sides. "It just goes to show you how short life is, I guess." Looking up, smiling sadly.

He knew where she wanted his gaze to fall, and he damned himself for doing it and damned himself again for liking what he saw. She gave him a neutral smile—the move was up to him—and he did his best not to clear his throat when he bid her good-night and walked out. Temptation, he thought, god deliver me from temptation, and laughed silently when he realized he was lying. Gayle would kill him if she ever found out, assuming there was anything she would kill him for.

Oh Christ, Graham! He stood on the pavement, tapping a finger against the camera's case. A group of teenagers swept by, glancing at him, the girls giggling, and when he turned to move on he saw himself in a window—T-shirt and cowboy hat, and a camera in his hand.

He grinned.

He shook his head.

Then he settled the hat lower over his eyes and swaggered a few steps down the street before telling himself to knock it off; making a fool of himself once in an evening was definitely his limit.

In the Mermaid Lounge, on the boardwalk, Stump sat at the bar and stared at the glass of scotch he'd been nursing for over an hour. Chuck Geller was perched beside him, scanning the crowded room for unescorted women, nudging Stump once in a while and chuckling to himself. His uniform had been replaced by a tight, short-sleeved shirt, plaid slacks, and pointed loafers, his hair slicked back and reflecting the colored bulbs that ran around the bar's mirror.

"Jesus, ain't it fine," the bank guard said finally, pointing to a young woman in halter-top and shorts. "What do you say, Stump? We up for it tonight?"

Stump looked at her—a child, hardly more than a child—rose, and dumped his glass over Geller's head.

In time there was the darkroom.

And in waiting patiently for the chemicals in solution to do their work, standing in dull red light, hearing nothing outside, he found himself glancing more often toward the filing cabinet, the bottom drawer.

i want my picture

It has nothing to do with anything else, he told himself as he looked away . . . and looked back again.

"Hell," he whispered, and knelt slowly, knees cracking, wincing at the scrape of warped runners as the drawer opened and he took out the folder, took out the picture, and held it up to the red light.

Black smoke and white fire, and the tip of his forefinger drifted across the surface until it rested on the spot where he knew Julie was.

i want my picture back

And in time, long past midnight, he stood in front of the open refrigerator, rubbing the back of his neck and staring at the shelves—cans of soda, cans of beer, cheese and vegetables and a half-eaten bar of chocolate. The door swung closed before he realized he'd released it, and he stepped back and surveyed the kitchenette without knowing what he wanted, knowing only that when he saw it, something would tell him.

In his left hand he held a folder, and he dropped it on the table before reaching up and opening the cabinets above the sink, one at a time, scanning the contents until he pulled out a box of cookies, sat, opened it, and put something in his mouth.

Chewing without tasting.

Swallowing, and chewing again.

It was cold in the house.

Only the lamp behind the couch was on, lifting a cone to the ceiling, drawing in the dark from everywhere else.

A sudden draught from the window frame rippled the draperies, and a sudden gust made the loops rattle on their rod. When the noise, bones colliding, sticks snapping, subsided, it took him a moment to hear the scratching at the door.

The sound of someone trying to put a key into a lock.

He tilted his head as if to hear better.

It was tempting to think it was one of the neighbors,

back from a drunken evening and trying to get into the wrong house. But the scratching persisted, slow and deliberate, stopping when he rose and wiped a crumb from his chin.

The wind gusted again, and the pattering of dry sand against the wall made him look sharply to the right. And back to the door just as quickly.

Someone was out there.

The drapes shimmied and swelled.

He stepped around the chair and table and walked as quietly as he could across the room, stopping at the couch to put a hand on it and listen. Hearing nothing. Staring at the door as if he could see through it to the stoop, the drive, the street; daring the doorknob to turn while he considered the possibility it was one of the kids visiting late; letting his hand fall to his side and into a loose fist, relax and clench again and press against his leg.

Someone was out there.

He didn't know why he thought that, but he knew it was true; there was a space beyond the door, he could sense it, and it was filled.

Someone was out there, trying to get in.

The scratching began again, lightly, timidly, and so very slowly that he knew it couldn't be just a stick or leaf trapped there by the wind. First it was up near the knob, then lower, near the threshold—something not very sharp drawn across the wood and nearly smothered by the wind that stopped gusting and began blowing, steadily through the fence across the tops of the dunes, bringing the salt tang of the marshes and the keening in the eaves and the sand that clawed its way across the blacktop and the stoop.

Scratching.

, And the wind.

And a surge of adrenaline that had him stride to the door and take hold of the knob. But he didn't turn it. He leaned instead against the door and put his ear to it. Listening—to the wind; feeling—someone out there.

"Hey," he called. "You've got the wrong house."

The grip on the knob tightened in case it tried to turn.

Scratching, so close to his ear he snapped his head away and swallowed.

"Hey!"

Scratching.

"Who's there?"

Scratching.

Finally he yanked the door open, standing quickly to one side with his free arm cocked and his free hand in a fist, and the wind bellowed into the room, knocking over the lamp, the light dying with a hiss-and-spark. Papers snapped and spiraled; the folder on the table whipped open, the pictures scattering to the floor.

Ducking his head, he stepped outside, caution gone, angry now at being trapped by himself, in his own house.

"Hey!" he called, and saw no one in the yard, no one on the street. He ran to the left and peered around the corner, ran back across the front and stared down the alley, all the way to the next street where a dust devil rose from the gutter into streetlight.

No one.

And when he looked up, the sky was dark—no stars, no moon, and the air filled with sand that made him squint and close his mouth and finally retreat to the house and slam the door behind him.

"Idiot," he muttered, both to himself and the trickster, and barked his shin twice as he hunted for the flashlight he kept in the bedroom. Once armed, he picked up the lamp and put in a new bulb, held his breath, and smiled when the switch brought back the light.

A glare at the door and still feeling foolish, he cleaned up the mess the wind had made of the large room, ending by slapping the photographs back onto the kitchen table and sitting down to check them.

They hadn't changed.

Mary facing the dark pier from several different angles, Mary going down though her arms were still high—nothing at all of consequence to show to Marty Kilmer. There was, as far as he could tell, no one within ten yards of her; the few who had somehow gotten into a number of shots were going the other way, toward the camera.

He shuffled them and fanned them out again; and when a second and a third check produced nothing but an exasperated curse, he fetched the magnifying glass from the darkroom and went over them one by one, starting with the old woman falling to her knees, ending with a shot that had her on the left and the face of the dark pier on the right.

Nothing.

Nothing; and the last one was flawed. Dust on the lens, or his haste in making the prints, had produced specks of light on the dark pier's entrance where the plywood boards had parted, as though the negative had been damaged.

He sighed and leaned back, massaged his neck, rolled his shoulders, and suggested to his stretching shadow that he really ought to go to bed and get some sleep. An early day tomorrow, if he was to get to the hospital to see what had killed Mary, then come back again and square things with Gayle. She was going to be angry that he had scotched her meeting; but the more he considered it, the more he doubted it would do any good. The kids might benefit; they would feel like something at last was being done. But he decided as he stood that not a damned thing would be accomplished.

"Tomorrow," he said as he gathered the pictures together, "you will call Ken and talk about the job, make sure he's not talking through his hat. That's your problem, you know. That's why you're making such a big deal about this."

He closed the folder and reached up to switch off the overhead light, and slowly lowered his arm.

"Dust?" he said to the table.

He reopened the folder, the damaged picture on top; he slid the magnifying glass over it and shaded his eyes.

The wind.

The smell of rain.

He stood there, bent over, until his spine protested; he ran into the darkroom and grabbed the negatives, found the one he needed, and brought it to the table.

There were no scratches on it.

But there was something in the gap where the barrier had been pried open.

He rubbed his eyes, rechecked the picture, rubbed his eyes again because his vision was blurring.

Light and shadow, black and white.

Something was in there.

Looking out.

A face.

TWELVE

T HE grey clouds lowered just before dawn, the temperature cooled, the tide rose, and the puffs and smears of mist lingering in the gutters and hovering over the tarmac were shredded by a drizzle that began falling at first light. A dim and unpleasant light that crept rather than fell across the living room floor, setting couch and chairs in relief, not reaching through the bookcase to the rest of the house.

The lamps were out.

Devin, one leg bent and swinging over an armrest, looked toward but didn't see the prints scattered on the cocktail table. They were the same picture, each a different size to the largest he could make without losing definition, and none made the face he'd seen any clearer.

Unexpectedly he yawned and dragged a knuckle across

his eyes, rubbed wearily at his chest and glanced to his right out the window. The shadow of his house still darkened the house opposite. A few gulls were aloft. The pane was streaked with running droplets.

Oh god, he thought; it was nearly a prayer.

He wanted to think, but his mind kept drifting, too drugged with sleeplessness to hold a single thought for more than a few seconds. He had already tried to get hold of Marty to tell him what he'd found, but the station's night shift had been no help at all, failing to raise the sergeant on his walkie-talkie or his cruiser's radio. He'd called at least three times that he could remember, and the last time whoever had answered the telephone had ordered him to stop bothering them: there was enough to do without Devin tying up the lines. When he mentioned Mary's name, the man had laughed and hung up.

Marty's home phone hadn't answered either.

And he'd known what Gayle would say if he'd tried to call her that long past midnight.

The face: peering out through the separated pieces of plywood, barely distinguishable eyes and mouth, blending with the black as if it were black itself; there was no indication what sex it was, impossible to tell what age it was. But he was convinced it was there, not in his imagination, and Marty had to know.

He shifted, pulling his leg off the armrest and letting it fall to the floor. His throat felt packed with mucus coughing failed to dislodge; his eyes had to be forced to stay open. His arms trembled slightly with a gooseflesh chill. Dear god, sleep. He needed sleep, but he didn't think he could, not as long as that face lay in so many forms on the table.

Sleep.

He yawned widely, wincing when his jaw cracked.

An hour or so, he finally decided as he pushed himself to his feet and swayed until he grabbed hold of the chair. Just an hour or so, to clear his mind. If he confronted Kilmer with the pictures, in the state he was in now, he'd probably be locked up in the drunk tank.

The telephone rang.

"Christ!" he yelled, taking a startled step away. A hand went to his chest; he checked the window and decided that whoever was calling at this hour didn't deserve an answer. Staggering slightly, he moved to the table and switched on the answering machine, turned up the volume and listened to his voice let the caller know he wasn't in. He hated the sound of it; he'd rather believe he was more sonorous, more Shakespearean. Then he started for the bedroom, slowly unbuttoning his shirt, not really listening until he reached the end of the divider.

"Mr. Graham"

He swiveled so quickly his shoulder struck the sharp edge of the bookcase, and he rubbed at it gingerly as he watched the winking red light that told him a call was coming in.

"Mr. Graham"

It was his imagination. He was groggy from too little sleep. His mind was still wandering.

"Mr. . . ."

". . . Graham, you busy?"

She stood hipshot and bold in the doorway, a shoulder bag on one arm, a cased camera in her other hand. The bathing suit she wore was pale enough to make him look again to be sure she wasn't naked, small enough to make him wish she was wearing something else.

He grinned, however, and stepped aside with a nod. "You wear an outfit like that when you come calling," he said, gesturing her inside, "and you damn well better call me Mister. Otherwise, the neighbors are going to talk."

She winked at him as she passed and dropped her gear on the couch before dropping beside it. Her arms spread across the back, and she crossed her legs, her right ankle resting on her left knee.

Devin was abruptly conscious that he wasn't wearing a shirt. He had been struck that morning with one of his infrequent bouts of cleanliness and had been single-mindedly attacking the house with mop and broom, vacuum cleaner and dustrags. When the knock on the door came, he'd been on his knees in the bathroom with a scrub brush, and the front of his cut-off jeans was damp with washwater.

"Something to drink?"

She shook her head.

"Eat?"

Again.

"Do you mind if I get something?"

She shrugged so slowly he wasn't sure she had moved. But when her expression told him to go ahead, don't mind me, he went quickly to the kitchen and pulled a soda from the refrigerator, looked back at her and puffed his cheeks. She'd been coming to the house off and on since April, since a week after she'd quit school. When he had been at the house, an occasional dinner date with Maureen, Julie had expressed interest in his work—not the photographs themselves so much as the taking of them. With Maureen's blessing, then, he'd begun showing her how to use the expensive camera she had, the tricks of lighting, the gimmicks of focus.

Her mother had once joked that Julie had a crush on him; he'd allowed the possibility but didn't think it mattered.

"So," he said when he returned, "what can I do for you?" He dropped into an armchair and leaned forward, trying to minimize the amount of bare skin he was showing. He felt stupid to be embarrassed, but embarrassed he was. "You want a lesson?"

"Why aren't you dating my mother anymore?"

The question so surprised him he leaned away from it, almost as if she'd struck him. "I'm sorry?"

Her smile was brief. "I just wondered why you weren't dating my mother anymore, that's all. No big deal. I think she kind of misses you."

He drank to stall his answer. "I don't know," he answered at last. "We just sort of . . . stopped. It happens."

"It's that woman at the shop, right? Cross?"

He lifted the can and drank again. "Sometimes." He was careful not to smile. "Julie, Maureen's your mother and all, I know, but—"

"It doesn't give me the right to butt in."

His answer was a gentle smile.

"You're right." She mimicked his position, holding her arms close to her sides to push in her breasts, bulge them above the top of her halter. "It was nice having you around the house," she whispered, looking at the floor. Then she looked up at him without lifting her head. "I lied."

He nodded.

"I don't care what my mother does."

He waited. It was, among other things, the tension in the Etler household that had driven him off. Maureen couldn't understand why Julie had thrown away a Princeton degree, and Julie for her part couldn't seem to make anyone understand that she'd just gotten up one morning with no clear idea of what life was going to be like after graduation. It had terrified her. It had chased her off the campus and back to her own bed.

"I want you to take my picture."

"Well, for heaven's sake," he said with a laugh, "is that all? You didn't have to go through all that just to ask for a picture. You know I'd be glad to."

She had told Devin of her fear the day he'd taken the Ferris wheel picture. And the only thing he could tell her was that fear was something you learned to live with, to wrestle with, to come to terms with before it drove you out of your mind. You had no choice. She hadn't been impressed, and neither had he. It had been as feeble a response as telling her that when she grew up she'd understand what he'd meant. As if she were no more than ten and asking about death.

"Naked," she said.

"Hey, now wait a minute."

She stood, slowly, still watching him, and ran her palms down her sides to her hips, one leg set slightly behind the other. Then she turned profile and looked over her shoulder. "You have to admit it isn't bad, right? Don't you ever wonder what I look like?"

"I know what you look like, Julie," he said sternly.

"You know what I mean, Mr. Graham."

"Julie, for god's sake—"

He didn't know how she did it—one moment she was by the couch, the next she had rolled her shoulders and was standing directly in front of him, forcing him to sit back. The halter was bunched around her waist, and her breasts were as tanned as the rest of her.

"Just for me," she said. "I won't show it to anyone else."

He shook his head. "No."

An inch closer, her legs touching his knees. "I'm not ugly, you know."

Pointedly, he kept his gaze on her eyes. "I know. And I also know you're either being particularly dense today, or you've had a hell of a liquid lunch. Either way, Julie, the answer is still no."

Her frown made her seem twenty years older, lines deepening around her eyes. "You hate me."

"Don't be stupid."

"You let me come here all the time, let me—"

"You wanted to know how I took pictures."

"—think you wanted me."

"I never did, and you know it."

"And now . . ." She flung her arms wide, daring him to look at her, at the sweep of her breasts, the flat of her stomach, the childlike hips she rocked slowly side to side. "You're going to pass this up?"

He stood so abruptly she was forced to back away, planting her hands on her hips when she realized he wasn't going to touch her, hold her, pull her against his chest. "Pass what up?" he said almost cruelly. Making it clear he didn't care if he touched her or not, he reached around her to pick up her bag and camera. "Taking your picture? Or taking you to bed."

"Whatever," she answered, glancing down at her chest.

"Neither," he said, deliberately flatly. He held her things out until she adjusted the halter and took them. "And if you want more lessons, I think we'd better meet on the beach."

"Okay, sure," she said, seemingly unconcerned at the rejection. "Whatever you say, Devin." She walked to the door with an exaggerated sway, opened it, and looked back. "I'll tell my mother you were asking about her."

"Do that, Julie. Tell her I'll call."

"And Mr. Graham," she added coyly, "I still . . ."

". . . *want my picture*"

The machine clicked as the connection was broken, and Devin found himself staring at the door. His shoulder ached where he'd struck it. A second later, a dial tone filled the room until he almost ran to the machine and turned the volume down. He didn't replay the message.

Instead, he made his way into the bedroom and stripped to his shorts, sat on the edge of the mattress and tried to decide how much of what he'd heard was real, how much was the stupor he found himself in. Had it been the first time, he would have known what to think; now, all he could do was stare at the couch through the doorway, to the machine on the other side.

Then he fell slowly backward and watched the ceiling lighten, until his eyes closed—

Dreaming of racing along the beach, the sand afire, the silent flames searing his legs and soles, and not feeling the pain when he finally stumbled and fell;

Dreaming of standing alone on a sandbar a hundred yards from shore, while the tide began to rise and the waves nudged the backs of his knees, and he could only watch the faraway beach because he'd forgotten how to swim;

Dreaming of a face in The House of Night that receded as he approached it, keeping to the shadows cast by no light that he could see, slipping over the debris like black water running backward, until it reached the mouth of a cave and vanished altogether, leaving him alone in the dark with nothing to see, hearing nothing but his own breathing, and the sound of claws on the floor behind him.

When he awoke, he was curled in the center of the mattress, knees drawn to his chest, hands clasped tightly under his chin. There was no transition—he was facing the cave, and he was facing the doorway.

It took him several minutes to realize that the phone machine's red light was blinking, a minute or so more to straighten his limbs and roll to stand beside the bed. With a deliberation that nearly caused his calves to cramp, he changed his clothes and went into the bathroom. He did not look at the light. Not then. Not when he grabbed his jacket from a kitchen chair and walked into the living room.

And not when he picked up one of the photographs from the table and slipped it into a manila envelope on which he scribbled Kilmer's name.

He didn't look at his watch.

He was going to drop the evidence off at the police station, then go on to the hospital.

Later.

Maybe later he would listen to Julie Etler tell him again what she wanted.

But not now.

If he did, if he turned up the volume and pressed the right button and heard that voice *i want my picture* he knew he would scream.

By nine the shops were open.

By ten Summer Road was an echo of November—few cars, fewer pedestrians, the streetlamps still on and the traffic lights haloed.

By a few minutes past twelve, the echo had faded, and it was Labor Day weekend, Saturday, the last day for most before the packing began. Though the sky hadn't cleared, the clouds had lightened considerably, and the temperature had climbed so rapidly that the puddles and stained sidewalks were already drying out. Traffic filled Summer Road as if it were the Fourth. Pedestrians hurried along the pavement, packages in their arms, while families and couples battled each other on the way to the beach.

In the Summerview Diner, its neon waves flickering just brightly enough to see, the clatter of dishes was brittle, the scrape of a fork like a nail dragged across iron; the coffee urn's hissing, the crack of a dropped plate, and whispering seemed more proper than normal conversation.

For want of something better to do, Mike tried to eavesdrop on what Charlene was saying to a customer at the far end of the counter, but all he could hear was a buzzing, a snapped laugh, the buzzing again. His lips curled in disgusted boredom, and he looked outside for the fifth time in five minutes, his attention caught for a moment by a large balloon bounced by a breeze along the sidewalk. It seemed too heavy to rise more than a few inches above the ground, and after ricocheting off a car bumper, it rebounded off the diner's steps, tried again to climb, then settled into a shrinking puddle where it shivered, and revolved, was finally slammed by a gust that carried it out of sight.

He sighed.

He cracked his knuckles.

He considered taking off his school jacket and changed his mind when the air conditioning whirred on.

He sighed again and moved away from the window as far as he could without bumping into Tony, wishing someone, somewhere, would say something before he started to laugh—like being in church, where things sometimes grew too solemn.

He guessed it was nerves, and the changing weather, and the fact that Miss Cross hadn't said more than a dozen words since she'd told them about Devin going to the hospital. He couldn't tell if she was angry or not, but he was more than a little bit relieved. He hadn't want to come here in the first place, had planned to spend his last weekend home lying on the beach, making sure his tan was good and deep before heading off for California.

But the damned weather had stopped that idea in its tracks, and then Tony had called and he was trapped.

He thought of Kelly, and after another look around decided he was marginally better off hanging around here. Because it was the season's final Saturday, there was no way Opal would let her have time off.

"I want you to know," Miss Cross said, a palm under her chin, partially covering her mouth, "that I have had better Saturdays in my life. I can probably think of twenty or thirty this year alone that have been better than this."

When he looked at her, she winked broadly, and he managed a smile back. She wasn't so bad, not really, though except for her figure and the way she wore her clothes, he still couldn't see why Devin bothered. She didn't seem . . . right somehow. He didn't know exactly why, but she didn't seem right. It wasn't the money everyone knew she had, and she was always good for a laugh the few times she had loosened up around them; yet there was something about her, something distant, he couldn't put his finger on. Something that made her not right for his friend.

Tony, hunched in his denim jacket over a barely touched glass of soda, shrugged with a tilt of his head. "Maybe he'll be back soon."

Mike saw her eyes then when she turned that half-smile on Riccaro—they weren't looking as much as they were watching—like she expected Tony, or him for that matter, to suddenly jump up across the table and try to rip her clothes off. No. That wasn't right. Like she didn't know what the hell either one of them would do next and wouldn't know what to do when they did it.

That puzzled him. According to Kelly's not always kind jibes, he was an open book, and Tony . . . well, shit, Tony was Tony, what was there to know?

"Nope," she said at last. "Not for a while anyway." Her gaze dropped to the cup of coffee she hadn't touched since Charlene brought it. "He'll be there until he gets some answers if I know him." A shake of her head. "I'm sorry. This is kind of a bust."

"Not your fault," Tony said. "You couldn't know."

Suddenly Mike pushed into the corner again, the pane growing warm against his shoulder. He had to do something, or someone was going to mention *her* name. "It's like the duster, Tony," he said, watching her, feeling Riccaro relax. "Remember?"

Tony grinned. "God, yeah. I'd almost forgotten about that."

"What?" Gayle asked, smile polite and confused.

"Devin," Mike told her. "Why he's at the hospital."

The smile remained; the eyes demanded an explanation.

He rubbed a finger across his brow. "When I broke my hip," he said, "it was when I was a kid, and Tony here, he was too young to come visit me. I mean, that was the rule, even though we were practically living in each other's house."

"I threw tantrums when my folks told me I couldn't go," Tony said, slowly turning his glass between his palms. "God, I thought my mother'd kill me."

"So his father, see, he was into westerns and stuff back then, and he had a hat and the boots and everything, he had this long sort of white coat, you know? All the way down to his ankles practically. They call it a duster, like in those Italian westerns."

"Oh, right," she said, nodding. "Sure."

"So one day, all four of them, my folks and his, they came to visit me, see, and Mr. Riccaro, he's standing at the foot of the bed looking like Clint Eastwood or something, and all of a sudden this head pops out of his coat and sticks out its tongue."

Tony laughed, leaned back, looked at the ceiling. "Mike almost shit, you know? God, he almost screamed."

"I did not," he said, punching Riccaro's arm. "Scared the hell out of the nurses though, when they found out." He giggled, laughed, giggled again. "He was on Mr. Riccaro's hip, see, and the four of them came down the hall all close together so the nurses wouldn't catch on."

Tony took a drink, laughed, and wiped his mouth and chin. "You never saw my dad look scared, Miss Cross, but when that nurse—"

"Fat as hell and twice as wide, no kidding."

"—started chewing him out, I thought for sure they were going to lock him up."

Mike couldn't stop the giggles. "He . . . they made him leave. Some intern comes along . . . he comes in and says, 'Hey, cowpoke, head for the north forty.'" A slap at the table that made Gayle jump. "My mother was going to sue, for god's sake, you should've seen her."

Laughter rose and fell, and Tony nearly knocked his glass over, until Gayle reached across the table and pulled it away.

"See?" Mike said then, trying to settle himself, trying to stave off the hiccoughs, and was surprised when Miss Cross shook her head. He cleared his throat several times, ordering sobriety and not doing very well. "Devin's like that, that's what I mean. Tony, he wouldn't take anyone's word for what was wrong with me: he had to see for himself. Right?"

"Right," Tony said, nodding.

"So . . ." And he lifted one hand, unable to understand why she hadn't figured that out for herself.

Her mouth opened but nothing came out. Then she

turned away to the window, chin back in her palm, and he watched the light sweep across her face. She still doesn't get it, he thought; she still doesn't get it.

Charlene came by and cleared the table of their dishes, took orders for more coffee and soda, and gave him a broad wink as she walked off. He hoped Tony hadn't seen it, that's all he needed now—Riccaro on his case just like Kelly.

But at least they weren't talking about—

"Julie," Tony said once Charlene was around the counter.

Shit, he thought, his lip curling again; shit.

But before he could think of a joke, swear, drop a spoon, anything to keep them off the track, a flicker of motion caught his eye, and he looked out the window. Across the street, a woman in a shapeless raincoat was standing under the striped awning of a drugstore, her back to the diner, a furled umbrella in one hand. It was slashing the air, chopping and slashing, as if she were engaged in a sword fight with her reflection, faster and faster until the umbrella was a blur, a smear of blood staining the air.

"Hey," he said, "look at that."

"Jesus, Mike—"

"No, look!"

He could feel Tony lift himself partway off the seat, saw Miss Cross turn as well, just as the woman stabbed at the store's window. He winced in anticipation. She leaned back, leaned forward, and stabbed again. No one else on the sidewalk paid her any attention.

"Loon," Tony pronounced, and sat down again.

"Loon is right. She's gonna break that—"

The woman turned around then, umbrella-sword now lifted over her head like a club.

The breath in Mike's lungs caught and felt like sudden razors. "My . . . god," he said.

Miss Cross cut him off by reaching across the table to grab his arm, squeezing it so tightly he stared. She was

171

pale, and a droplet of perspiration broke on her forehead and slid to the bridge of her nose.

"No," she denied in an almost laughing whisper, and before he could tell her she wasn't seeing things, she released him and slid out of the booth. Tony complained when Mike shoved him but got out of the way so he could follow at a trot, ignoring Riccaro's demands to know what the hell was the matter. A second later, Mike heard him following, and they reached the street just as Gayle reached the curb.

"Miss Cross!" Mike said, coming up beside her. "Miss Cross, I don't think we'd—"

"Look," she said, pointing.

He did.

The woman was still there, the umbrella still in her hand, but it was open now and low enough to prevent them from seeing her face. She walked briskly to the corner, shoulders turning as though she were looking both ways, then crossed over and moved on. Faster. Nearly at a trot.

"But I don't get it," he said, squinting through the drizzle. "I mean . . . I don't get it." He looked down at Gayle anxiously. "I *saw* her. I . . . Miss Cross, it was her, I saw her."

"A trick," Tony said, standing behind them. They looked at him. "Of the eyes, I mean. She kind of looked like Mary, so we thought it was her, right?"

Mike almost shook his head, but a stray raindrop splattered on the back of his neck and he shivered instead and followed Gayle back into the diner. She was moving fast and was halfway down the aisle before he passed through the inner door.

It wasn't a trick; there was nothing wrong with his eyes. That woman, until she'd opened the umbrella and somehow grew smaller, was Prayerful Mary, he would swear to it, bet on it, and refused to believe it because that would mean that the voice on Devin's machine was real, that Tony's ghost was real, and he knew damned well that

172

ghosts didn't stand in the middle of the street in the middle of the day and swordfight with a store window.

Things like that didn't happen.

They just didn't happen.

Devin stood in front of the Jeep and tried to act knowledgeable as he poked around the engine, tugging at this wire, tapping that chunk of metal, all the while chanting charms to himself in the hope that the goddamned thing would start without his having to swallow his pride and call a garage.

No one stopped to help him.

He was on the sandy shoulder of the road, at the west end of the bay bridge, and the line of traffic stretched all the way across to Oceantide and a good two miles inland. It moved at a fair pace, just fast enough to blur when he stared at it and wondered where the hell they had all come from, and where the hell they were finding room to park. Station wagons, pickups, sedans, the occasional convertible, packed to the gunwales with children and beachballs; shouting, laughing, rock music, guitars, snatches of it all snatched away by their wind as he finally rounded the Jeep and leaned against the metal railing that separated the shoulder from the water's edge.

He was warm. Perspiration clung to his shirt collar. He hadn't brought his sunglasses and had to squint to keep his eyes from stinging.

I am not, he thought glumly, one of God's chosen.

When he reached the county hospital just before nine, he had planned to hunt for someone in charge, ask a few simple questions and leave; what he had found was chaos—the consequence of a multi-vehicle accident on the Garden State Parkway just a few hundred yards away. None of the nurses or interns either wanted or had the time to speak with him.

When he finally decided to locate the morgue himself

and corner someone, anyone, who worked there, he had gotten lost in the tangle of hallways and poor directions given him by harried staff. And though he knew he wasn't helping his own cause by losing his temper and snapping back at those who snapped officiously at him, he couldn't help it. The nap he'd taken had been worse than no nap at all, and he felt as though he were carrying sandbags on his shoulders.

And when, at last, he had found his way into a subbasement, cool and silent and echoing and narrow, the morgue attendants had been nearly as busy as those upstairs. He was told to have a seat in the hall. He sat. He waited. He lost his temper again after more than an hour and slammed through the swinging double doors into the outer office, where a beefy man in soiled white told him to take a hike without even looking up.

"I want to know about Mary Heims," Devin demanded.

The attendant, scrabbling through forms and chewing on the end of a ball-point pen, waved him away. "She's dead."

"How?"

"How should I know? I'm no doctor."

"Look it up."

The man almost rose as he leaned across the table that served as his desk. "You family or something?"

"No."

The man rolled his eyes. "Beat it."

"Damnit," he said, taking a step forward, "a woman was killed last night, and I'm—"

"Hey, you a cop?"

Devin shook his head.

"Then screw off, pal. The old woman's dead, and we haven't got the room to keep her, okay?" His eyes narrowed. "Hey, you a reporter?"

Devin shook his head again. "A friend."

"Well, look, *friend,* you'll just have to ask the cops. I haven't got the time—"

A gurney was wheeled in then, a bloodied bare foot dangling from under a blood-stained sheet. Devin gaped at it and left, one hand to his stomach, his anger all but gone as he tried to find the elevator without stumbling.

In the lobby, a woman was screaming for her son.

In the parking lot, a man was bent over the hood of a car, weeping.

And almost as soon as he joined the eastbound traffic, the Jeep began making noises. It stalled at two of the four lights before the bridge. It bucked when he tried to race across an intersection to keep from being trapped in a rapidly forming gridlock. And just as he reached the bridge, it sputtered so badly that he pulled over with a shouted oath and watched helplessly as it died before he had a chance to turn off the ignition.

He kicked at the round pebbles poking through the sand.

Over an hour just to get this far, and the stupid machine couldn't make it another couple of miles.

He should have stayed home. He should have waited at the police station for Marty after dropping off the picture. He should have gotten some decent sleep before charging out of the house. And he supposed he should have known all along that no one really cared about Prayerful Mary except her friends. It was clear that the hospital only wanted her out as quickly as possible; there was no curiosity, no sense of something being wrong. She was dead, and they wanted her out and buried, and the form with her name on it jammed in some cabinet.

"Shit," he said softly.

A car honked its horn at him.

With a sigh and gesture dramatic enough for everyone on the highway to understand, he slammed down the hood, made sure the keys were in his pocket, and stepped up to the narrow pedestrian walkway that led to the other side. First thing he had to do was find a garage and have the Jeep towed in for fixing. Then he'd walk down to the Summerview, drink four or five gallons of iced tea, and bitch to anyone who wanted to listen.

After that, he would call Marty and hope that the sergeant was impressed enough by the picture to do something about it.

Not that he thought the man would. The way things were going today, Marty would probably pat him verbally on the shoulder, tell him to take a vacation, and hang up just before he started to laugh.

Midway across the bridge, a gust of wind from a passing van nearly knocked him into the low railing.

Just as he took off his jacket and slung it over his shoulder, someone tossed an empty paper cup at him.

And he lowered his head stubbornly when he reached the other side, and a horn blared at him several times, keeping pace with him until finally he swung around—one hand in a fist.

It was Gayle, leaning over the front seat of her car with one hand on the steering wheel while trying to stay in her lane.

"You need a lift?" she called.

Several seconds passed before he relaxed enough to climb in, immediately adjusting the grille on the dashboard to blow the air conditioning into his face.

"Are you all right?" she said, speeding up to close the gap between her car and the one ahead.

"You don't want to know."

"Wonderful."

He looked over, then reached over to still a tic at the corner of her eye. "The big meeting didn't go well?"

"It didn't go at all," she said. "I mean, the boys were there, but . . ."

He sat up. Her chin was trembling, and the muscles of her neck were taut, as if she were clenching her teeth.

"Hey," he said quietly, "are you all right?"

"I'm not sure yet, Dev," she answered. "We saw . . . I mean, I *think* we saw Mary."

He blinked once, slowly. "What?"

She nodded.

He looked through the rear window. "I see."

Her foot trod on the brake pedal, shifted to the accelerator. "Devin Graham, if you say you believe me, I'm going to drive off this damned bridge."

At first he said nothing. He only slumped down in his seat and folded his arms across his chest. The sound of the traffic, the sound of the sea.

"I got a call this morning," he said at last. "It wasn't a joke. It was Julie."

THIRTEEN

M IKE sat uneasily in the booth, bewildered and somewhat frightened as he ordered himself not to squirm. More than fifteen minutes ago, Gayle had grabbed up her purse, and they had gone, Riccaro telling him to stay put while they chased after the woman; and though he thought Gayle had waved to him as she backed into traffic, he couldn't be sure.

"Boy, what was that all about?" Charlene asked at his shoulder, making him jump.

"Nothing," he answered absently, craning his neck in hope of seeing them return. "Just someone we knew."

"Whatever," she said. She gathered up the plates and crumpled napkins. "You want something else?"

With an effort he knew made him look stupid, he gazed

at the abandoned cups of coffee, the full glass of Tony's soda. "No," he said. "Yes. French fries."

"Super," she said sarcastically, one hip cocked. "You don't order lunch, you probably didn't have any breakfast, and now you want french fries. You call yourself a doctor?"

He snapped his head up to glare, but she was already gone, calling out the order to the kitchen. Then he looked at his hands, they were trembling, and he gripped the edge of the table as hard as he could.

No ghosts, he told them.

picture

It was a trick, like Tony said.

want my

He was going to be a doctor, and as a doctor he knew that the dead stay dead, that's all there is to it, and the woman just walked away, didn't vanish into thin air, so what was the big deal?

His hands ached, but he didn't let go, not even when Charlene slid into the booth opposite him. After a moment, she covered his hands with hers, warm hands, and when he looked at her he saw nothing but concern in the way she scanned his face.

"You sure you're all right, Doc?"

He wanted to snap at her again, yell at her to mind her own goddamned business, but he didn't; her skin was soft and somehow smelled of talc. The smile he gave her instead was strained. "Yeah. Yeah, I think so. I just got a chill, that's all. It's the weather."

She nodded to the plate of french fries. "I think you'd better eat something, Doc. How about a side order of hot dog to go with them? On me."

The smile relaxed. "Okay. You talked me into it."

A gust of wind spattered sand against the oval window, and he looked out with a grimace, and gasped when he saw Kelly on the diner steps, one hand on the door, looking straight at him. He wanted to wave, but Charlene's hands were still on top of his.

Kelly saw.

Immediately, she yanked up the collar of her open raincoat and stomped down to the sidewalk, paused to glare up at him, and stalked away.

Charlene looked out the window and pulled away quickly. "Oops," she said.

Mike knew he ought to run after her and explain what had happened, but when he imagined her response, the fight that was sure to follow, he only shook his head in resignation and popped a french fry into his mouth. "It doesn't matter," he said. "Hell, it doesn't matter." He glanced outside. "Women," he muttered.

Charlene chuckled. "You're learning, Doc. You're learning."

The plate was almost empty by the time the hot dog arrived *(mary no it wasn't)*, and the hot dog was nearly gone when Gayle's car *(dead don't walk)* parked again at the curb. As he chewed, he waited for someone to get out, but no one did. Shadows in the front seat. The doors remained closed. Fearful of what was wrong now, he headed for the exit, smiling thanks at Charlene as he went out to the tiny lobby and waited, snapping his fingers and willing them to hurry up.

Then Gayle got out, and from the other side, Devin.

He waited, but Tony wasn't there.

"Going someplace?" Devin said with a strained smile as he pushed through the door. He took Mike's arm and led him back inside, yelled to Sal for a gallon of coffee, and disappeared into the men's room as soon as Mike promised he would wait.

"So what happened?" Mike asked Gayle as she dropped into the booth. "Where's Tony? What's going on?"

"In a minute," she said.

"Well, I can't wait a minute, I gotta go," he told her impatiently, reaching for his windbreaker. "Kelly—"

"I know," Gayle said with an exasperated look that told him she had other things on her mind besides teenagers' lovers' spats. "I know."

"You do?" He sat down. "You do?"

She was angry, he could see that, and his own temper began to unravel while she took her time fishing through her purse for a cigarette. She lit it, blew smoke at the ceiling, and stared at the men's room door.

"We couldn't find her. The woman, I mean. We drove practically all the way to Seaside and didn't see a trace."

Mike fidgeted.

"After we turned around, Tony saw Kelly. I stopped. He got out and talked to her, told me she said you were fooling around with a waitress and went off with her. To calm her down." She raked a hand through her hair. "Are you sure you guys are going to college?"

Mike didn't answer. He was wondering just how comforting Tony was going to be, and had to be prodded several times before he pushed himself to the window to let Devin have a seat.

"And you didn't see . . . that woman?"

"I told you she wasn't there," Gayle said.

Mike looked to Devin, back to her. "But we saw her. She couldn't have gotten that far away. She couldn't have."

"By the time we got as far as the police station," Gayle said patiently, through a cloud of smoke, "she was already gone. We tried a couple of side streets, but she . . ." She leaned away from another puff of smoke that hovered in front of her face. "She must have gone inside somewhere along the way. One of the stores, maybe. I didn't stop to check them."

Mike nodded doubtfully. "Yeah, I guess."

"Of course," she said, nodding once, sharply.

But he could see that she didn't believe it, and her expression pleaded with him not to contradict her, at least not just now.

Then Devin sighed loudly and tried to light a cigarette

from a pack in his shirt pocket. It was split, and when he finally realized it, he slammed it angrily into the ashtray. "Great," he said. "Y'know, this whole goddamn day has been one great joke. Jesus, I should have stayed in bed."

Mike stared at the crumpled remains of the cigarette, not listening when Gayle mumbled something about the weather, and Devin answered with a barking laugh completely without mirth. And when Charlene brought the coffee, Devin blew across the cup while Mike watched the steam curl away, watched him take out another cigarette and roll it between thumb and forefinger.

"I guess Riccaro's not coming back," Devin said.

Mike stared out the window, grunting an answer and trying not to smile. His hands were fists in his lap, pressed into his thighs.

He knew. God, he knew what was going on.

Gayle lit a match and held it out. Devin stared at it dumbly for a second, then shook his head and put the cigarette away.

"What are you going to do about the Jeep?" Gayle asked.

"Shoot it," Devin grumbled.

Mike finally allowed himself a grin. "You must've run out of gas, huh?"

"I wouldn't be surprised, pal, believe me." He shook his head, inhaled slowly, and checked his watch. "Right about now, that overpriced sonofabitch is sitting in a garage, and before it's over, I'll probably have to ransom my mother to get it back. Christ!"

Finally Mike could stand it no longer. He excused himself twice before Devin moved out of the way, and only gave Gayle a knowing smile before rushing out of the diner. Though the air was warm and growing hot, relief soon had him in an easy trot.

Devin had said it: it was a joke.

Tony and Kelly, maybe even Gayle, getting back at him for all the times he'd led them into disaster. A fitting end, they probably thought, to their last summer together—let's get Mike, teach him a lesson.

He laughed aloud.

Beautiful.

It was beautiful, so well done he couldn't believe he'd fallen for it. He didn't know who they had gotten to play Mary's part, but if he ever found out, he was going to buy her dinner, flowers, and anything else she wanted.

Once on the boardwalk he went straight to Harragan's.

That might have been their joke; now it was time for his.

"I don't know what to tell you," Tony repeated for the fourth or fifth time. "I wasn't there, but it can't be what you think."

"The hell it can't," Kelly answered through clenched teeth. "He was screwing around with that . . . that cousin of yours. I saw it, Tony. I wasn't imagining things."

She was moving fast, very close to trotting, and he felt as if he were trying to rein in a runaway pony.

"Hey, slow up, Kell, huh?"

She paid him no heed.

He had no idea what the hell Mike had done now, but he was positive the girl's mood had been dark even before she'd seen whatever Charlene had been doing with his friend. He could tell by the tightened cheeks, the thin lips, the way she slapped her bangs away from her eyes.

"I'm not going to California," she said suddenly.

A slow line of cars moved between them and the boardwalk block, and a flock of people were trudging up the ramp.

"At least not with him."

"Kelly, c'mon, let's go back to the diner, okay? They're waiting for us. And—"

"That campus is never going to be big enough, Tony. Never."

He didn't say a word. He'd seen this coming for over a month, and was surprised only because it had taken her so long to realize what a mistake their going to school together had been in the first place. At the bottom of the ramp he stopped her and turned her around. Her cheeks were red, and the tip of her nose, and her lower lip quivered from either outrage or indignation.

She was beautiful.

"You were going to tell him today?"

She shrugged. "I don't know. Sometime."

"He's gonna shit, Kell."

"I don't think so. He'll mope a lot, but he won't get mad."

He smiled. "You taking bets or what?"

And before he could move, she laid her forehead against his chest and wrapped her arms around his waist. His own hands didn't know what to do, and he glanced side to side, hoping no one who knew them could see them standing here. Not like this.

"Kell . . ."

She raised her head; there were no tears in her eyes.

"Julie was right," she told him, the anguish of the admission all too clear. "She predicted it, I guess."

He didn't know what she was talking about, but the name reminded him of the umbrella woman, and he was about to pull away when surprise took him again—she kissed him. Not a long kiss, not a short one, but enough to let him know that there was something else on her mind.

When she leaned back, there was no embarrassment; she took his arm and started up the ramp. Saying nothing. Squinting in the sea breeze, turning him south when they crossed to the benches and kicked idly at the boards. He tried twice more to get her to turn back, but she was adamant—she wasn't going until she was good and ready—and he finally resigned himself to hoping neither Gayle nor Mike would do anything without him.

"So, what was going on?" she asked, nodding in the diner's direction.

He had the feeling that if he didn't tell her, she wouldn't lose any sleep, but he did anyway, alternately defensive and aggressive at the accusing darts of her expression. He gave her no explanations because there were none to give. The woman had been there, had gone, and he had frighteningly little trouble believing it really was Prayerful Mary. Kelly glanced over her shoulder at the dark pier, shook her head, and gripped his arm tighter.

"It's nuts."

"Tell me about it."

"Miss Cross . . . she saw her too?"

"Everything. The whole thing. It was Mike who—"

"You said that already. I don't want to hear about him, I want to hear about you."

"What about me?" He stepped around a child chasing ahead of its parents. "I've already told you everything."

An empty, parked stroller parted them; the little boy who belonged in it was at the railing with his parents, pointing excitedly at the ocean—grey and roiling, the breakers slamming against the beach and hissing over the drop to deposit its dead and dying.

"You know what I think?" Kelly said. "I think we're all going crazy, that's what I think. We've got only a few days left here, and we're acting like it's the end of the world. We're driving each other nuts. We're making each other climb the walls." A hand punched toward the clouds. "And that's not helping either."

They paused to allow a gang of squealing kids swarm in front of them and down the steps to the drying beach. Their laughter was loud, and they instantly sorted themselves into raucous teams for a game of touch football. Tony watched them with a frown, then looked along the line of concession stands—all of them were open, and there were customers at every one. Lines of them, and none of them seeming very patient.

He pulled Kelly closer.

The growls and shrieks from Harragan's Pier overrode the surf and the wind; music from open bars clashed and battled; and he had to check the sky again, just to be sure the sun hadn't snuck out while he wasn't looking.

"It's the end of the year," Kelly said, poking him gently on the chest.

"What?"

She gestured toward the rapidly thickening crowd. "The end of vacation, I mean. They're determined to make asses of themselves because on Tuesday they have to go back to work." She drew a coat sleeve under her nose. "Like we have to go to school. God, won't it be great when we don't have to go to another class ever again?"

The lights were on, all of them, the day still gloomy enough to give them halfhearted sparkle.

The clowns at Harragan's cackled from a tape.

The wind died abruptly. The heat returned without the sun. Shirts were opened, jackets stripped off, and Tony carried his over his shoulder.

They had walked the length of the boardwalk from Harragan's to the dark pier twice, and still he couldn't convince her to go back with him. He wanted to know what Devin had learned about Mary's death; he wanted to know if any of them had come up with an explanation for supposed ghosts; and increasingly desperately, he didn't want to be seen here with Kelly. She had taken off her raincoat and folded it into a plastic packet she crammed into her hip pocket; now she was in jeans, tennis shoes, and a man's plaid shirt with pearl snap-buttons. Her hair was undone and occasionally blew into his face; her face had lost the pinch of cold, and for a moment, while she ran to a stand to buy them cans of soda, he damned Julie for teaching him what it was like to make love.

As she walked back, he deliberately shifted his gaze away from her chest.

When her fingers brushed his knuckles handing over the can, he pulled away too quickly and almost dropped it.

"I have to go back to work in a little while," she said, taking hold of his elbow. "Let's go someplace else."

186

Devin lit a cigarette and stubbed it out almost immediately; the smoke tasted foul. And when Charlene brought him a second cup of coffee, it nearly burned his tongue. Lousy, he decided, was absolutely the wrong word for this day: disaster, on the other hand, seemed to fit just right.

With Mike gone, grinning like an idiot without explaining the joke, he couldn't help wondering what was going on in the heads of the kids. "I think," he finally said, "young love must be a pain in the ass."

Gayle didn't respond, and he stared down at his cup. She hadn't said much since picking him up beyond telling him about the woman. She hadn't asked about Mary, and after Nathan had left, she was more quiet than ever.

He shivered as the air conditioning kicked in and blew over his head. "Are you going to talk to me or what?"

Gayle barely managed a smile. "Sorry."

He reached over to touch her hand. "Go ahead," he said softly. "Go ahead."

Her right hand pulled absently at her shirt collar, her left tapped her cup before picking up a soon and spinning it slowly. "I'm trying to decide," she said firmly, as if each word had to be just right, "if I saw what I saw, or if all that nonsense at your place has me seeing what isn't there."

He didn't know what to tell her.

"I am not," she continued, "an unreasonable person. You know that. But . . ." She dropped the spoon and hugged herself then, and Devin quickly switched around the table to sit beside her, an arm around her shoulder she didn't shrug off. "If Mike hadn't seen—"

"What were you going to do?" he asked.

She looked at him, puzzled.

"This afternoon," he reminded her. "If all this hadn't happened, what was your great plan?"

"Oh." A lopsided smile and a quick laugh. "I was going to mount an expedition to the pier."

"You were what?"

"To prove there's nothing wrong there. No ghosts, no zombies, no nothing." She leaned into him. "I was going to try to scare Kelly shitless so she'd confess to making that call. Then you'd see what you were doing and get back to work." She grunted a laugh. "It seemed like a good idea at the time."

He stared over her head at the street, at the pedestrians rushing past with bundles piled in their arms, at the cars and motorcycles and vans and trucks filling the lanes, blowing their horns; at the shoppers ducking in and out of the stores. As he did, he could hear Sal and Charlene and Paula rushing from booth to counter to kitchen and back, conversations high and excited, the electronic *ping* of the cash register as the girl working there toted up the checks and made change.

"And now?"

She followed his gaze to the street. "Now, Graham, I think you've finally gotten me scared."

They sat for a few minutes, saying nothing, watching only, until Devin fumbled in his pockets for enough money to pay the check. He dropped the bills on the table and took Gayle's hand.

"Let's go."

"Where?"

"First to get the Jeep. The way things are going, I wouldn't be surprised if Mike was right, that it was only out of gas and I didn't even notice."

And on the street, standing in front of her car, she said, "Then what?"

"Then you and I are going on that goddamn pier, and we're going to see for ourselves . . . whatever there is to see."

She didn't respond until she was behind the wheel and they were finally, after a half-dozen frustrating minutes, in the northbound lane. At several intersections there were police guiding traffic, but traffic moved slowly anyway— jaywalking pedestrians, cars turning from the wrong side, an overheated station wagon being pushed by two young men laughing so hard they could barely stand up.

Devin tossed his jacket into the back seat, rolled up his sleeves and wondered who'd turned on the heat. It was what his mother always called "pneumonia weather," temperature swings that confused people into the wrong kind of clothes. He supposed, considering his luck, that tomorrow he'd wake up with a summer cold that would last until the middle of December.

Gayle leaned on the horn to hurry a family dawdling across the street. The man peered at the windshield and smiled; the youngest child gave her the finger and giggled.

"I could walk faster than this," Devin complained a few minutes later.

"You in a hurry or something?"

The fingers of his left hand were drumming on his knee. "I don't know. I didn't think so."

"Then relax," she told him, "and tell me why the pier."

"You were going to go," he reminded her.

"Sure, because that's where Julie died."

"That's where Mary died too, Gayle. Someone's in there." And he told her about the picture, about the face he had seen. It wasn't clear, wasn't defined, but someone had been there.

"Well, for god's sake," Gayle exclaimed, almost shouting, almost ramming the car ahead. "Jesus, Devin, why don't you show it to the police?"

"I did. I stopped in on the way to the hospital and showed it to them, to one of the guys who'd been there. He claimed he didn't see anything." He put a hand lightly on the dashboard when she had to stop quickly to avoid a convertible turning right from the middle lane. "When I told him to get a magnifying glass, he politely suggested I was wasting his time."

"A magnifying glass," she said flatly.

He reached over the back of the seat to grab his jacket, dug into the breast pocket and pulled out a folded print.

"It's hard to see. I almost missed it myself. I left a copy for Marty to look at, maybe he's—"

She glanced over when he held it up, and shrugged. "Devin—"

"It's there, Gayle," he insisted calmly. "It's there."

"Then we'll find Marty," she said, speeding up so rapidly he was taken by surprise. "We'll show it to him and let him decide if anything else has to be done."

"The woman," he said.

She leaned on the horn.

FOURTEEN

HARRAGAN stood to one side of his pier's entrance, hands deep in his pockets. The crowds shoved past him, most of them not even bothering to give him a look. Men with loud voices, women shrill, the young ones dancing and tugging and demanding attention. There were two of his crew in the ticket booth, two at each of the rides, and more than once one of the latter had asked if the ride times could be shortened, the lines were growing too long. Earlier he had refused, but now he was worried. If one red-faced father got too impatient, one hopped-up kid tried to jump ahead, there was going to be a riot.

It unnerved him. He'd seen Labor Day crowds before, had lived through three decades of watching the last of summer's energy get spent in one-day explosions; but this was different. This was more than an end-of-the-season party, and he was frustrated because he couldn't find the right name.

Slowly then, favoring his aching back by leaning over more than usual, he made his way along the pier, one ear tuned to the sounds of the engines, the rest of him watching for cheaters, for thieves, for the idiots who tried to use the crowds to cover their dealing and their drugs.

By the time he reached the wheel he was panting, sweating heavily, and he leaned against the railing and wished he could jump over, into the sea. It was surely cooler down there, where the waves were dragging the tide in behind them. It had to be. And surely it was more quiet, even with the waves' thunder.

He plucked his shirt away from his chest, wiped his face with a sleeve, and squinted out over the water. Swimmers were risking the undertow today, many of them easily a hundred yards from the shore. Inner tubes held others. Rafts still more. Beyond that a handful of sailboats daring the wind to tip them over.

The shadow of the Ferris wheel raked over him. He sniffed, scratched his head, shifted until he was tucked in the corner, looking down at the beach. The day was bright again, and the blankets were out, the umbrellas, the flesh.

Lord, he prayed, make me twenty one more time, that's all I ask, just one more time.

"Looks like you'll get through the winter after all, Stump."

He didn't look at Planter. He didn't have to. The man would still be in tailored clothes, even on a day like this. And somewhere among the concessions would be Laureen, cool and slim and flirting like mad until her husband reclaimed her and brought her back to the house raised on thick pilings, keeping her there until the next time he wanted to show her off.

Planter snapped his fingers to no rhythm at all. "They're a little high-strung, wouldn't you say?"

Stump grunted.

"Got a feeling the police are going to have their hands full today, wouldn't you say?"

"I guess."

Planter touched his arm. "Stump, you mad or something?"

"No. Just hot. Thinking about all that peace we're going to have come Tuesday."

To his surprise, Planter agreed with him. "It's a bitch, Stump, you know that? You get the hell out of the city, and that goddamned city just drags itself right after you, like it was your goddamned pet dog or something. Shit and damnation, I think Laureen and I'll move to the goddamn mountains."

Stump pushed away from the railing without taking his hands off. "You drunk or something, Dumbo?"

Planter laughed—an open mouth, a quick sound. "No, but what I am, I think, is damned tired of this place."

Before Stump could say anything, the banker winked once and pushed back into the crowd, a leaf vanishing in a whirlpool that soon made him dizzy and turned him back to the beach. Two lifeguards were standing up on their seats, a third marching along the edge of the water, blowing his whistle like a madman and no one paying him any mind. Just below him, a young man was leaning back against a piling, his girlfriend leaning toward him, trailing one hand along his chest. A little girl was crying. A dog chased the waves.

Above and behind him he could hear the cries of those on the wheel, calling to their friends, calling to the gulls that swooped like hawks above their heads. The generator coughed. A curse as someone tripped over a loose cable.

And when he felt a twinge of pain in his left wrist, he looked at his hands and realized he was wringing them—around and around, an old woman fretting.

I know what it is, he thought suddenly, eyes wide, then narrow; I know what it is.

A finger tapped his shoulder.

"What?" he demanded angrily without looking behind him.

"Stump, have you seen Devin today?"

A sideways glance; it was Marty Kilmer, his uniform stained with sweat, his hat pushed up to the back of his head.

"Nope."

"You sure?"

"Yep."

"Damn." Kilmer scowled down at the bathers. "The jerk left me a picture of Mary's killer and then ran off, the idiot. What the hell is he thinking of?"

But Stump didn't care. "What do you mean, Mary's killer?" He didn't release the railing, but his head turned until Kilmer moved over to stand beside him. "What I heard, it was a heart attack."

"Yeah, well, maybe it was, maybe it wasn't. But there was somebody over there when she died. Maybe threw acid into her face, I don't know. And I won't know until I find Devin. The idiot."

Stump licked his lips. "I see him, I'll tell him." He licked his lips again. "Acid?"

Kilmer shrugged, and Harragan wanted to grab his throat and strangle him, gripped the railing more tightly and held his breath as long as he could.

"I might have spoken out of turn," Marty said then. "Don't let this get around, okay?"

"Sure."

Acid? Mary's killer?

He stared over the beach to the dark pier and had to squint in order to see any detail. The heat shimmering off the beach, off the water, was blurring it, making it shift, giving it a depth it shouldn't have had. He thought then of the way the air was before a storm—suddenly so damned clear you could see every detail on a house or tree a hundred yards away, then suddenly so dark you'd swear it was midnight.

Just before the rain.

Just before the lightning.

"Stump, you all right?"

He nodded after a moment.

"You'd better get some water, old man. The sun ain't out, but you can't be too careful when the temperature's up."

He nodded again, and kept his head down.

Marty watched him, waited for a word, then turned quickly and strode through the crowd. He'd been hoping the old guy would offer him some of that bug juice, to help clear his mind, but today it was like talking to a tree, for god's sake. Just what he needed. First Devin's little surprise, now this, and he'd probably have to break up a dozen fights before he reached the boardwalk proper. That was the way his day was going—every creep and asshole in the state was crawling out of the woodwork to make Saturday his private hell.

Less than an hour ago there'd been a coke bust right in front of the station; someone had thrown a couple of softballs through the stained glass windows at the Methodist church; Chuck Geller had been brought in drunker than ten sailors, claiming he'd been rolled and robbed by nymphomaniacs under the boardwalk; and there'd already been four traffic accidents, six reports of missing persons, and a bomb scare at the Salvation Army's day care center on Summer Road near the bridge.

He'd had to get out of the station before he went nuts and used the picture as an excuse. Not that he believed the note Graham had left. It had taken him nearly five minutes just to imagine he saw a face there. But the note had added there were others, ones perhaps clearer, and there was no sense taking the chance the photographer was trying to pull a fast one, maybe making noise so whatever lawyers there were fly-crawling over poor Mary's estate would give something to him.

"Oh, Christ," he muttered in disgust at himself. If anyone would try something like that, it would be Geller, not Devin. Devin, for his sins, was too damned honest, too earnest, to even think of a stupid scam like that.

An elbow caught him in the middle of his back. He whirled, and held back just in time not to slug a young woman struggling with three children barely out of their diapers. He smiled. She shrugged an apology. One of the kids threw up, and Marty strode away.

Through the crowds. Slowly. Scanning the benches, the beach, the people jamming the ramps and the front of the concessions. He'd gone less than a block before he told himself to take his own advice, and he ducked into a bar where the bartender offered him a quick, short beer to cool him off, speed him on his way without checking the IDs of the kids drinking and laughing at the tables.

Marty accepted.

And once on the boards again, mopping his face with a handkerchief, he called himself twenty kinds of a fool. If Devin was sure that the killer, or whoever, had been hiding on the other pier, then it stood to reason that he'd probably try to do something even more dumb—like go there himself and check it out.

Even though it was condemned.

Even though whoever it was might still be there.

A half-block later he gave up trying to dodge skateboards and squalling brats, and retreated down the steps to the beach. He stayed close to the boardwalk, and though walking wasn't easy, it at least gave him a chance to check out the bathing suits more closely. Especially those on the women who eyed him just as frankly as he passed them.

Perks, he reminded himself, sucking in his stomach and straightening his hat; take the perks where you can, Kilmer, and maybe you'll get lucky.

He laughed and turned his head quickly so that no one would see him, just as quickly sidestepped under the boards into the grey shadows when he saw a body lying up against a concrete wall on the far side.

Great, he thought.

His hand drifted to his revolver.

He moved slowly, using the pilings to push him on, waiting for his eyes to adjust to the slants of light and dark that split the air and barred the sand.

Then he stopped and said loudly, "Jesus Christ, can't you at least wait until after it gets dark?"

Tony, who had been slumped against the wall in shadow, Kelly's head in his lap, shoved her away with a hissed warning and scrambled to his feet. Kelly only sat up, carefully brushing the sand from her T-shirt. She looked at Kilmer as though he were something she couldn't bother with just now.

Kilmer ignored the look and rubbed a heavy hand over his face. "Y'know, Riccaro, don't I got enough trouble on a day like this without having to roust you and your girlfriend?"

Tony slapped at his jeans nervously. "We weren't doing anything."

"I know," the policeman said. "And she's only your cousin, right?"

Kelly laughed as she stood, laughed harder when she saw the look on Tony's face, and put her hands over her face.

"I say something funny?" Kilmer demanded.

Tony, suddenly feeling laughter of his own swelling in his chest, shook his head, then nodded and said, "You should see my cousin."

"Oh, Jesus God, just get the hell out of here," the policeman ordered wearily, waved his hand at them once and marched on, angling toward the sunlight, not looking back.

"Oh my god," Kelly gasped, leaning heavily against him, pushing away and kissing his cheek wetly. "Oh my god, Tony, did you see his face?"

"But we weren't doing anything!" he insisted.

"No shit, Sherlock," she said flatly, and looked up at the dark figures walking over their heads. "Look, I gotta get to work. Jimmy's gonna kill me anyway, but a buck's a buck, right? See you tonight?"

He shrugged and didn't move when she kissed him again and ran off, fading into the bright light like a suddenly dying shadow. He waited for several minutes to be sure she wouldn't return, then started walking, keeping under the boardwalk, trailing his hand along the foundations of the buildings that held the concessions and game parlors.

This wasn't working out at all.

This last day wasn't working out anything like he'd planned, and he was going to be in damned big trouble with Mike as soon as he found out. Which he would, because the mood Kelly was in, he knew she was going to say something the first chance she got.

And it wasn't fair, because they'd only sat here the whole time. Talking. Dreaming. Wishing. Trying to figure out how things were going to change in only a few days. She'd even let him talk a little about Julie and the umbrella woman, though the way her hands slapped at the sand made it clear she still wasn't having any of it.

Then she'd slid down and lain with her hands folded over her stomach, her head on his lap, and he'd had to sit as straight as he could so she wouldn't feel the reaction her hair across his groin had created.

Once, only once, did he wonder if he had the nerve to let his hand slip down onto her breast, but a sweep of kids playing tag between the supports stopped him just in time. And before he could get up the nerve again, Kilmer had come along and busted their chops for doing nothing.

Nothing was going right.

He grabbed up an empty beer can and tossed it hard against the wall, veered toward the first set of steps he saw and climbed up to the boards. The heat was worse, much worse, than before; and by the time he found the nearest ramp, he was sweating so hard he felt his hair clinging to his temples, to the back of his neck. His mother would have a fit if she saw him now, but he had no choice but to return to the diner. There was no chance Gayle or Devin were still there, but maybe his father would know where they'd gone.

FIFTEEN

"LEFT!" Devin ordered suddenly. They reached the intersection just before the police station, the traffic moving not much faster than a walk. He sat up suddenly and pointed over the wheel. "Left, now!"

Without thinking, Gayle snapped down the turn signal lever and only glanced at the rearview mirror when someone behind began sounding an angry horn. "But we're almost there, Dev." The corner of her mouth lifted. "You want to park in back? There's no entrance there, remember?"

"No," he said, a hand to his cheek, rubbing slowly. "Forget it. Marty isn't going to be there, not now. All this mess, he's bound to be working."

She said nothing. A beleaguered, hatless traffic cop saw her signal and, when he couldn't stare her into changing her mind, shrugged and tried to clear the southbound lane enough to let her get off Summer Road. Pedestrians ignored his directions and flowed between the cars, glaring at them, grinning, daring them to move.

"Damnit, it's going to take an hour before we get another inch," she complained. "Why don't you get out now and I'll meet you?"

"I told you, we're not going. If he'd wanted to get in touch, he would have left a message or something."

"Dev, for god's sake."

He shook his head; he didn't care. He wanted to get home and pick up some things before they went to the pier. Kilmer wasn't going to be able to help him, and he had been crazy to think the policeman could.

In the car the only sound was the turn signal—click-*click*—and it was getting on his nerves.

It had occurred to him only a few minutes earlier, while watching a pair of young men standing on the corner taking pictures of the gulls over the stores, that if he had more conclusive proof that someone had really been on the pier at the time Mary had died, Kilmer would be moved to do something, now, not later when he had more time and fewer distractions. He suspected that the police who had searched the place before hadn't done a thorough job; after all, who was Prayerful Mary that an already overtaxed police force should haul out all hands?

The car inched forward.

Click*click*.

Besides, whatever he'd seen was probably just a derelict. Some poor homeless bum barely living among the ruins. It certainly couldn't be comfortable, not to mention hardly appetizing, under the boardwalk would have been better, but the bad weather had probably made it awfully tempting. Maybe Mary had been in there before and had disturbed his hiding place, and the guy had panicked when he saw her again. Maybe.

The car moved again, the engine catching once, nearly stalling.

Maybe he had stuff there, from shoplifting and petty theft, maybe he had all he owned in brown paper bags he considered his treasures.

Maybe.

He stretched his left arm along the back of the seat; his right hand pressed lightly against his chest. His thumb beat his sternum, click*click,* his right foot tapped the floor, click*click,* and when he switched on the radio to get some music, some noise, there was nothing but pulsing static.

"Sunspots," Gayle muttered as she switched it back off. "The damned thing hasn't worked since I bought it."

The light brightened though no sky could be seen.

His left thumb now click*click* tapped the back of her neck until she jerked her head away. He could see her knuckles white on the steering wheel, saw the stiff way her lips moved as she swore under her breath, urging the sweating policeman to give her more room to maneuver.

"There," he whispered, and pointed to a gap.

Before the cop could wave her on, she was moving, faster than she ought to, speeding when she swung into the nearly empty street and paid no attention to the exasperated warning whistle blowing shrilly behind her. Devin watched her profile. She refused to look away from the road. Then she turned left again and headed for the dunes.

Brightlight.

A pair of gulls swooping low over the blacktop, landing with a flurry on a toppled trash can. Their heads were up, their eyes unblinking.

He squinted and leaned forward; it was like driving through a fog.

"Slow down a bit, Gayle."

The car swerved slightly to the left, dipped over the center line before swinging back.

"Gayle."

Brightlight.

White knuckles.

He put a hand on her thigh and squeezed gently. "Gayle, you're going to end up in the marshes. Take it easy. We're in no hurry, remember?"

A gull fluttered in front of them and swerved away, calling.

The dunes were straight ahead and the fence a black band above it that made him look away, look back, and swallow when he realized that its uneven silhouette resembled The House of Night.

Take it easy, he cautioned himself; take it easy, it's just the heat.

A baseball on the street. Gayle ran over it.

Trails of sand blew across the blacktop, swirling toward them, swirling away.

The dunes appeared to swell, and the gaps in the fence became startlingly wide.

"Gayle!"

She jerked and gasped, stomped on the brake pedal, and he was thrown against the door as the car fishtailed, skidded, finally stopped across his driveway, facing the other way. A trembling hand switched off the ignition.

"I don't . . ." she began. "I . . ."

With exaggerated flailing he sat up again, hoping she would laugh and banish the tension. When she didn't, he touched her shoulder and she looked at him, wide-eyed, licking her lips and swallowing. He gave her a shaky, one-sided smile, and she leaned into him for a moment before straightening, and straightening her hair. A crooked finger brushed over the wheel, back and forth, back and forth.

"I must have . . . my mind was somewhere else," she offered as apology.

"Where?" he asked lightly. "Canada?"

Her own smile was nothing more than a quick pull of muscle.

"Wait here a minute," he said. "I'll be right back. Only a second, okay?"

A long second passed before she nodded, and he touched her again before easing the door open.

Brightlight.

The bellow of the surf as if it were only just behind the house.

And the noise—tinny music, muffled shrieks, carried by the westward breeze so clearly he had to convince himself that the motes that danced darkly before him weren't going to turn into ghosts.

After ducking down to check on Gayle and give her a reassuring wink, he shaded his eyes and hurried to the door, fumbling in his pockets for his keys before he remembered that he hadn't locked up when he'd left. And once inside he hadn't taken three steps toward the darkroom when the telephone rang.

He looked.

It rang again.

A stern shake of his head, and he straight-armed the door open, went straight to the filing cabinet and yanked out the folder that contained Julie's picture. He didn't know why he wanted it, but he wasted no time folding it twice and jamming it into his pocket.

And froze when he heard a voice in the front room.

I didn't leave it up, he thought as he stepped out of the darkroom; I know I didn't leave it turned up.

"Devin, are you there?"

I didn't.

It was Viceroy, and there was no friendly cajoling left in the man's voice.

"Look, Devin, this whole business has gone on too long, and you know it as well as I do. I have to have a decision from you soon, do you understand? And since I don't want to lose you, I'm coming down to see you on Tuesday. Tuesday afternoon, and you'd better be there."

He headed for the door, his eyes on the camera bag sitting on the table.

"Devin, *mr. graham* this is ridiculous. I *I* want *want* only the best for you, you know that. I *I* want *want* you for my *my* magazine, and I'm going to have *picture* you *back*. See you then, pal. Tuesday afternoon. *Now!*"

He nudged the coffee table aside with his leg, picked up the machine and yanked it high over his head. The wires grew taut. He yanked again, spinning away until it came free of the wall, almost free of his hands.

mr graham i want my picture back

Then he threw it as hard as he could against the baseboard, watched it bounce and skid back to his feet. The cover had popped up, the cassette had sprung free. He lifted his left foot and brought it down, heel first, once, twice, until his leg began to ache.

mr graham

Then he grabbed the camera case and ran out of the house.

SIXTEEN

TONY braced himself against the counter as he leaned over and looked down at the top of Charlene's head. "Are you sure?"

With an extraordinary sigh she dumped the rest of an armful of dirty dishes into the plastic pan Sal would take into the back for washing later, and nodded as she looked up. "I am positive. They just up and left, and there wasn't any message. Why? Should there have been?"

"Damn."

She stood, blowing hair out of her eyes, putting a hand into the small of her back to massage her waist and spine. "Christ, it's been murder around here, you know it?" She gazed around the diner, puffing her cheeks, rolling her eyes. "I'm gonna ask the old man for a raise for next year.

If he doesn't give it to me, my mother'll move in with him."

He didn't smile, didn't laugh. He looked for his mother and saw her trying to placate a straw-hatted customer who was pointing angrily toward the air-conditioning vents, then down at his bowl of soup. From the expression on her face, he had the feeling that if the guy kept it up, she was going to empty the bowl over his head.

There was no sense trying his father again; he was helping in the kitchen and had already told him twice he didn't have time to stop and answer questions.

"You want to leave a message yourself in case they come back or something?" Charlene said.

Mike wasn't home either; he'd already called.

"No," he said. "I don't think so."

She shrugged, grabbed up an order pad and made her way deliberately slowly down the length of the counter when a woman in a business suit tapped her spoon against a glass.

Damn, Tony thought; and he hurried outside again, turning his head away from the light that nearly blinded him, finally reaching into a pocket and pulling out his sunglasses. They helped, but not that much, and he tried to avoid the glare on the sidewalk and the glare of the sky as he hunted for a promising gap in the traffic. He moved slowly north in side steps, tensing when he thought he found a way over, blowing exasperation when the cars closed up again.

His right hand tapped his leg.

At the corner he danced in place, hopping off the curb, hopping back on.

They were going to the pier.

He could feel it in the way the hairs on his arm began to stand up, the way his palms began to itch.

They were going to the pier, they were going inside, and they were going to do it without him.

207

The moment the light changed and the cop thumped on cars' hoods to get them to stop, he dashed to the other side and moved straight on toward the beach. It wouldn't do him any good to stop at Gayle's shop again; he'd already done it after he'd left Kelly, and it was closed.

A woman several sizes too large for her bathing suit collided with him, snarled, and hurried on. He gaped after her, ignoring the elbows he was taking and the garbled comments that drifted back. Then he moved on, unable to believe the number of people on the sidewalk, so damn many of them that a couple of times he had to swing into the street to keep from slowing to a walk. It was like everyone in the state had come here today. Probably the whole East Coast.

On boardinghouse porches, all the rockers were taken, the elderly fanning themselves with magazines, not speaking, dark glasses without reflection.

And at the beach itself he saw as many people ducking under the boardwalk as were using the ramps. Pushing. Yelling laughter. Arms and legs moving, he thought, like old-time films on television, as if steps or frames in between were missing.

Without hesitation he headed up the ramp when a fight broke out between two couples who were trying to get their umbrellas and baskets between pilings at the same time. He shook his head and tried to stay alongside the building, snapping around the corner as soon as he was able.

He didn't look north.

He didn't want to see the dark pier, not yet.

If Devin and Gayle had really gone there, he had no intention of going in alone and couldn't for the life of him say why.

He passed a crowded, noisy food stand and swallowed to keep from gagging at the smell of hot dogs, mustard, sauerkraut, catsup; a game that had dozens of kids lined up to shoot water into the mouths of clowns with balloon heads; the narrow boardwalk entrance to an arcade that took up most of the building behind it; a bar that floated raucous music and what might have been boisterous laughter out across the beach on the back of beer-fume waves.

Someone called his name, and he waved without looking around.

The surf was loud, full-throated. He didn't have to check to know the waves were higher than normal, the storm pushing at the tide, the water colder and deeper and grabbing for legs.

Frankie Junston spinning his wheel, face red, beard dark with perspiration.

Tony stopped, panting, and pressed against the narrow partition that divided the wheel of fortune from Balloon Heaven. A dozen Hispanics were handling the darts, hefting them, turning to each other and trading, joking, all of them with headbands made of folded bandannas, the Spanish so rapid he couldn't distinguish a single word.

He poked his head around the corner.

Kelly was on her stool, T-shirt clinging damply to her, a can of soda in one hand.

"Hey," he said, and she jumped, raised a fist and mouthed a threat to take off his head.

Frankie screamed that he had a winner and pressed the button of an air horn.

"You seen Mike?" Tony asked, raising his voice to be heard.

Kelly shook her head.

"You know where he is?"

She turned away for a moment, long enough for him to wish he hadn't asked the question.

"I think—"

The air horn blared again.

The Hispanics began throwing. All of them at once. A dozen darts in a whooping fusillade that thunked into the boards and didn't hit a thing. They shrieked with laughter and spilled more quarters onto the counter.

Tony gave up and moved away, trying to signal to her

that he'd be back later. Either she didn't see him, however, or she was ignoring him, and suddenly he couldn't be bothered with her tantrums. Her moods. Her goddamn trying to play with him while his goddamned best friend in the whole world was going to drop out of his life in only three days.

A man with a pearl-encrusted accordion played in the center of the boardwalk, a bowler at his feet, a German shepherd lying panting beside him. The tune was fast, and people's heads were nodding though none stopped long enough to drop him a coin.

A headache blossoming at his left temple made Tony slow down once Balloon Heaven was behind him. He rubbed at it with the heel of his hand, dislodged the sunglasses, and he cursed as he grabbed for them one-handed and snatched them out of the air.

He had to find Mike.

He damn sure wasn't going to the dark pier alone, even if Gayle and Devin were there. He wanted someone with him, someone to watch his back.

At Harragan's he swung sharply left and shoved his way through the crowd. Stump was sitting on the end of a bench, a row of children beside him eating ice cream and cotton candy and swinging their legs.

"Hi, Mr. Harragan," he said when he reached the old man.

Harragan looked up, one eye nearly closed against the brightlight. He nodded.

"You see Mike?" Tony asked, craning his neck to scan the crowd. "Mike Nathan?"

"Nope."

"Nuts."

Harragan laughed. "You mean 'damn,' right? Maybe 'shit'?"

He didn't know what to say.

Stump ran a palm down his chest, across his lap, slapped his knee. "Free rides, you and your gang, y'know. Last day, all that crap. Free rides if you want them."

Tony waved a hand helplessly. "Gee, thanks, Mr. Harragan. Maybe later, okay? I gotta find Mike now. I think—"

There was a shout, hundreds of voices cheering, and he looked over the railing. Toward the dark pier. People on the far end of the beach were milling about, but they were too far away for him to see what was happening.

Harragan rose and walked stiffly to the railing. Tony followed him, curious, until he stood beside him and realized that the people racing along the sand up there were also racing under the pier. The rope barricade was down, and he spotted one of the warning signs being flung into the sea.

"Idiots," Harragan muttered. "That damn thing, it's gonna fall down any day now, and those idiots are gonna get themselves squashed." He scratched the back of his head furiously. "Idiots, boy. Every goddamn one of them are idiots, and damn if I don't give a shit."

Tony blinked. The glare off oil and sand and water brought tears to his eyes in spite of the glasses. But even when he turned his head and looked back sideways, the lines of the pier remained indistinct, as if it were fading.

"I gotta find Mike," he said by way of leaving.

Harragan nodded. "I'll tell him if I see him. Remember, free rides."

Tony hurried away, sticking close to the railing and watching the people, pausing at each ride to see if Mike was on one. He snapped his fingers. Each time he stopped, his heel tapped the planks.

*Son*ofabitch, he thought when he reached the Ferris wheel and couldn't find him.

God*damn*, he thought as he cut through the lines, parted trios and families, and stood indecisive for a moment under the high-pitched laughing clowns.

Heel tapping.

Brightlight.

Fingers snapping.

Jumping in place a dozen times before breaking into a run that brought him back to Balloon Heaven.

"I'm going to The House of Night," he told Kelly before she could turn away from him again. "If Mike comes, tell him I'm there, okay?"

Kelly stared at him dumbly.

"Kell, you hear me?"

"You can't," she said.

"Damn right I can. See you later."

"Tony!" she called after him. "Tony, it's condemned, you'll get hurt!"

He ran again, slowly, slipping, sliding, easing his way through the crowd.

When his glasses were knocked off, he didn't stop to retrieve them.

When he saw Angie walking with Fran Kueller, ice cream cones in hand, he dodged to the other side, as far away as he could get, then chanced a look over his shoulder to be sure they hadn't spotted him.

And he stopped, colliding with a bench that had him sprawling against the railing.

It wasn't Mrs. Kueller.

It was Julie holding his sister's hand.

Julie Etler, and she was laughing.

SEVENTEEN

CHARLENE snared Mike's arm and dragged him to the end of the counter before he could protest, and pushed him through the swinging doors that led to the narrow tiled passage to the ladies' room and employees' restroom. He had no time to say a word, but for a moment, there in the silence of the short cool hallway, he thought she was going to rip off all her clothes and throw him to the floor.

He backed up against the wall.

Despite the thrum of the air conditioning, her face was flushed, a gloss of perspiration giving her cheeks and brow a faint shine. "This place," she said between deep breaths, swatting an errant curl away from her eye, "is a fucking madhouse, you know that? This place is a loony bin,

Nathan, and I ain't no information operator, you understand? I don't run no service here, okay? You got it?"

She was breathing heavily, licking her lips, turning her head as though ready to spit and looking back at him again.

"I am getting tired of being yelled at by rednecks who think they can grab my ass every time I bring them a cup of coffee. I am getting sick of goddamned fathers—*fathers,* for Christ's sake—trying to look down my tits while the little wife counts her goddamned postcards."

"Charlene," he said, "listen, I'm—"

She waved him silent with an angry chop of her order pad. "I am tired of my uncle looking at me like I'm ready to die any minute just because I don't have a sonofabitch husband like those creeps out there. And I am sick and tired of my mother sending me down here every year because she thinks I'm gonna find some goddamn millionaire or something."

"Char—"

"And," she said, poking his chest with her finger, "I am sick of waiting for you to ask me out, okay, Nathan? Hey, I am not a beautiful woman, you know. I know that. I got eyes and a mirror. I am not what you call your prime piece of ass, believe me, I know that. But Jesus, Nathan, I ain't old enough to be your mother either, so how about it, huh? What do you say?"

In a panic he looked to the door, looked through the two fake portholes, and prayed for Mr. Riccaro to come and save him from this woman who'd been out in the heat too long.

No one came.

He held up his hands, and to his astonishment, she stepped right into them, letting him feel the give of her breasts. His arms snapped to his sides, his fingers rubbing furiously at his palms.

"Well?" she demanded.

"Look, all I wanted to know—"

"I know what you wanted to know," she said tightly.

214

"And I want to know something too, okay? I mean, am I that fucking ugly or what?"

He wanted to run, couldn't look away from her eyes that jumped side to side as if she were checking each square inch of the skin on his face. There were lines there beneath the makeup and a weariness about her lips. And he didn't dare look at her chest because of what she'd just told him.

"No," he said at last, when her chin jabbed toward him, demanding a response.

"Good. Then buy me a hot dog tonight, okay? One shitty hot dog on the boardwalk and I'll die happy. I'll never bother you again, which you know I won't because you're out of my life come Tuesday, in case you forgot."

"Charlene, I . . ." A mother and daughter came through the doors, the woman staring at them oddly as she hustled the child into the restroom. "Jesus, Charlene."

There was a tear.

He didn't believe it.

It shimmered in the corner of her left eye until she blinked and it was gone.

"Okay."

"Fine," she said curtly.

"Right." And he nodded.

"He went looking for you."

Mike lifted a hand again, remembered just in time, and let it drop. "He did what?"

In exasperation Charlene looked to the restroom door, to the exit, back at him. "Are you deaf or something, Doc? I said, he went looking for you."

"Did he say that?"

She took a deep breath and pushed closer to him when mother and daughter returned to the hall. Mike smiled at them politely, started to follow them, but Charlene took his arm with a look that told him to freeze.

"No, he didn't say that," she whispered harshly. "But the way he was asking, the way he ran out, I figured that's what he's doing."

"Do you know where he went?"

"What, you think I'm a magician or something?" she answered, almost yelling. "Christ, Nathan, no. He comes in, he asks for Devin and that lady, asks for you, then runs out. You guys on a scavenger hunt or what?"

Mike knew then, and he yanked his arm free.

"You remember my hot dog, Nathan!" she called as he banged through the doors. Her voice cracked. "Goddamnit, don't you dare stand me up!"

Mr. Riccaro looked at him askance as he hurried down the aisle. Mike waved him a goodbye and closed his eyes briefly as he practically ran out onto the street, slowing only when he reached the corner because the heat and the press of strollers refused to let him move faster.

The pier.

Tony was going to the pier.

The way Devin and Gayle had been talking when he'd left, he figured they were going to go there sooner or later, and it had to be that Tony was going with them. Or after them. It didn't matter which now. That idiot was probably going there, the hell with the fact that the place was falling apart, and something had to be done before the jerk got himself killed.

Besides, Tony was going to spoil the last gag, the one he'd arranged with Harragan, who thought he was nuts but was willing to try it as long as no one got hurt.

The traffic cop blew his whistle.

Mike grinned to himself. It was going to be great. Not as spectacular as he would have liked, but it was going to be great anyway. A little ride on the Ferris wheel that would, once at the top, just happen to break down. And after a few minutes, Harragan would tell them they'd have to climb down.

Tony would shit.

Kelly would demand the national guard.

Mike actually planned to start down and see how long it took them to talk him out of it.

216

Jesus, it was childish.

But it was going to be fun.

Once across the street, he headed straight for the beach, thinking that maybe Kelly knew something about it, going to the pier, would maybe want to come with him if only to keep Riccaro from breaking his stupid leg. But he hadn't taken more than a dozen long strides past the corner when something stabbed through his hip. He gasped and stopped, his eyes wide in shocked surprise. Tears blinded him until he cleared them away with the back of his hand.

"What the hell?" he said, looking down at the hip as if waiting for an answer. "What the—"

The pain came again, and his knee nearly buckled. Quickly he grabbed for the closest telephone pole, wrapping his arm around it and hanging his head.

No, he thought, swallowing, rubbing the hip with his palm as hard as he could.

"Disgusting," a voice said.

He glanced up as a man and woman hurried by arm in arm. The woman's lips were pursed, the man's mouth puckered as if he were going to spit.

Like a needle. Probing through the bone, heated by a flame, turning slowly, slowly, until he finally dropped to the ground and leaned against the pole, still hugging it, ignoring a splinter that dug into his shoulder.

"God, oh God."

He sobbed.

Slowly. Slowly. Now a dull-edged sword that worked on the seam where the bone had once split.

He tasted blood.

"Jesus God, please!"

He swallowed a scream.

The sidewalk beneath him vibrated as a truck grumbled past.

One leg curled up, the other straightened and the foot braced against the tire of a parked car. He pushed, hard.

217

Trying to force the agony through his thigh, his calf, through his sole and out.

And it was gone.

It took him a moment to realize the pain was gone, and when he did, relief doubled him over until he was almost lying on the pavement. Sweat dripped off the tip of his nose, the round of his chin, raced down his back and chest and made him shiver when the breeze finally blew again. His throat was dry when he swallowed, and he couldn't feel the arm that held him to the pole. The inside of his cheek stung where he'd bit it.

"God," he whispered.

He waited until he was sure the pain wouldn't return, then hauled himself to his feet. A surge of dizziness kept his arm around the pole, a belch brought up bile he spat into the gutter. Then he pushed off toward the boardwalk.

Limping, and not caring.

Shivering as the perspiration dried on his skin as his hand rubbed his stomach lightly, calming it, settling it, while he took increasingly deeper breaths to slow his heart down.

And it was only when he finally reached the nearest ramp to the boards that he realized how manic the crowd was behaving. Darting from rail to concession stand, laughing with mouths wide open and hands flailing the air and each other, walking just shy of a trot from one place to another, as though someone had posted a closing time for the beach and they were determined to make sure they didn't miss a thing; taking the steps up two at a time, leaping down to the sand without bothering to look.

He stood for a moment and watched them, puzzled, before moving on to Balloon Heaven, people packed three deep waiting for their turn.

His expression must have announced his astonishment because Frankie Junston, momentarily without a customer, leaned on the counter and jerked his head toward the stand.

"Incredible, ain't it?"

Mike looked at him stupidly before the words penetrated. "Yeah, I guess."

"It's been like this since the rain stopped, y'know? I haven't even had a chance to grab lunch."

Applause for a breaking balloon.

A quartet of teenagers shouldered Mike aside and placed their quarters on the numbered squares. Junston shrugged at him and spun the wheel, his chatter as mechanical as the sound the wheel made.

It took almost fifteen minutes before the crowd thinned enough for him to get to the end of Opal's stand, another twenty before Kelly was able to acknowledge him. The shelves were almost bare, all the larger stuffed animals were gone.

"I've been waiting for you," she said, gathering the darts together, avoiding his look, clearly uncomfortable at seeing him here.

"Tony," he said shortly, as another group moved up.

Kelly collected the money and handed out the darts. "He was around a little while ago. He was looking for you."

Mike leaned closer. "What did he say? Did he say where he was going?"

She was almost in tears.

His hip throbbed again.

"He said he was going to the pier." She pointed. "I tried to stop him but . . ." A frustrated hand waved at her customers. "I tried, Mike, honest to god I did, but he took off before I could do anything."

The darts flew. Balloons popped.

A high shriek from the beach and the lifeguard's whistle, a surge toward the railing, the clack and clatter of the rides on Harragan's Pier.

"Come with me," he said suddenly, holding out his hand.

"Mike, I can't—"

She was interrupted by a man demanding a gift for his child. She stared at him, looked at Mike, then swept the few remaining prizes from the shelf and handed them out to everyone she could reach. Then she scrambled over the counter and reached for the cord that would bring the corrugated metal shade down.

"Sorry," she said, over and over. "Sorry, we're closed. Mike, grab the other end, it's heavy. Sorry. Closed. Sorry."

No one complained; they simply moved on.

"Kelly, are you sure? You're gonna get killed, you know." He helped her drag the cover down and watched her lock it. "You might lose your job."

"No I won't. Jimmy'll love it. Besides, it's almost the last day, remember?"

"The money," he reminded her.

"It'll be safe." She tugged on the shade until she was satisfied, then jammed the key into her pocket. "Let's go." Three steps later she looked down at his leg. "My god, you're limping."

He nodded.

She gnawed on her lower lip, put a hand on his arm. "You okay?"

He looked toward the dark pier. "I don't know," he said. "You tell me."

EIGHTEEN

D EVIN wanted to say something. He wanted to remind Gayle about the attractions The House of
Night had once offered, how the kids and their parents would flock here in the evenings to scare themselves
laughingly to death riding the spinning barrel, avoiding the
trap-door ramps, walking the tilted path through Midnight
Hall; feeling bats tangle in their hair, spiders walk their
cheeks, cool air from nowhere curl around their legs and
climb toward their waists; watching the dark suddenly
lighten and a vicious ape lunge toward them, a caped man
with a dagger, a monster whose face was shadow and fang,
a vampire, a werewolf, a ghoul with wide eyes and a claw
for a hand; listening to the eerie, sometimes atonal music
that followed them everywhere once they passed through
the doors at the top of the staircase, the screams of those

who had gone deeper into the dark, the nervous laughter of those who finally thought they were safe; feeling the sea surging beneath them, slamming the pilings, roaring for victims who chose the wrong exit, bellowing during storms and making the walls tremble no matter how thick they were.

He wanted to show her, over there on the left between a mechanical fortune teller and a strength-measuring device, the little shop where magic was sold, from coin tricks to scarf tricks to crystal balls in which waited the face of a gypsy woman who mouthed the future and cackled and winked; and there, on the right, midway along and next to the tiny booth that sold ice cream, a stand that sold Halloween masks, full-sized, with real hair, of the Hunchback and King Kong, the Phantom and the Beast, and creatures who never lived outside the pier's doors save in dreams that never came until the time was past midnight; and up there, just before the steps that led to Midnight Hall, a booth he remembered used to sell food to those who wobbled back through the exit—ice cream and cakes and candies handmade, all molded in the shapes of limbs and organs and unidentifiable *things* that were saved for much later, when hands and lips stopped their trembling.

He wanted to tell her about the time he'd come in here with Maureen, on a whim, for a lark, to find out how young they still were, and they'd stood patiently in line at one of the three double doors and listened with tolerant smiles to the faint trailing screams, with feigned shivering to the groans and chains, and watched the lights flash through chips in the black paint on the glass. They hadn't gone in. Maureen had finally had enough when a brief power failure darkened the entire building and all that was left were the stars dimly glowing through the faceted domed roof. It had unnerved her. She began fretting about what would happen if they were trapped inside. With the monsters. Nothing he could say changed her mind, and they had left and spent the rest of the long night in a lounge, listening to a bad jazz

222

quartet and drinking watered cocktails while they talked about anything but the place they'd just left.

He took a deep breath and shivered at the cold that invaded his lungs and made him believe for a moment he could see his breath in the air.

His left shoulder ached a bit with the weight of the camera case, and he shifted it, rolled the shoulder, and looked behind him at the gap in the plywood barrier, looked ahead at the ticket booth and the brass plaque on the floor.

He began to wonder, and he narrowed his eyes.

It was dark.

Not so dark that they couldn't see, but dark enough to hide the edges, the corners, the places where the floor might have collapsed after the fire. It shouldn't have been. Daylight should have glared from all the holes in the roof, from the gaps in the wood, and the stacks and deadfalls of debris should have been revealed, and any evidence of anyone who had used the pier for shelter.

It was quiet.

Not so quiet that they couldn't hear themselves breathing, but quiet enough to dampen all sound from the boardwalk. It shouldn't have been. Sections of the outside walls had been split, in places fallen, in other places tilted outward. They should have been able to hear the voices, the music, the footsteps, the rides' rumbling.

All they could hear was the ocean.

In his right hand he held the camera, electronic flash ready, strap wrapped loosely around his wrist. He looked up, he looked side to side, and he looked at Gayle, who had jammed her hands into her pockets and was blowing as if she were trying to stay warm.

"What do you think?" he said at last. Softly. For the sound of his voice more than the answer.

She glanced at him, looked away. "I think I'm wishing you hadn't talked me into this." Softly. For the sound.

"Me?"

"You. If I get out of here alive, I'm going to claim I was kidnapped."

He smiled without feeling it, took her hand and led her forward. She resisted for a second, then sighed and moved with him, muttering to herself, her heels coming down hard.

The floor here was relatively clear, nothing too large to step over or around. A piece of wood, a rusted bolt. She blew one last time and took a flashlight from her hip pocket. She had insisted they buy one at one of the souvenir stands. It was plastic, its head narrow, but she didn't turn it on yet, only tapped it against her leg.

They stopped first at the ticket booth and wondered aloud how the front glass had broken only in places, leaving jagged holes without collapsing upon itself. It was dark inside. He hunkered down beside the plaque. The space where it had been bolted below the sill was the plaque's ghost, and he realized that the fire had barely scorched the wood, hadn't touched the brass at all. A finger pushed at it. He stood, wincing when his knee popped, a gunshot in the silence.

Then he pointed toward the center, beyond the booth and slightly to his right. "She was over there," he said.

A slide of ash in the dark, the hiss of a wary snake.

"Swell," Gayle said.

"Look," he began.

"No," she said, dropping his hand and turning on the light. "I'm not here for that. You said there was a face, and we're supposed to find a bum. Okay. Let's look for the poor slob and get the hell out."

The beam rode the dark, melting white over black and revealing nothing but ash and ashen wood, charred beams in tangles, piles and platters of shattered glass. All the stands and shops were gone, burned back to the outer walls, a few studs standing, nothing more. The flooring was bare in spots where the wind had swept it clear, cluttered with chips and splinters the wind had loosened from the roof.

Devin followed half a step behind her, the camera up at his chest. Stepping around darkforms. Ducking under angled timber. Being careful not to push anything too hard, nor step too strongly where he felt rather than saw separations in the floor.

Once, he paused and let Gayle move ahead. He wanted to *feel* something, *sense* something, perhaps pick up emanations of something that would give him a clue. But he felt nothing but the damp chill, sensed nothing but Gayle's anxiety, and knew that was wrong.

It shouldn't have been.

In a place where sound and light were smothered, that shouldn't have been.

Gayle aimed the light at him then, and he threw up a hand to shade his eyes. "C'mon," she said. "This place gives me the creeps."

"It's dead."

"I don't care."

A pane from the buckled dome was standing out of the floor, its corner like an arrow's tip deep in the wood. He walked around it several times, scratching his jaw, not wanting to touch it, then moved on until he found himself at the place where he thought Julie had died. He touched his pocket. He looked down, softly biting the inside of his lower lip, trying to reconcile what he saw now with what he had seen through the lens. He looked straight up, but the roof was gone; he tried to peer through a gap he found in the wall, but several beams and other clutter prevented him from moving closer.

He couldn't see the outside.

He couldn't see the beach.

"What do you make of it?" he said, pointing when Gayle turned to the shattered ceiling, the crumpled walls—the failure of summer to make its way inside.

225

A soft breeze, warm but not uncomfortable, pushed a fall of hair into her eyes. She shook it back with a curse. It blew again.

"I don't know," she said, voice close to cracking. "Devin, this is dumb. There's nothing here. Let's go."

"Not yet." He nodded toward the opposite side and walked in that direction, the camera ready, Gayle beside him with the light.

"You know what this reminds me of?" she said, close to his shoulder.

"What?"

"A barn."

"You're kidding."

A door split in half lay over a vanished threshold, its brass knob gleaming when she dropped the beam on it.

"Any minute now," she continued, "I expect to be charged by pigeons that are hiding up in the loft. They're going to scare me senseless, and a zillion violins are going to play from somewhere outside and scare the audience too."

He looked at her quizzically.

"For god's sake," she said, "don't you ever go to the movies?"

The urge to scold her died when he saw the look on her face, the way the beam danced though her arm was perfectly still.

"Barns," he said.

"Right," she told him.

When he accidentally bumped into a piece of timber propped against the wall and it didn't fall over or bring the place down around his head, he felt himself relax and felt Gayle relax too. Safe, he thought; for the moment they were safe.

He pushed then at other beams, other piles, directing the light with a grunt and nod, or pointing with his camera hand. Searching for signs that someone had been here, someone who had a face he had snared through his lens.

226

A gull screamed.

The sea.

A section of wall held a half-dozen shelves, but he couldn't remember what had been there before. The shelves were empty, and he realized there wasn't a single spider web in the place.

By the time they reached the staircase, Gayle was kicking at piles of ash, and he had decided that the reason the pier hid the daylight had something to do with all the dust in the air—it was beginning to make him cough and make his throat feel coated, and he supposed that the light was refracted somehow and made to appear as if it weren't there.

"Well," she said, hands on her hips, "that's about it, wouldn't you say? I didn't see a damn thing. If he was here, he's gone now."

If, her tone said, *there was anyone at all.*

He nodded toward the doors above them. "What about up there?"

"No, not a chance."

"Why not?"

She looked at him sideways. "Were you ever in there?"

"Sure."

"Okay then."

He waited, then understood what she meant—that there were too many trick floors, trick doors, trick windows, trick mirrors back there, and even if any of it had survived the fire, no wanderer was going to take the chance that something soon wouldn't give. If anyone was staying or hiding here, he would have to be in the main hall.

"Yeah," he said, and put the camera away. When he was done, he felt her watching him, saw the half-smile. "What?"

"Y'know, Graham, I really think you're disappointed."

He couldn't help but return the smile. "It's kind of anticlimactic, I have to admit."

"What did you want to see?"

227

He sobered. "I don't know." And he took out Julie's picture, didn't unfold it, tapped it against the heel of his hand. "I'm not sure."

"Well, whatever it is, it's not here," she said, taking his arm and leading him away. "We've done the dumb thing, now we're going to do the smart thing."

"Which is?"

"We'll give that picture to Marty, forget the voices and all that other stuff, and you're going to take me out to dinner."

He grinned. "Again?" Though he wasn't so sure about the picture.

"You weren't there the last time, remember?"

He nodded, shrugged, and covered her hand with his as he stopped, suddenly, and looked over his shoulder.

"Now what?" she asked.

"Listen," he said.

She cocked her head. "I don't hear anything."

"Yeah," he said. "I know."

They should have. They should have heard something, but the main hall was silent.

The chill became cold.

The breeze began to gust.

"Devin," Gayle whispered.

Not even the sea.

Tony took a hesitant step toward the barrier, stepped back and turned around in a quick tight circle. Finally, he snapped his fingers in anger at himself. This was dumb. There was no reason why he should be afraid to go in there, for god's sake, no reason at all, and besides, Devin and Gayle were there so he wouldn't be alone.

A step forward.

Dumb.

A step back.

The whole thing, he thought; the whole thing's just unreal. He was acting like Angie, for Christ's sake.

And in thinking of his sister, thought of her walking along the boards with Julie. He'd almost screamed. If he hadn't stumbled and stopped, he probably would have, and then they wouldn't have passed him, and he wouldn't have seen that it wasn't Angie after all, just a kid he didn't know.

And it wasn't Julie.

Yes it was, something told him.

He shook the voice away and stared at the plywood, at the gap that would let him in.

A step forward; a step back.

It wasn't Julie.

yes it was

He didn't have to pretend anything for the shills in the stands because there weren't any; all the stands were closed, those facing the pier. He didn't know why, didn't give a damn right now, but the folded metal shades were down and locked, and no one was there.

Not even the crowds.

He sniffed, hunched his shoulders, and took four long strides to the steps leading to the beach. The tourists were there in force, more as the day brightened, and the rope that marked the danger area had been trampled into the sand. Kids were running around the pilings, a few men stood at water's edge with their cameras, the lifeguards had given up trying to keep them away.

There were no police that he could see, though he'd spotted Marty Kilmer ducking under there only a few minutes ago. He'd expected some shouting after that and some kids racing for the open air, but there was nothing, and they pressed closer as if teasing the pier like teasing a chained dog.

He rubbed his nose.

He stretched his neck and rolled his shoulders.

Hands in pockets, he returned to the front and stared at the gap where Devin must have gone.

I am, he thought then, a truly dumb shit. This has got to be the dumbest thing I've ever done in my life.

His parents were back at the diner, working their asses off so he could go to college next week, and instead of helping them, instead of pitching in, he was standing here in front of a goddamn wreck, too chickenshit to go inside because he thought he'd seen a ghost.

Jesus.

I mean . . . Jesus.

He stared down the boardwalk to his right, puzzled for a moment when he noticed that the crowds weren't coming his way. People were gathering at the nearest open concession, one that sold souvenirs, but they were coming no closer than the steps he'd just looked down. They were curious, they pointed at the pier, but not one of them looked at him or anywhere near him.

I must have crud or something, he thought sourly, and ordered himself to make up his mind before he grew old here and died.

Then he saw Mike, and Kelly was with him. Nathan was limping more than usual, and Kelly looked mad. For a moment he wanted to run—down to the sand, up the beach toward home, he wasn't sure he could face Nathan because of what he'd almost done.

Then Kelly waved a frantic arm and hurried toward him, Mike following as quickly as he could.

"Don't even think it," she ordered sharply, grabbing his wrist and turning to Mike. "Tell him, Mike, for god's sake. Tell him not to go in there."

Mike said, "Are they there?"

Tony shrugged. "I don't know. I haven't gone in yet. I think so, though."

"You guys are totally nuts," Kelly said, her voice high. "What if they changed their minds, huh? What if they didn't go?"

Mike strolled over to the barrier and poked at it with his

230

finger, gripped the edge of the gap and peered in. "Dark," he said.

Tony joined him. "I already looked. You'd have to go in to see anything."

Kelly clamped her hands on her waist. "Jesus! I mean . . . Jesus!" She stalked over and yelled, "Devin! Gayle! Hey, you guys in there?"

Tony looked at her as if she'd lost her mind, feeling incredibly stupid because he hadn't thought of it himself. Then he called as well, and Mike did, once, but there was no answer, no echo, and the voice of the crowd began to sound like the sea.

"What the hell, what can it hurt?" Mike said.

"The goddamn place could fall down, that's what," she snapped, slapping at his arm. "Are you totally out of it, Michael Nathan? Do you want to bust your other hip too, you jerk?"

Tony couldn't understand why she was so hyper, why she was dancing in place, why she looked ready to cry. He peered in again. "I guess," he said to Mike. His shoulder lifted in a question.

"Sure," Mike said, and before Kelly could grab his arm, he slipped through the gap.

Tony waited.

Kelly started to walk off, and walked back, her face flushed, her chest rising and falling with the effort not to scream.

Then Mike poked his head out and grinned. "Dark as shit, Riccaro, but I ain't dead yet."

Tony grinned back and had taken a step forward when Kelly grabbed his arm. He yanked it away and glared at her, ready to cut her down, when he saw how her eyes kept shifting to the right, toward the beach. Her mouth opened, closed, and she tugged until he followed.

"Hey!" Mike said, squirming through the gap. "Hey, what's up? Where you guys going?"

Kelly stood at the head of the stairs and pointed, then used that hand to take hold of Mike's.

"What?" Tony said.

The people were still there. More of them. Old men with open shirts and sandals, older women with straw hats, girls in string bikinis, men sporting tans against brilliant white trunks. And halfway to the water a large, wire-haired woman in a straw hat and spangled boots.

She was singing, and the people were dancing in time to the hymn.

"It's her," Mike whispered. "Jesus Christ, we were right."

They couldn't hear the words, couldn't hear the melody, over the surf that slammed the beach and the hands that clapped over the shouts and the laughter.

Tony saw the teardrop on Kelly's cheek, saw her shake her head as she tried to back away.

Mike looked at them both. "What . . . what'll we do?" And grimaced with pain, clamped a hand on his hip.

Dancing in a great circle whose northern arc dipped beneath the pier.

Singing along, arms waving, heads bobbing, knees and feet high while Prayerful Mary nodded solemnly and opened her arms as if embracing them all. Turning slowly as the circle wound about her, turning slowly until she faced the boardwalk.

She stopped.

The people danced.

Tony saw her mouth beneath the brim of the floppy hat, but he couldn't see her eyes, and suddenly didn't want to.

Dead, he thought; she's dead.

"Tony," Mike said hoarsely.

Brightlight.

Tony looked up and squinted, the clouds now a haze that turned the whole sky to sun without giving an edge to the shadows, or shade beneath the boards and under the umbrellas.

"Tony," Mike said, and tapped his arm, hard.

Kelly released them and backed away. She swallowed several times. Her gaze shifted to the boardwalk and the tips of her shoes.

Dancing.

Slowly dancing.

"Tony, look."

"I can see," he snapped.

"No," Mike said, and Tony realized that Nathan was pointing somewhere else. At the pier. "Look. Down there."

He held up a hand to block the sun and couldn't see what his friend was trying to show him. It was just the pier. Charred and crumbling and . . . he blinked and wiped an eye with his finger. Blinked again and leaned to the side to give him a better view of the place where Devin had seen Julie during the fire. A gap in the wall that wasn't there anymore.

None of them were.

And the black became blacker as the brightlight increased.

Dancing.

Mary singing, and turning again.

When Kelly began to whimper, Mike hurried to her and put an arm around her waist. She leaned into him and hid her eyes against his chest, her legs straining to push him though he wouldn't be moved. Tony hesitated, wanting to join them, wanting to figure out how much of what he saw was heat, how much was real; and in the hesitation he saw the first board come loose.

"My . . . Jesus!" he shouted.

It peeled away from the wall as though it were being pulled, a twenty-foot plank that pulled two others with it.

Slowly.

And slowly dancing.

Cupping his hands around his mouth, he screamed a warning, but no one heard him, not the women, not the men, not the children who had joined the circle swinging pails and sand shovels and dragging colored tubes in the shape of horses and mermaids.

A frantic look to the others, and he raced down the steps, leapt to the sand and started to run. Looking up at the timber peeling away from the pier, knowing that when it fell it would hit at least a dozen dancers, maybe more.

He stumbled, caught himself and straightened, and was knocked to the ground when someone charged out from behind a piling and collided with him, arms pumping, feet sliding, nearly falling himself just before he reached the circle.

Tony pushed himself to his hands and knees, ready to run again, when someone else ran past him in pursuit. Marty Kilmer. And Tony recognized the first man as one of the guards at the bank where he kept his college savings. The man was obviously drunk, couldn't move in anything near a straight line, and Kilmer, hat off and uniform jacket open, wasn't doing much better.

Chuck Geller reached the circle just as the first plank ripped loose.

Falling slowly.

Dancing slowly.

Prayerful Mary singing as the wood struck the bank guard square across the back, end first, driving him into the sand, legs kicking, blood quickly spreading out from the base of his neck. Kilmer skidded and fell to a halt beside him. Tony stood, gaping, and heard above the noise the policeman scream, "Get help! Someone get help, this man is hurt!"

Dead, Tony thought as he half-turned toward the stairs; the old guy is dead.

A second plank fell, glancing off Kilmer's shoulder, striking half a dozen others. They sprawled. They bled. No one stopped to help them.

The circle never broke.

The ground began to tremble. Slightly. So slightly he

barely felt it and at first thought it was the dancing, the stomping of feet, hundreds of them in time, all them moving deeper and deeper beneath the pier. Others joined them, and for the first time he was able to see their faces clearly.

"Oh Jesus," he whispered, and bolted up the stairs. "It's falling apart!" he screamed to Mike. "C'mon, we gotta get Devin!"

Kelly shrieked at them not to go.

Another plank fell, another twelve dancers were replaced by twelve more.

Harragan leaned against the railing, ignoring the rides, the customers, the press and chatter of passersby at his back. His hands were cupped around his eyes; his left foot was on the bottom rail. Six blocks. Sometimes it might as well be six miles. Yet still he could see something going on up there. Even at this distance he could tell something was attracting large numbers of bathers under the dark pier.

Too many heads in the way, too many moving bodies.

He wiped his face with a palm, wiped it again, rubbed his nose; he backed away and felt his stomach telling him not to be stupid, it was none of his concern; he backed farther until he came up against a bench, then whirled and began moving as fast as he could.

As fast as the heat would let him.

Something going on.

Marty knelt beside Geller, trying to shake off the dull ache where the board had struck his shoulder. He tasted salt. His stomach bubbled with acid. He blinked fiercely several times to clear the tears from his eyes. Christ, he hurt. Christ. He tasted iron now, and bile, and he rolled Chuck over, knowing he was dead. He looked up at the dancers, saw their faces, and looked away.

The whole goddamn beach is on drugs, he told himself, rocking away from Geller's body; every goddamn one of them. They're crazy. Dancing around like idiots; the chief is gonna shit. But he wouldn't look more closely at the woman in the center, only wondered where she'd gotten poor Mary's boots.

Idiots.

On drugs.

Which was one reason, he decided, why they looked scared to death.

Tony squeezed through the gap, wincing when an edge scraped along his spine, narrowing his eyes against the dim light while Kelly came behind him, Mike bringing up the rear. Frantically, he looked to the right but saw no gap where the planks had broken loose, and it stopped him. He frowned. He looked straight down the main hall and saw the ticket booth, the plaque, and someone beside it.

"Devin," he said, taking a step forward.

Kelly hissed at him to be careful.

"Devin?"

His voice was flat; there was no echo.

The darkform moved toward him, face shadowed, shadows giving it bulk. He glanced at his friends, felt his hands fold to fists and again he said, "Devin?"

Another darkform from the other side of the booth, and Mike pushed Kelly behind them, though she held onto his waist. Tony exchanged glances with him, and they stood their ground, up off their heels in case they had to move quickly—though they weren't going to leave without Devin and Gayle.

Then the first figure was close enough to see without squinting, and Tony opened his hands, flexed his fingers, tried not to let his relief out in a sigh. "You didn't answer," he said to Devin. "Are you guys okay?"

Devin nodded. "I didn't hear you."

Gayle stood beside him. "We didn't hear anything."

"But—"

"The pier's falling apart," Mike interrupted. "I think someone's already hurt, maybe even dead."

Devin stared at them all, and Tony pointed to the south wall. "Some chunks of wood fell from over there just a couple of minutes ago. It hit a guy, some kids, I don't know." He took a few steps closer, to show them exactly where the wood had fallen, but Devin stopped him by taking his arm.

"Don't," he warned. "There's too much stuff around here."

"For god's sake," Kelly burst out, "we've got to get out of here, you guys! This whole place is falling down!" She took Mike's hand and started for the exit, swearing when he didn't move as fast as she wanted.

Then Tony said, "Look."

He was cold, he was frightened, and though he wanted to leave with the others, he couldn't turn away from the light that began shining behind the entrances to Midnight Hall. White light. Brightlight. Flaring through each gap where the doors had been, without touching the shattered ceiling. Intense enough to make him squint against it, yet soft to let him see the blackshadow of a woman at the top of the stairs.

He ran toward her without thinking, without listening to the shouts that exploded behind him.

He ran without looking and heard Mary ask, *do you know any prayers to save you from death?*

"Go!" Devin commanded, spinning Mike around and shoving him toward the exit. "Get the hell out, all of you. I'll bring him back."

He ran after Tony, cursing the boy's stupidity, wondering who the hell was playing tricks with the lights in Midnight Hall. Between one stride and another he thought it might be something Michael had dreamed up, and dismissed it because he didn't think Mike would dare risk

237

coming here just to set up one of his gags; he thought it might be the sea air, salt and damp, playing havoc with the electricity and dismissed it because the power had long since been switched off.

"Tony!" Kelly shrieked.

Devin dodged a fallen timber, cracked his shin against another and spun around, cursing, pausing long enough to see that the others were following. He almost shouted. He raised a fist to signal them away and ran again just as Tony leapt over the last step and reached the first entrance, the one on the left.

"Tony!"

The boy stopped and shook his head, as if puzzled.

"Tony, wait!"

He looked over his shoulder at Devin, and Devin saw the tears. "I'm scared!" the boy cried. "Devin, I'm scared!"

And Devin skidded to a halt at the bottom of the staircase when Tony stepped through the glassless frame and vanished into the light.

Whitelight, and cold, and splitting into beams as if shadows were passing through.

Mike ran past him before he could whip an arm out to stop him, diving through the center gap, shouting for his friend.

Whitelight, and cold, waxing and waning like the pulse of a dying man.

He managed to throw his arms around Kelly's waist and spin her to a stop before she could chase Mike. She screamed and kicked at him; and before Gayle could arrive to help, she bit his forearm and he let her go.

Into the whitelight, no shadows at all.

And a voice whispered over his shoulder, *you can bring my picture now.*

NINETEEN

FIRE.

There had been a fire.

The newspapers said the flames had jumped and spat over a hundred feet into the air. The smoke could be seen for miles. More than a dozen people had received minor injuries trying to flee.

And a young woman had died.

In the fire.

Devin knelt in the main hall, clutching the camera to his chest. Rocking back and forth. Staring at the light.

Gayle was down beside him, an arm lightly around his waist, crooning something, whispering something, wet matted hair making her forehead look cracked. He could feel her. He could smell her. What he couldn't understand were the words she was saying; they were nothing but jumbled sounds, and she was nothing but a dark shape because the lights behind the doors didn't reach this far down, into the black.

I'll call Ken in the morning, he thought. I'll call and we'll talk and maybe I'll take the job. What the hell. If he thinks I can do it, maybe I can. What the hell. I can always come back and go to weddings again. What the hell.

Whispering. Holding him.

The fire.

I can . . . I am . . . I . . .

Rocking back and forth.

Oh God Oh God Oh God Oh God

Oh God, please help me, I'm . . .

He could feel the flooring shudder as the sea rose against the pilings; he could feel the cold deepen as the light that was merely dim shaded slowly toward black; he could feel splinters digging into his knees, Gayle's arm against his shirt, a sharp corner of the camera stabbing his breast.

Oh God I'm . . .

The first light, Tony's light, flared and died.

He froze, mouth open.

Gayle held him more tightly, her free hand pushing back through his hair, pausing to massage his nape, flowing over his shoulder to touch his cheek, his chin. When he looked at her, and it hurt to turn his head, she was still moving her lips; and he knew the words were there, but he still couldn't hear them.

The center light, Michael, sighed and faded.

I could propose to you, he said to her, not saying a word; we could get married, I suppose, and I know you well enough that you'd take some of that money you have and let me go on my own, me and my lenses and the tripod and the flash and all the rest of it on my back, wherever I wanted. I could do that. What the hell. I could do that, and maybe I could show Ken what I'm doing and he could pub-lish a few photographs, what the hell, and maybe get me a gallery that would get me a show. What the hell. I could do that.

Oh God, I'm . . .

He started rocking again, more quickly, and she held his shoulders with both hands, tightly, nails close to hurting; and he stopped and stared at her and asked what the hell she thought she was doing? But he couldn't move. Oh God. He could barely breathe. Oh Jesus. He couldn't tell her that for all the talk he couldn't do it.

He couldn't follow the kids.

Oh God.

"I'm afraid," he said.

"Don't be afraid," she said at the same time. "It's all right, Dev, it's all right. Don't be afraid."

Whitelight finally died, and finally there was black.

She half-rose and tugged at him until he was standing, finally swallowing, finally hearing, and feeling so goddamned ashamed that he couldn't look at her. Not even when she tried to grab his chin and turn his head.

"C'mon," she urged. "We'll get Marty. He'll help us."

He shook her away and let the camera dangle by its strap from his hand. He was terrified, he couldn't move, but neither would he leave while the kids were still in there. Lured. Driven. What the hell did it matter? They were in there, and he couldn't leave them because they trusted him too much.

Jesus, I'm scared.

"Damnit, Dev, we've got to go, now! We can't wait here for them to come back. They're in trouble, don't you get it? We have to get help."

"The lights," he said, as if thinking aloud. "The lights are . . . something. God damn, I can't think!"

She moved to the other side of him, stood in front of him, a dance of frustration, and cupped his cheeks firmly in her hands. "Listen to me, Devin, listen. This place, there's something wrong. You know it, you know I'm right. It's

241

this place, Dev. For god's sake, let's get out of here and get some help."

He looked at her and saw her eyes fill with tears, saw the skin taut across her cheekbones, saw over her shoulder the lights flash once before vanishing again.

"The kids," she said. "Dev, the kids."

He tapped her shoulder lightly, rapidly, using the contact to help him clear his mind, until he reached into his pocket and pulled the photograph out. He unfolded it and told her to get out the flashlight. When she balked, he glared until she switched it on, and they looked at the place where Julie's face was, so tiny they saw little more than a blur, a smear of white.

Yes, he thought.

"Yeah," he said, and jabbed at the spot. "Yeah, yeah, that's got to be it."

"What?" Gayle asked, looking from the photograph to his face, and suddenly behind her when the lights returned. And left. "What's it?" And she raked at her hair with fingers stiffened to claws.

"She's not laughing," he said.

"What?" Her voice was high. "Devin, what the hell are you talking about?"

"In the picture, Gayle. In the picture. Jesus, I was wrong."

A hand lifted as if to slap him, and lowered when he shook the picture in her face. "Okay," she said. "Okay. But how can you tell? You can't even see her."

"I'm here," he explained, nodding to the hall, to the place where she was found. "I'm here now. I know."

She hugged herself and looked to the ceiling, licked at her lips and chewed them. "I'm leaving, Devin. I am. I'm going out to get Marty." She waited for an answer; he had none to give her. "Okay. You stay here, all right? Stay right where you are, don't move, and we'll be right back with enough people to search every inch of this place."

The flashlight was slapped into his hand, and he swiveled

as she walked past him, but he didn't try to stop her. She was afraid too, and he understood that nothing he could say would make her follow him into Midnight Hall.

He smiled briefly.

Midnight Hall.

What an inanely obvious name, and how it used to make the kids make themselves shiver, make the adults grin, transform the whole garish place into something more sinister than it was. A fun house. A house of mechanical and plastic horrors. Lights flashing. Gears grinding. Recorded screams that sounded tinny, and monsters' growls like wire being pulled through a long tin can. A tunnel of love for pedestrians. And at the exit you could buy a candy in the shape of a human heart.

He watched until the dark of the hall erased her, turned back toward the staircase and looked down at Julie's picture, folded it, and stuffed it back in his hip pocket. Then he started up, a slow shuffling stride that clouded dust and ash around his ankles until the bottoms of his jeans were stained a pale grey. He was going to have to go in now, no matter how he felt, and unless Gayle had decided to run, and Marty was right outside with an army, he was going in there alone.

He couldn't wait.

Julie wasn't laughing.

And she hadn't killed herself.

Gayle ran into the ticket booth before she even saw it. The collision with its corner knocked her to her knees, a splinter rammed into the heel of her left hand, and she kicked out at the structure as she struggled back to her feet. The move faced her the other way, and she couldn't see Devin. She couldn't see the flashlight. A sob wrenched into a curse. There was ice beneath her breast. Hatred at her desertion whipped her through the gap, and she staggered at the blast of light, the blare of sounds that knocked her back against the barrier as if she had been struck.

Gasping for air, trying to shake the tears from her eyes, she stepped away and sobbed aloud. The splinter. She held the injured hand up and tried to pull the wood out, but her fingers wouldn't close, her nails wouldn't grip it, and she closed her eyes tightly in an effort to find calm.

Someone took her wrist gently.

The pain was sharp and short as the splinter slipped clear.

"God," she said in relief, and saw Stump Harragan watching her as she sucked at the swollen skin. She almost kissed him. "Stump, we've got to get somebody. Devin . . . the kids . . ." And she pointed behind her. "There were lights all over the place and Tony, I think it was Tony— god, I can't remember—he ran into it, the light I mean, and then Mike and he was limping and—"

Stump took her wrist again and squeezed until she quieted. "Fear," he said.

"What?"

Oh god, she thought; oh god, another crazy.

He started walking and she followed, allowed herself to be led to the beach stairs. She saw the dancers then—more of them, hundreds of them, she couldn't count—and policemen in uniforms coated with sand and blood kneeling over dozens lying beside the pier. There were two ambulances down there, and as she watched two more pulled up on the boardwalk.

The dancers—clapping and singing hymns and waving their hands in the air.

The sight took her breath away, and she sagged against Harragan, let him take her away again, backward to the line of stands where she ordered herself to stop shaking, took such deep hurried breaths she thought for a moment she would faint.

"I saw it," Stump said as he watched attendants race with stretchers to the beach. "This morning I saw it clear as I see you now. All of them, all those fools. I couldn't place

244

it before, you know. I tried but I couldn't place it for the longest damned time."

"Stump," she said, "we've got to get Marty. Devin's—"

He looked up at her, head tilted, eyes wide. "They are afraid, young lady. You know what that means? Afraid. You can see it in their eyes. Every one of them, afraid." His head swiveled toward the pier. "In there is where it is. And it's going to kill them."

"Jesus Christ!" She slapped the man's shoulder as hard as she could. "Jesus Christ, you idiot, will you listen to me?"

"I heard," he said calmly.

"Then for god's sake—"

"He's in there?"

"I just told you he was."

Harragan looked up at the arches and shook his head. "Oh my," he said. "Oh my."

Gayle leaned toward him, feeling her arm tense and her hand become a fist that quivered at her side.

"Oh my."

She swung away and returned to the steps. The police were moving quickly through the injured. The dancers wove in and out among the pilings. Marty Kilmer wasn't there; at least, she couldn't see him. And when she shouted for help, no one turned around.

Her teeth began chattering.

One of the dancers saw her and waved.

Brightlight, and she saw the sky, featureless and white. Dancing slowly.

And she realized Harragan was right—every one of them looked scared to death. And all those she saw on the boardwalk as well, standing at the railing, puzzled by the commotion, some of them shrugging and turning away, others climbing over and jumping to the sand, still others slowly taking the other steps to the beach to join those already there.

She knew it should have unnerved her, sent her running for home, but instead she ran her hands down her sides and stepped away, back to Stump.

"I can't stay out here," she said without looking at him. "If I can't get any help, I'll have to go back. Devin . . . I have to go back."

He didn't answer.

"Come with me, okay?"

Stump shook his head.

She didn't argue. Nor did she jump when a section of the pier down by the water split off from the rest.

Falling slowly.

Dancing slowly.

"You know what it is," Harragan said as she left him.

She nodded without looking back.

"Then you know if I go in there, I'm going to die."

She nodded again.

It didn't matter.

And she wasn't surprised when a shadow abruptly chilled her, and she saw beneath the ornate arches the pier's name glowing black.

Stump watched her go, and he beat his chest for his cowardice, then broke into a run, back to his own place, back to the wheel.

Marty saw the plank hit the beach just as a wave curled and crashed on the sand. The wood was lifted and spun and tossed and whirled, and at least four people had their legs smashed before it stopped and floated. He didn't try to help them. He kept thinking he ought to dance.

Angie held Mrs. Kueller's hand, a teddy bear towel around her neck. She thought she saw her mother. It didn't matter. She was dancing.

He stood at the center entrance and stared into the black. Motes of color sparked before his eyes; the jamb was wood, and he thought it was ice; the camera swung on its strap, a pendulum he stopped when it felt as if a magnet were pulling it inside.

He had to go in.

He had to get the kids.

Although he tried to remember, he didn't know what lay just beyond this particular threshold. All he could picture were the short narrow hallways people took when they stepped through the door—on the left, where Tony vanished, he thought it might be the spinning barrel; the one on his right was the trap-door path; this one led to the monsters and murderers who popped out of alcoves and dropped from the ceiling.

Maybe.

Maybe not.

The only thing he was sure of was that sooner or later they bled into one another, so that all one could choose was which thrill one had first.

All right, he thought; all right. Let's get on with it, boy, before the Bogeyman eats you up.

Carefully, still watching for signs of movement beyond the doorway, he wrapped the strap around the camera and set it on the floor. There was no need for it in there, and he would need both hands free for whatever came along. He didn't look behind him either—Gayle was coming or she wasn't, and it didn't matter at all whether or not help was with her.

i know, Mary had said.

Oh lord, Mary, he thought, not even your hymns could save you.

He was positive now she hadn't been talking about *who* had killed her that afternoon; she was talking about *what* had done it. She was talking about the pier. She must have come inside as he had and had seen whatever stayed here; and she had died because the pier didn't want her—not her, but someone else. Because until she came inside, Prayerful Mary wasn't afraid.

What was it?

He wasn't sure.

Ghosts and voices. Dark and light. Fanciful enough to be impossible; real enough to kill.

What was it?

Maybe nothing, he thought. Maybe he was just going crazy.

With a touch to his hip pocket for luck, and still holding onto the jamb, he stepped over the threshold and waited for something to happen.

Nothing did.

The light here was as dim as it had been in the main hall, yet still enough to let him see the streaks of black on the walls, the scuff marks on the floor, and the bend just ahead where he knew the first trap lay.

"Tony!" he called, not expecting a response. "Mike? Kelly, it's me, Devin."

As he let go of the jamb, he wondered, can fear be alive?

Out there, on the beach in the hot sun where children played in the water, it was impossible . . . out there. Fear was an emotion, a reaction, a sometime protection against danger, sometimes an excuse to run away. It didn't live. It didn't breathe. It didn't leave tracks to follow in the sand.

But he had heard Julie's voice, and the others had seen Mary Heims, and no one could explain why she'd died the way she had.

But Mary knew—*i know*.

And Julie had known at the last, because Julie wasn't laughing. He touched the pocket again.

"Julie?" he whispered.

The mouth, the eyes, the attitude she'd taken—in the fire she wasn't laughing.

In The House of Night she was screaming.

TWENTY

JUST over the threshold he heard the voice of the dark pier: boards and canted walls and twisted planks and weakened beams, creaking and groaning in irregular rhythm, softly, sometimes loudly, and sometimes with a muffled low grinding as if a hollow millstone were rolling slowly over rock being slowly crushed to gravel; and the counterpoint of a soprano wind that keened and hunted behind the walls, above the low dark-painted ceiling, around the bends he couldn't see, darting as if running, lingering as if waiting, and in the distance far deeper, as if a storm expected a summons at the first sign of a scream; and the sea constant and surging, a herd of beasts beneath his feet, pacing, marking time, thundering against the pilings and hissing against the sand.

Pacing.

Marking time.

With the fingers of his right hand brushing the near wall, damp and smooth, he moved quickly toward the sharp turn in the corridor several yards ahead, the corridor itself barely five feet across. There was just enough light to see by, to see he had no shadow and no shadow followed, but it was like walking through autumn dusk—details were blurred or missing, shapes drifted and vanished, and he kept snapping the wood with one finger to be sure it was still there, came down hard on his heels to be sure he wasn't floating.

Or falling toward the sea that was waiting to catch him.

He stopped—*easy, Devin*—and ordered himself just to move, not to take the time to think; that way lay the rest of his madness, and the terror he had admitted to and had somehow held at bay. For the moment it was sufficient that he was here, that he was trying; yet when he reached the turn he hesitated, breathing deeply through his mouth, his feet shifting without carrying him forward or back, leaning out and looking down a diminishing tunnel of black.

His palms were cold. The back of his neck was stiff. Something banded across his chest and didn't ease until he bent over and pressed his fists against his breast. He felt his heart; it was drumming. No matter how rapidly he blinked, he couldn't rid his eyes of a faint watery burning. A thumb rubbed beneath them, pulling at the skin, contorting his vision, bringing tears he wiped away though they washed away the burning.

He shivered and his stomach began to feel queasy; his tongue wouldn't stop moistening his lips.

Oh God.

The sea; and he knew without the grace of contradiction that he was in the throat of a great beast, slipping toward the boiling acids in its belly that would reduce him to nothing. No way to stop. No time to turn around and flee. Slipping forward, and downward, and his body shook from an ice storm that raged briefly in his chest.

"Take it easy. Take it easy."

His voice so suddenly loud he almost laughed when he imagined the expression on his face.

Pressing hard against the wall calmed him. He expelled a loud breath that bordered on a growl, scrubbed his face with his palms, wiped them dry on his shirt. Urgency nudged him, but he resisted for a time, and resisted as well the goad to form a plan. That was impossible. How could he plan against what he didn't know? How could he predict action when he was fumbling in the dark? Instead, he shoved away from the wall and began walking boldly, much more boldly than he felt, searching the floor for signs of the spring-locked trap doors that in better times would open underfoot and send him laughing down a slick and curved metal chute into a room filled with pillows and the roar of a laughing clown.

Maureen, he remembered, had been frightened of the monsters.

But there was nothing now but the fading scuff marks of other peoples' shoes, islets of stirring sand, low clouds of grey dust like ground mist in spring that swirled away and re-formed behind him with every step he took.

A draught through a ceiling crack, an icy tendril down his spine. He massaged his shoulders to warm them and rolled his sleeves down, buttoning the cuffs and feeling not the slightest bit warmer.

Ten paces, and he stopped again, frowning to himself, puzzled, tapping a hand thoughtfully against his thigh. He stared unseeing at the floor. No; by this time he should have reached something, some trademark of Midnight Hall—a trap door, the revolving barrel, the first alcove with its leaping monster and shrieking music. But the walls and floor remained unbroken, not a seam nor an outline, the darkness receding as if he himself were faintly glowing.

Behind him there was black.

Beneath him, the sea.

A step forward.

251

Before he knew what he was doing, his hand drifted to his hip pocket where it tapped the photograph without feeling—*she was screaming.*

The wind blew without touching him, still hidden behind the walls, stalking him overhead as the ceiling creaked and snapped and streamers of dust curled over his shoulders.

He rubbed the side of his left hand under his nose, hard as if scratching, and began to wonder what it took to make whatever lived in here make itself known. A scream? A name? Should he look to superstition and find a spell, a chant, a way to conjure a demon?

The face.

Another draught, chained around his ankle.

Can fear be alive?

His eyes closed for a second while he tried to bring back the face he had trapped in the picture of Mary; but as in the picture, he saw nothing but pale dots and faded spots that indicated where the eyes were, perhaps the nose, perhaps the mouth. A face watching Mary dying in convulsions on the boards. Watching him, then? Waiting for him?

Who the hell was it?

What in god's name was it?

His mouth tightened, lips bloodless and thin, and another step forward, another, and he was walking. Almost strolling this time because he was beginning to lose his temper. He didn't like playing the mouse, didn't care for being It. He'd been playing tag with his own dreams for most of his adult life, and he was growing weary of the game.

Julie, he called in silence, why the hell don't you help me?

The tunnel reached another corner.

He turned it without pausing.

"Kelly!"

His voice lost against the voice of the pier and the grind of the sea; her name fell without echo.

And if it was alive, or some portion of it, what brought it here, to a small town beside the sea?

Now urgency overrode caution, and he broke into a slow trot, wisps of black breaking away from ahead, blackfog he chopped aside with a swipe of his arm, blackfog that rose and drifted and clung to the ceiling, gathered into spidershapes, ran in rivulets down the walls.

"Tony, it's Devin!"

No echo.

Soles against the floor without making a sound.

And the cold . . . the touch of fear . . . the whisper of a child hiding under bedclothes against the coming of the night.

He shivered, shook it off, bit down on his lower lip just shy of tasting blood.

Too big, he thought as the trot became a run, it's too big for the pier, something's wrong, something's here.

The third corner and he took it, rebounding off the far wall when he slipped and lost his balance, regained it within a yard, was racing within two.

The wind seeping through the walls now, coming at his back.

The *crack* of a burning splitting plank.

"Mike! Mike, where are you?"

No echo.

The sea.

And he slammed against the wall again, grabbed at his shoulder and turned around, walking backward, frowning, until he realized the floor was tilting, rocking, slowly side to side, front to back, not frighteningly so but enough to prevent him from running anymore unless he wanted to stumble, wanted to fall.

It's breaking up, he thought; Jesus, it's breaking up.

He envisioned The House of Night folding like a pack of cards in slow motion, toppling in upon itself until there was nothing on the beach but stacks and piles of crumbling ash; he saw himself trapped and falling, saw himself buried alive and drowning, saw himself dead before he hit the sand and something giggling behind him.

The ache subsided, but he kept on rubbing. It gave him something to do while he watched in amazement the black shred and re-form. Closer now. The walls running damp and the floor streaked with clear slime and the sound of slow dripping water filling the gap behind.

He stopped.

He swallowed.

He wished he had a gun, or a club, or a cross he could hold up to fend off the night.

Oh God, I can't do it. Jesus, Tony Kelly Mike, I can't do it, I'm . . .

And when he stepped into the dark and the dark swarmed around him and the rocking and the wind and the sea and his hoarse breathing, he closed his eyes and waited, thinking *this is it, boys, this is it and i'm sorry ken that i didn't return the call; sorry gayle i couldn't return the favor.*

"Tony," he whispered. "Kelly, it's Devin."

Silence.

He moved again, shuffling his feet because he couldn't see a thing, though he sensed he was in a room much more vast than the main hall. He ought to feel claustrophobic; instead he felt like he was flying.

"Mike, are you there?"

And suddenly he was blinded by an explosion of brilliant white, beams and shafts of it from above him, sheets and spirals of it from either side, the only dark left in the center where he saw the bodies of his friends.

He grunted as if punched, didn't move, only stared, until something pushed his legs, and he moved lock-kneed toward them. Shaking his head. Glancing around. Feeling his temper shred again and not caring again and taking rapid deep breaths again to keep himself from screaming.

They were lying atop each other, arms and legs akimbo, Tony's face the only one visible, eyes open and staring.

Quickly, not daring to speak, Devin knelt and grabbed a hand; it wasn't warm, wasn't cold, and he chafed it as he whispered each of their names, over and over and over an over until it was chanting and a chant, until he felt someone watching and looked up and saw her.

Slender dark against the white.

Long hair blowing as if in a slow breeze.

Mr. Graham—

"My god, Julie."

—I'll take my picture now.

Here, in this place, it wasn't a threat, it was calm, the expectation of a promise kept with just the faintest hint of pleading.

Though he guessed it wouldn't do him any good, he couldn't help but stare at her, trying to fill in all the black with the woman he had known—the color of her eyes, the flush of her cheeks, the shoulders and upper chest freckled like her mother's. And when he failed because the black was too solid, like a mask and gown, he astonished himself by only shrugging instead of demanding an explanation.

Please, Mr. Graham.

He looked down as he stood—he'd been holding onto Kelly—then reached into his pocket and pulled the picture out. He unfolded it and pressed it flat against his chest, rubbing at the creases, watching Julie waiting.

"Why?" he asked at last, the only question he could think of.

I want to die.

He looked around him, squinting into the brightlight for signs of something, someone else, looked back at Julie and saw her take a gliding step toward him, brightlight behind her, wavering and flickering as if it were white shadows of fire. Then he looked down at the crumpled picture and touched her face with a finger. Looked at Julie. Looked down. Not believing she was here, and here simply because of him. It didn't happen that way, he hadn't captured her soul, but for the moment he could think of nothing else, no other reason, and when he lifted the picture in both hands and made to tear it in half, Julie screamed.

Something screamed.

And the white began to vanish like candles blowing out, leaving gaps of black, a black fence being raised to block out the sun.

Instantly Devin dropped back to his knees, leaning over the kids as if he could protect them, though from what he didn't know, except he knew it wasn't Julie. The picture in one hand. The other shading his eyes, trying to maintain his vision, keeping his gaze on Julie who was still moving toward him, moving without growing closer, hair blowing, hands beseeching, her face still in shadow and her feet skating across the floor.

A punch of wind thrust him forward, and he put a hand out to keep from falling and felt a heartbeat when he realized he was bracing himself against Michael's chest. He yanked the hand back, then stared at the others, leaning as close as he could without losing sight of Julie. Chests rising, falling, something gurgling in Kelly's throat.

Julie called his name.

Something called his name.

Trapped, Julie whispered.

After a moment he nodded. He thought he understood. At the moment of her dying, he had somehow frozen her in time. She wasn't screaming at the fire; she was screaming at him for denying her her death.

Not a ghost. Not a soul. Not in limbo or in hell or on the midpath toward heaven.

She was here. Because of him. Because he wanted a break and wanted pictures of . . .

trapped let me go i want my picture let me go

Don't think, Graham; you think too goddamned much.

Trembling, he pushed back to his feet and stepped around the kids, his face slightly turned from the brightlight still behind her. Wishing he could see her face and ashamed when he was glad he couldn't. A glance down at the others and a faint relieved smile when he spotted Michael stirring. Then he held out the picture, and she reached out a hand

256

and above the keening and the sea he thought he heard her crying.

"Julie," he said, trying to see through the dark to her face, "Julie, I'm sorry."

The picture left his hand.

Mr. Graham, I'm afraid.

"Julie," he said, and all the lights went out, all the sounds died, and something screamed, something laughed, and Devin knew he was wrong again.

She could feel the pier begin a slow warping turn, begin to settle, the pilings reluctantly giving way beneath her like arthritic legs losing strength; and with a glance at the gap behind her, she raced as best she could down the hall toward the staircase. Stopping, almost skidding, when she reached the ticket booth and what glass remained in its face shattered and fell in spinning fragments that caught the light from the gap and turned it into sparks.

Tiny flames on the floorboards, winking shades of blood.

"Jesus," she muttered; and *Jesus,* she prayed, when the tiny flames became fires that flared toward her like torches and forced her back, flared upward and died. Just like that. Without fading. Without smoke.

Devin, she reminded herself as she wove through the debris. Devin's in there, you jackass, Devin's waiting Jesus Christ.

But when she finally reached the staircase, she shrieked once in frustration because he was gone.

"Devin!"

Her hands cupped around her mouth; she would not look up, to the gaps of the doors above her.

"Devin!"

The creak of fallen beams shifting to fall farther; the scrape of nails loosening their hold; a wind she couldn't feel soughing somewhere above her and skimming ash and dust across the floor, holding dust and ash in the air, dark clouds in the dark that blotted out the light.

The sea.

Without echo.

She took the first four steps at a run, the next four at a fearful walk, and stopped with fists hard against her sides as she waited for something to tell her he was fine. Breathing in, smelling dust; breathing out, smelling fire. Finally holding a hand in front of her as though parting a spider's web, and seeing the camera on the floor just outside the center opening.

"Oh god, Devin," she said, nearly whimpering. "Oh god, don't make me do it."

The last four steps were like slogging through mud. She could barely lift her feet, could hardly feel her legs; at the top she began to stagger, and at the door she finally dropped, ignoring the sharp pains in her knees and the cold in the hand that grabbed the door's frame. She picked up the camera and wept at the strap so neatly wrapped around the casing. It was heavy, heavier than she remembered, and as she stared into the corridor dimly lighted, she wondered if she ought to bring it, just in case.

"Devin!" she screamed.

Just the sea.

There was no echo.

It's not fair, she thought as she pushed herself up and leaned against the jamb. It's not fair; it's not my fight, god damn you, Devin.

"Damnit, Devin, where are you?"

Then she screamed when a hand took hold of her arm and turned her around, screamed again when a dark face leaned toward her and hissed at her to be silent. Raising a fist to knock it away, and lowering it when she caught her breath and saw Stump flinch at the expected blow.

"Jesus Christ," she gasped, dropping the camera and wincing when it bounced once and settled. "Jesus God, Harragan."

"I couldn't," he said, looking around her to the corridor. He shook his head. "Some woman, the wife of a friend, she asks me to dance, and I couldn't do it." He looked back at her and shrugged. "I might have made three minutes, y'know. Graham's gonna pay, I might've made three minutes."

She hadn't the slightest idea what he was babbling about, but she didn't care. She almost hugged him. Then she heard a distant screaming, a distant rumble, and the hand on her arm dropped away.

"He in there?" he asked, pointing at the door.

She nodded. "I think so."

"We gonna wait for him?"

She shook her head. "No."

Another scream, like a hurricane tearing through an alley a hundred miles away, and she cursed Devin for leaving her and stepped over the sill. Stump stayed beside her, swaying as the pier swayed and the rocking grew more pronounced, muttering to himself so softly she thought he might be praying.

He took her hand.

She managed a smile.

A fine thing, Cross, she thought, when you need a geriatric knight.

There were blotches on the walls, remnants of old paint until she touched one and her hand came away black. Soot. Ash. And over her she heard the wind, below her she heard the sea, and somewhere around that turn just ahead she could hear the sound of someone laughing, something laughing, and she gripped Stump's hand harder until he tugged at her arm to make her stop.

Something clear and slippery on the floor.

Blackfog obscuring her vision in drifting spinning patches, though some of it seemed to hang from itself from the ceiling, and parts of it seemed to cling in blotches to the walls and huddle at the baseboards where here and there the floor was buckling and the prowling of the sea leaked through in throated grumbling.

When it touched her, she was chilled; when she batted at

259

it, it parted; when she blew at it once, it sailed to one side and settled lower, writhing.

At the second turn, she knew it couldn't have been. They should have arrived somewhere else, not another stretch of tunnel. But when she looked the question at Stump, he only looked straight ahead, his white hair dull, his bent back a weight, his legs unable to straighten, keeping him shorter than she.

At the third turn she stopped and closed her eyes and took a breath.

"You said you knew what was in here," she said, knowing full well she was stalling and not giving a damn. Not now. When ahead there were sounds she couldn't identify, a black wall at the end, and smells she thought she knew and didn't want to, and the pier was still twisting around upon itself without actually coming apart.

Stump hooked his thumbs in his suspenders, peered down the tunnel, lifted his chin as if testing the air. "They were afraid out there."

"I know, but—"

"There was places like this. Other places. They come and go. You've seen them."

"Stump, I haven't the faintest idea what you're talking about."

"You said you did." He looked at her. "You said you knew."

"I thought I did. I mean, Devin, he was talking about fear and things, and I figured . . ." She closed her eyes tightly. "Shit. Damn. I don't know what the hell I'm talking about."

He took her hand and pulled her away from the wall. "We'd best be going, okay? We can't wait here for the place to fall down around our ears."

He led her down the tunnel, toward the unmoving black, and she whispered, "Are you trying to say this is some . . . I don't know, some kind of place where fear attracts fear, something like that?"

He didn't answer, and she didn't press him because it was too fantastic to believe and too fantastic to disbelieve, now that she was here, in the place where Julie died. He didn't answer until they reached the black wall and she imagined she could see shadows moving deep inside.

"Fear don't attract fear," he said then, making her jump. "Devin knows that. It ain't fear that lives here. It ain't fear, it's worse."

Then he let go of her hand and stepped into the dark, and before she knew it, she had followed.

He held them all as best he could, kneeling on the floor and listening to Kelly weeping, Michael cursing, Tony demanding in a quavering voice to be allowed to go home. Children. They were children, and Devin's arms reached and gathered and pressed around their shoulders, holding them tightly while he searched the dark for the way to escape. It wouldn't be back the way they'd come—though how the kids had come here, he didn't know—because he'd lost his direction, could hear the louder grinding and knew the pier was falling down.

There was no light.

He was blind.

Then he felt the huddling ease, and he eased his arm away, though they kept their shoulders touching and kept their hands moving to touch what they could.

"I saw Julie," Tony whispered. "She was standing . . . there was a door . . . she . . ."

"It wasn't her," Devin told him.

"I *saw* her."

"It wasn't her."

"It was Mary," Mike said, straining to keep his voice calm. "She showed me this . . . this place where all those trap doors and things were. I thought she was showing me the way out, y'know? I thought she wanted me to get away or something."

"It wasn't her," Devin told him.

"You weren't there," Mike snapped. "Jesus, I ought to know, I saw her."

"It wasn't her."

There were hands on Devin's cheeks, damp from tears, cold from fear, and he traced them to the wrists and gently pulled them away. Then he reached out and found her hair and stroked it, pressed her neck, and when she tried to speak, to tell him something, he only said, "It wasn't her."

At last he knew them, recognized them—the places; he had seen them often enough and hadn't thought about them one way or another because, at the time, they were no concern of his. A stretch of road where accidents happen no matter how often the road is fixed, the shoulder widened, traffic lights established, or policemen put on duty. A mountain or a plain or a forest or a river, plots and plains that armies sweep through with the regularity of a timepiece and leave the dying behind—the excuse was strategic location, the reality something else. A village, a part of town, perhaps even a single building where people died, people vanished, the injured screamed in pain, and lurid headlines wondered if a curse was at work, and reasonable men pondered the awful tragedy of circumstance.

Places like The House of Night.

It had nothing to do with evil, or magic, or curses, or random chance.

It had nothing to do with jinxes.

It had everything to do with death, and the lures it used to call its victims.

"Listen," he whispered, and the others became silent. "Hold hands, all right? Everybody grab somebody's hand and don't let go. We've got to get out of here before the whole pier falls apart."

Kelly sobbed once and sniffed.

"My hip," Mike said, voice tightened with pain.

They gathered closer and took hands and found themselves in a huddle, awkwardly bunched, facing each other. Devin nodded to himself as he turned around, nodded again when he was sure the hands he held were the hands of a friend. Behind him was Tony, Kelly and Mike left and right, pressed close, and the dark straight ahead where he hoped the tunnels were.

"Don't pick up your feet," he said then. "You'll trip. Just shuffle along and take it easy. If you start running, you'll pull the rest of us down. If we get separated . . ."

"What is it?" Kelly asked then, "where are we?," and Mike grunted.

"If it wasn't Julie . . ." Tony began.

Devin began moving, feeling Kelly pressing timidly against his arm, Mike trying not to touch him. Shuffling. Scraping. Every few feet Tony bumping up against him. Shuffling. Scraping. It was an effort not to stare, but there was no sense attempting to make sense of the dark; he'd only give himself a headache, strain his eyes, and eventually make him see things that weren't there.

Sing for me, Mary, he thought; Jesus, please sing.

The pier groaned and shifted.

In a low voice not meant to be heard, Kelly asked Tony if they were going to die.

Tony said no.

Devin wanted to agree, but he didn't know; it was difficult enough convincing himself he hadn't gone completely crazy, thinking about places Death marked as its own. Maybe it was all futile—shuffling, scraping—and they should sit down and wait for what was bound to be; maybe those who escaped were the ones who fought back; and maybe, he thought, escape was really no escape at all.

Shuffling.

Stopping, his head cocked, squeezing the hands he held to tell the others to be silent. Listening to the cautious footsteps somewhere out there—in front or back, he couldn't tell. Feeling Kelly grow rigid, smelling their fear, sour and bitter.

It occurred to him that a show of bravado might be the answer, that feigning courage, whistling a happy tune, snapping fingers against the demons, would build them a shield and see them through safely; and it occurred to him that bravery had never stopped men from dying before.

"I hear something," Tony whispered.

Despite his own admonition, Devin stared into the dark, blinking away the sparks and swirls, shaking his head to clear his vision, swallowing when the footsteps finally stopped, surely no more than a few feet ahead, directly ahead.

"Who is it?" Mike demanded loudly at last, and Devin wanted to strangle him—useless, of course, death knew where they were.

"Free rides," a hoarse voice answered. "But this ain't one of them, boy."

And: "Goddamnit, Nathan, where the hell is Devin?"

Stump leaned into Devin and whispered "Death" in his ear.

Devin held him for a moment, nearly wept, and said, "I know."

He held her tightly and kissed her cheeks while she swore at him, trying not to cry, and the others remained close, still touching, chattering nervously and clapping when Stump told them he'd taken only a few steps into the dark before bumping into Devin. A few steps, he insisted when they pressed him just to be sure, and Devin reluctantly eased Gayle's arms from around his waist. Once again they held hands, bunched like sheep against a storm; once again they began to move—shuffle; scrape—Devin praying they hadn't been turned around during the commotion.

And when they stepped from dark to light, into the tunnel, they sagged against the walls and gulped at the air no different than the air they'd just left. Kelly was in Mike's arms, Tony beside them; Stump's head was bowed, his hands braced against the wall; Gayle was staring at Devin as if she were trying to put the face to a name she thought she ought to know.

Blackfog coiled around them.

Devin touched Gayle's hair, then walked over to the kids. Tony's face was unnaturally pale, his shirt torn at the shoulder, and he stared blindly at the ceiling, gulping, swallowing, blinking rapidly, trembling. Kelly's face was smeared with soot that gave her a raccoon's mask, her hair in damp straggles over her forehead and cheeks. And Mike, holding her, looked over her shoulder at Devin, eyes too wide, lower lip quivering, a hand gripping his hip in a spastic massage.

"We have to go," Devin told them gently. "I don't know how much longer the pier's going to stay up."

"I can't," Kelly said into Mike's chest. "I can't move. I don't want to."

Mike tightened his hold on her. "We're dreaming, right?"

Devin managed a brief smile. "I wish we were."

"We have to be," he answered angrily. "I'm gonna be a doctor, y'know? I can't—"

The pier lurched sharply.

Kelly cried out, and Gayle grabbed Stump's arm and forced him to start moving. Devin, refraining from looking over his shoulder, brought up the rear, prodding when he had to, nodding when someone checked to be sure he was still there.

The sea.

The wind.

He thought: this isn't right; and a section of the tunnel began revolving, without warning, without a sound.

Slowly at first, so slowly he thought the motion was merely the pier moving again. But when they were toppled to the right and slid to the floor that became a wall, became the ceiling, became the opposite wall, he hauled himself to his feet and tried to blot out the screaming. All of them, screaming, unable to gain their feet, rolling in a huge rolling barrel while he forced his way through them until he was at the head. Then he stood, bracing himself with his palms, shouting at them until they listened, watching as he faced the righthand wall and walked with the barrel's motion—feet and palms—and moved sideways at the same time, toward the barrel's end. Progress was slow, measured in inches, but they soon caught the trick and followed him toward that part of the tunnel he could see remained unmoving.

Until Gayle yelped, and he snapped his head around and saw the walls begin to pucker with what looked like tiny blades. He gaped and looked between his hands, saw the protrusions and saw that they were shells—ragged, sharp, glittering as if flecked with mica, forming bands around the inside of the barrel.

And the barrel began to move faster.

Michael cursed at the top of his voice.

Kelly screamed for help; Tony nudged her, forcing her to watch her hands, watch where they fell against the wall, straddling the shell-blades.

Devin couldn't see them anymore; he was too intent on keeping his own hands from being shredded, watching the blades come around, watching his palms barely miss them, every few inches glancing at the barrel's rim and the stable tunnel beyond. He breathed through his mouth raggedly. His knees felt lined with pins. He misjudged once, the side of his right hand nicked at the base of the thumb, and he hissed and resisted pulling the hand away to wipe the blood clear.

Gayle shouted.

The sea, the wind.

And then the wall was square, and he fell to his side, rolled to his knees, to his feet, and waited.

Watching.

Grabbing Tony's arm and yanking him free, then Kelly, Mike, dancing impatiently and waiting for Gayle whose hands were smeared with blood.

All of them watching Stump several feet behind, grunting as he moved crabwise, shaking his head in despair, his forearms bulging, his legs visibly trembling . . . and the blades began to lengthen and the mouth of the barrel began to close and Gayle threw her arms around Devin's waist when he shouted Harragan's name and tried to run to him.

"No!" Gayle said. "No!" She glared at the kids. "Get going, keep moving, damnit!" To Devin: "No! You can't, it's—"

Harragan grunted.

The barrel shrank.

Glittering shells.

And Stump looked at him and smiled sadly before the mouth finally closed.

Gayle tugged at him, her arms snug around his stomach, but he felt nothing as he moved, heard nothing but the wind and the groaning of the boards. He sucked at the cut on his hand, spat out blood and sucked again. He looked down and saw the blackfog in ribbons, in puddles, in layers. A rumbling he could feel through the soles of his feet; a humming that centered just behind his right ear. Gayle urging him on, the smell of her, the touch, and he straightened just a little and let his legs take him. Around the corner. Shadows just ahead, stumbling side to side, someone unashamedly sobbing and he thought it was Mike.

The sudden crash of a wave as though it had struck the wall just behind them.

The stench of the seadead laid too long in the sun.

An image of the barrel's mouth, a look down at the floor, and he jerked away Gayle's hand and began to run toward the others. He called their names, the shadows stumbled and turned, and the floor lurched again as an al-cove suddenly opened in the wall.

With arms spread he threw himself at them, his shoulder striking Michael's hip, his left arm shoving Kelly to her hands and knees. Tony wasn't touched, and he stumbled backward, struck the wall, and shrieked when something reached out from the dark and grabbed his shoulder.

Devin was on his feet immediately and saw the claws sleek and shining as Tony pummeled them, tried to pry them loose, spittle spraying from his mouth as he continued to scream while he was dragged toward the dark hole by something that growled and howled and laughed like a maddened clown. Devin tripped over someone's leg as he lunged forward, but when he landed, he grabbed Tony's ankle, held on despite the flailing, and called out for help. A toe lashed him under the chin. The side of a foot thud-ded against his temple. He tried to pull himself to his knees and pull Tony free at the same time, but the boy's other heel clubbed his forehead and snapped his head back.

His hand opened.

Tony vanished.

There was blood on the wall.

And there was no silence when the wall closed—the sea was louder and closer, the wind shrill and demanding, the pier's convolutions more insistent, like the prolonged snap-ping of thick bone.

Kelly threw herself at him, a fist catching his chin. "You let him die!" she screamed. "I don't want to die!"

He grabbed her, pinned her arms to her side, and dragged her along as he headed for the next corner. He didn't listen to her, nor did he look back as Mike kicked and punched the wall in an effort to find a way through. Kelly found her feet and no longer fought him. He dead-ened himself and looked at Gayle with so little expression when she joined him that she seemed afraid for a moment, before she took the girl and held her as they walked.

No one wants to die, Kell, he thought at the turn, but some of us don't have much choice anymore.

"Almost there," he said aloud. "C'mon, we're almost there."

The women stumbled into a run, bumping against each other, thrown once against the wall when the floor rose and fell in eerie undulation. Mike passed him, limping badly, not looking, without a word; his hands were bleeding. His stomach jumped when something—a plank, a portion of wall—crashed in the dark behind him. But he moved on. Feeling nothing. Not even elation when the doorway appeared less than ten yards ahead.

Kelly shouted, Gayle hushed her, Mike came up behind them and urged them to keep moving.

Please, Devin prayed then; please, God, don't let her die.

But when he stumbled through the doorway to the head of the staircase, he knew that God had nothing to do with it. This wasn't a god's house, not a god's domain; this place belonged to Death, and Death knew what it wanted.

Mike was waiting for him at the bottom. His face was blotched with dirt and speckles of blood; his hair was soaked and tangled, and his clothes were damply dark.

"I'm sorry," he said, and held out a hand.

Devin shook it, biting his lip, not stopping, still walking. "No sweat," he said. "I'm sorry I couldn't." He nodded toward the exit, and they hurried on, catching up to the women who had slowed down as if waiting.

"Move," he said quietly.

They could see the opening in the plywood; they could see the light.

"T-tony," Kelly said.

"Move," was all he answered.

And the pier began its collapse into the sea.

They were slammed to the floor when the staircase pulled itself apart and vanished in a boiling cloud of what looked like black steam; and what remained of the roof soon followed in diving sections and pieces, a hail of wood and splinter, a storm of glass and nail, all of it shrieking like the tunnel wind, bouncing off the beams already fallen and driving them through the flooring, opening gaps for the surf to lift through in fanlike sprays; the water surged in a flood tide, receded, and dragged the pier with it, surged again and twisted the outside walls, pulling them inward as the pilings buckled, pulling them down as the pilings snapped and sagged one by one.

Devin was the last to get back to his feet, choking in the raised dust, clearing his eyes of salt water with a vicious swipe of his hand. A glance upward—where the hell is the sky?—and he rushed forward, seeing Mike just ahead of him, stumbling and twisting forward, dragging Kelly by her elbow.

The ticket booth folded and fell.

"Gayle!"

"Mr. Graham, c'mon!"

He whirled to head back toward the seaward end of the pier, and stopped at the edge of a debris-jumbled gap, black crooked teeth, a solitary nail glinting.

"Gayle!"

He was thrown onto his back when the board he was standing on pitched up, then dropped away, and he scrambled frantically on hands and knees, half-blinded by the dust, spitting ash, spitting blood, not feeling the splinters gouging and ripping at his hands, rolling instinctively to one side when a glassless section of the roof crashed not five yards away. He couldn't call her name; his throat was clogged. He couldn't find a prayer *do you know a prayer for death i don't i know,* and when something glanced off his shoulder and paralyzed his arm, he only rocked to his feet and kept on moving.

Not thinking.

Watching the exit and the light.

Shoving aside a beam instead of going around it.

"For god's sake, Gayle!"

And falling with a despairing, enraged wail when his legs were smacked into from behind, knocking him down, pinning him so that he was unable to turn over and push aside the debris. Yelling now, his voice taken by the wind, the sea, the dying of the pier, and smothered. Feeling the floor tipping, feeling himself sliding, feeling something someone take his wrists and try to pull him free.

Feeling the edge of a board rip open his chest.

Feeling nothing.

Feeling the sun.

Hands rolling him over and a shadow covering his face. Fingers dusting his cheeks and brow while voices yelled, shouted orders, and a siren low and high tore through the darkening light.

He couldn't focus, he could barely breathe.

But he could hear the silence behind the rest of the noise.

The shadowed face leaned toward him.

"Gayle," he whispered.

"Mr. Graham," Kelly said.

TWENTY-ONE

THE November breeze cooled long before the lights died, and those walking the beach slipped on their gloves and buttoned their jackets and tucked in their chins and walked a little while longer, watching the tide pull away and the night rise from the horizon. The concession stands were boarded up. The doors to the bars were shuttered. The arcades remained open only on weekends for the locals who hadn't the energy to travel to the mainland, and for those who came down here to avoid the summer crowds and watch the sea make its change from sky mirror to winter.

Gulls wheeled and cried.

A dog raced along the sand, snuffling for treasure, barking at the birds.

And the sun paused at the rooftops, gathering armies of shadows to creep into town.

On the boardwalk, Devin sat on the bench opposite Balloon Heaven, hands deep in his coat pockets, hat low across his eyes. Beside him was his camera, lens capped, strap wound, and the tripod was propped on the lowest of · the three railings.

To his right he could hear the whipsnap of the canvas sheets that covered the rides on Harragan's Pier, the sough of the wind through the wires and cables, the creak of the Ferris wheel the wind gave a quarter-turn; to his left, whenever he looked, there was nothing but beach and boardwalk all the way to Seaside Heights. The rubble of the dark pier had long since been cleared away, the sand raked and sifted, and last month the last of the police warning signs had been taken down and stored, when the tourists stopped coming, and the newsmen, and the mourners.

He looked at his watch; it was just past three.

He puffed his cheeks and settled lower, crossed his legs, released a sigh.

All the little fears, he thought for the hundredth time, for a time beyond counting; all the goddamned little fears. If he had been clever enough, believing enough, he might have been able to save them. He might not have had to watch Sal turn off the diner's waves, or listen to the minister say the words about Gayle, never found. He might not have wept. He might not have the dreams.

He cleared his throat and sniffed, adjusted his hat when the wind tried to take it.

All the little fears. The ones that made up a life—not the big ones, not the terrors, not the ones that throttled you at midnight; just the little ones, the daylight ones, the ones that stalked and walked with you, not the ones that stopped your heart.

He shifted.

He watched an old man with a metal detector hobble

273

just above the sand's wet apron, his floppy cap tied down around his ears, his overcoat slapping at his shins when the wind finally rode in ahead of the night. He stopped once and dug, stood and stretched his back, moved on. Bent over. Listening to his machine tell him the beach's secrets.

The dog was gone; the gulls wheeled and were silent.

Devin heard the footsteps then, picked up the camera, put it in his lap, and looked over with a smile when Mike Nathan sat beside him. "You made it."

Mike, twice as large in a bulky sheepskin jacket, grinned back and shook his hand. "This, I have to tell you, is not California. God, I'd almost forgotten how cold it gets around here."

Devin laughed. "What? You've only been gone three months, for god's sake. What are you going to do when you come back for Christmas vacation?"

"You ever been to California?"

He shook his head.

"Believe me, it's like amnesia for the rest of the world."

They talked then of his studies, life on campus, the Pacific Ocean; they talked a little bit about Kelly, who hadn't written Devin since she'd left, and had done her best to avoid Mike since they got off the plane. Mike wasn't worried. He was positive she would come around sooner or later, when the trauma was taken care of and she could look at him again without seeing Tony's grave. Empty. Never found.

Devin suspected he was lying.

"You went to Arizona," Mike said then. "I hear it's pretty neat, all that cactus and stuff."

Devin nodded. After he'd been released from the hospital, stitches out, bruises fading, Ken Viceroy had been waiting. They'd talked. Devin had wept. They'd talked some more and decided that work was the cure; and if not the cure, then at least part of the healing. He had spent most of October wandering the desert and mountains outside Tucson and had returned with what Ken had called the best photographs of his life.

He didn't know.

Not even when Ken called this morning and left a message on the new machine—that there was a book offer and another plane ticket, just waiting for him to grab.

When he finished, the younger man grinned and slapped his shoulder in genuine congratulations; when he stood, Mike took the tripod and tucked it under his arm.

They walked.

The boards were empty.

"I've been thinking," Mike said after a few minutes in the wind. "About what you said in your letter."

"And?"

"I don't know."

All the little fears. The trite advice he'd given Julie about wrestling them into a shape she could cope with, but not defeat. Mike had his hip, Kelly had her parents, he had the fear of growing up and losing art—little fears that wouldn't die, that wouldn't be beaten into submission, that had by persisting somehow offered them sufficient protection to live. Them, but not the others—all Tony had, at the last, was the untried fear of leaving home; and all Gayle had, from the start, was the untried fear of being wrong.

"I don't know," Mike said again. "I keep looking through my books, y'know? There's got to be a clue or something in there, but I can't find it."

Devin took his arm briefly and squeezed it. "This isn't something you research, Mike. You either believe it or you don't. If you have another explanation, please God, I'd like to hear it."

They reached the former site of the dark pier; the only sign that it had been there was a section of new planks to replace that which had been torn away. The metal-hunter was scouring the sand, his head cocked like a bird's.

"I don't feel anything," Mike said after a few minutes standing at the new railing.

Devin questioned him with a look.

"I mean, shouldn't we feel something? Spooky, maybe, or a vibration or something? You know what I mean."

He grinned. "If you're asking me how I know that this is one of those places I told you about . . . I don't. I don't know if they even have a feel to them, or signs of some kind to point them out. Maybe it was just all godawful bad luck. Maybe we were just in the wrong place at the wrong time, and we were lucky to get out with . . ." He stopped and swallowed. "We were lucky to get out."

The old man glanced up at them, scowled, and knelt.

"He thinks we're gonna steal his treasure," Mike said, nodding toward him.

"Don't laugh. Even now he finds more loose change in one day than some people make in a week."

"No shit."

Devin grinned.

The old man dug with one hand.

"I miss him," Mike said at last. "Jesus, Devin, I miss him."

Devin lowered his head. Even while he was in the desert, lost in the world his lens defined, there hadn't been a night when he didn't wake up and see Gayle standing in the doorway. Just standing there. Waiting. For him to save her.

He hadn't seen her since he'd returned to Oceantide and had noticed the newsstand with a new name over the door.

Mike shrugged. "I have to go," he said. "My parents . . . it's Thanksgiving, y'know? They . . ."

"Sure," he said.

They turned to head the other way.

Then Mike stopped with a shake of his head and looked down at the old man, who was digging now with both hands.

"If this . . . I mean, this is just hypothetical, you understand, but if this is one of those places, maybe we shouldn't stick around. I mean, maybe . . ." His grin told Devin how foolish he felt, and how frightened he was.

"I don't know," Devin said.

Mike looked away, to the sea.

The old man shouted in surprise. Devin looked over, wondering what he'd found this time, and saw him throw something away, toward the boardwalk. Then he got stiffly to his feet, picked up his detector, and hurried north, almost running.

Curious, Devin walked back to the railing and leaned over, trying to find whatever it was the old man had tossed away. Probably, he thought, it was the shell of a horseshoe crab, which would turn anybody's stomach if he came across it unexpectedly.

Mike stood behind him, shifting from foot to foot.

"Hey, Devin?"

Devin saw it then, just beyond the deep shadow of the boards.

"Devin, I think . . . I don't think I'll be back for Christmas."

It was brass.

It was a plaque.

"I . . . my parents are gonna move out to San Francisco. I . . . actually, I came around to say goodbye."

And on the plaque, *The House of Night.*

Devin closed his eyes and told himself it was only a reflection of the setting sun.

The House of Night.

Etched in red.

THE BEST IN HORROR

HEATHCLIFF

AMERICA'S CRAZIEST CAT

☐	56804-4	HEATHCLIFF AND THE GOOD LIFE	$1.95
☐	56805-2		Canada $2.50
☐	56802-8	HEATHCLIFF AT HOME	$1.95
☐	56803-6		Canada $2.50
☐	56806-0	HEATHCLIFF: ONE, TWO, THREE AND YOU'RE OUT	$1.95
☐	56807-9		Canada $2.50
☐	56816-8	HEATHCLIFF: SPECIALTIES, ON THE HOUSE	$2.50
☐	56817-X		Canada $3.50
☐	56808-7	HEATHCLIFF: THE BEST OF FRIENDS	$1.95
☐	56809-5		Canada $2.50